PRAISE F(

NICHOLAS NICASTRO

On THE ISLE OF STONE: *A Novel of Ancient Sparta*:

"With *The Isle of Stone*, Nicholas Nicastro joins the illustrious pedigree of Mary Renault, Valerio Massimo Manfredi and Steven Pressfield with great style and enormous panache. His hero's checkered lifestory is used to frame a dark and darkening history of Sparta between a hugely destructive natural disaster, a great earthquake in 464 BC, and a self-inflicted, man-made debacle during the prolonged and even more destructive Peloponnesian War. Nicastro knows his ancient sources intimately, but also has the born novelist's instinct to flesh out their bare bones all too plausibly. Nicastro's antiheroes of the isle of Sphacteria are the dark side of Pressfield's heroes in *Gates of Fire*: both demand and repay the attention of all lovers of expert historical fiction."

—Paul Cartledge, Professor of Greek History, University of Cambridge, and author of *Alexander the Great: The Hunt for a New Past*

"From its explosive first pages, *The Isle of Stone* draws you into the gritty reality of Sparta during the Peloponnesian War. Nicastro writes powerful prose, but this is no exercise in debunking. With drama, passion, and a sure touch for the facts, Nicastro reveals the heroism behind the humiliation of the shocking day when some of Sparta's unconquerable soldiers surrendered. His images of life and death under the Mediterranean sun hit you like the glare of a polished shield."

—Barry Strauss, author of *The Battle of Salamis: The Naval Encounter that Saved Greece - and Western Civilization* and Professor of History and Classics, Cornell University

"Reading one of Nicastro's books has the same fascination as staring at a terrible car crash. The scenes he constructs force us to grapple with the disturbing roots of our own cultural assumptions. Each of these characters spins into a series of bloody events far beyond individual control. Nicastro lays naked the complex web of collective motivations that shape the events of history.

The Isle of Stone shows Nicastro's intimate understanding of this distant time and deeply foreign culture. By giving human faces to the dry bones of ancient battles, he goes a long way towards making ancient motivations somehow explicable. Once again, Nicastro proves his talent for capturing the attitude of historical times while spinning a passionate drama."

—Pamela Goddard, *Ithaca Times*

On EMPIRE OF ASHES: *A Novel of Alexander the Great*:

"*Empire of Ashes* is great historical fiction. Nicholas Nicastro paints an entirely believable portrait of the world of Alexander the Great, with the period detail and nuance that gives the reader a true feel for the time period. Even better, he resists simply regurgitating our common understanding of Alexander, and instead presents an unexpected and at times startling picture of a hero we thought we knew, but perhaps did not. *Empire of Ashes* is both fast-paced and scholarly, a difficult combination to achieve, but Nicastro succeeds beautifully."

—James L. Nelson, author of *The Only Life That Mattered* and *The Revolution at Sea* saga

"*Empire of Ashes* is a great read. I loved the style and thought the framing device of the court case was fascinating and gripping. The sights, sounds and social life of ancient Athens came to life for me in a way that few historical novels seem to manage. The characters were carefully and convincingly created and forced me to make various judgements about them, and then revise them, just as real people do. The action scenes were great too. Grim and gritty and vividly brought to life. All in all a great achievement..."

—Simon Scarrow, author of *The Eagle and the Wolves* and *The Eagle's Conquest*

"*Empire of Ashes* manages to be many things at the same time. The book is a grand historical epic combined with a courtroom drama and political intrigue. Believable characters rise off the page in clear, evocative language. Nicastro has a talent for capturing the attitude and motivations of historical times, and creating stories which tell us something about our current time and situation. The result is a captivating and compelling pageturner."

—Pamela Goddard, *Ithaca Times*

On THE EIGHTEENTH CAPTAIN: *The John Paul Jones Trilogy* v. 1:

"Nicastro takes you by the scruff of your neck and yanks you into the action of history. From the moment the spine is creased, you are there, on board the ship, like Jim Hawkins in the apple barrel listening to Long John Silver's most secret plan. . . . Kudos to Nicholas Nicastro and even more kudos to McBooks Press for adding this finely wrought novel to their armada of Maritime literature!"

—Eric Machan Howd, *Ithaca Times*

"This maritime historical novel fairly shimmers with furtive lustiness and wry humor. Embellishing John Paul Jones' early naval intrigues and sexual liasons, Nicholas Nicastro preserves the true spirit of a mercurial and moody hero."

—Jill B. Gidmark *University of Minnesota Professor of English*

"In *The Eighteenth Captain*, Nicholas Nicastro gives us a nuanced, insightful and thoroughly believable portrait of an American hero that few know beyond his saying "I have not yet begun to fight" which, in fact, he probably did not say. Nicastro does what the artist can do and the historian cannot; probe the inner mind of the historical John Paul Jones, guess who he really was from the empirical evidence, and then present that portrait in words and deeds that are on the one hand often fiction, but on the other true to the spirit of Jones. And he does it very well, showing us our American Tragic Hero, great but flawed, a conqueror brought down by his own faults. *The Eighteenth Captain* is beautifully framed by the fall-out of the French Revolution which represented the end of much that Jones loved but was a consequence in part of Jones' own actions, a lovely metaphor for the man's life and deeds. Carefully researched, accurate in tone and detail, *The Eighteenth Captain* is an insightful portrait of a man, a hero and his times, and what each of those things, in their essence, truly mean."

—James L. Nelson, *author of the* Revolution at Sea Saga

On BETWEEN TWO FIRES: *The John Paul Jones Trilogy* v. 2:

"By turns comic, gruesome, beautiful and devastating. Certain images are unforgettable...others laugh-aloud funny...a clean, swift, luscious read [that] assembles a provocative cast of characters in a story that resounds in the world today."

—Anne Campisi, *Ithaca Journal*

"*Between Two Fires* is at once a cautionary take and a great period yarn with extraordinary characters...the final chapters are filled with as many twists and turns as a tacking frigate."

—Pamela Goddard, *Ithaca Times*

ANTIGONE'S WAKE

A Novel of Imperial Athens

NICHOLAS NICASTRO

BellaRosaBooks

BellaRosaBooks

ANTIGONE'S WAKE
ISBN 978-1-933523-26-2

This book is a work of fiction. Names, characters, places and incidents
are products of the author's imagination or are used fictitiously. Any
resemblance to actual events or locales or persons, living or dead, is
entirely coincidental.

First printed: April 2007

Library of Congress Control Number: 2007925094

Printed in the United States of America on acid-free paper.

Book design by Bella Rosa Books

BellaRosaBooks and logo are trademarks of Bella Rosa Books.

10   9   8   7   6   5   4   3   2   1

This book is dedicated to my friend, Todd Yellin:

verus amicus est is qui est tamquam alter idem

TABLE OF CONTENTS

HISTORICAL NOTE	xi
PROLOGUE	1
I. NOTHING TO DO WITH DIONYSUS	4
II. A TASTE OF RUE	27
III. THE HIPPOCAMP SEES HIS SHADOW	49
IV. SHIELDBREAKER	69
V. THE SANCTUARY	94
VI. TUNNELING TO GLORY	113
VII. THE SOUND OF THIRST	137
VIII. THE BACK HAND OF FORTUNE	157
IX. HYDRA	176
AUTHOR'S AFTERWORD	206
ABOUT THE AUTHOR	211

HISTORICAL NOTE

Sophocles of Colonus (c. 496-406 BC) was author of some of the finest tragedies (*Oedipus the King*, *Antigone*, *Oedipus at Colonus*) of classical antiquity. What is less known is that Sophocles the playwright also had a military career, serving as a general in Athens' war against the island state of Samos in 440-39 BC. The date of this service means it was not some ephebic prelude to his productive years. Indeed, it puts him "in uniform" at the very prime of his creative life, close to the time of the premiere of *Antigone* itself. This novel represents an attempt to imagine what happened in this curious episode, when the histories of dramatic art and military science briefly intersected.

A mixture of ancient and modern units of measure is used in the text. For the sake of convenience, modern units are used when they are more or less similar to their ancient counterparts (e.g., feet, hours, months). Verisimilitude is served by including a number of antique units common in the relevant historical sources. Most prominent here is the *stade*, a Greek unit of distance approximately equivalent to 600 modern feet (and from which our word *stadium* is derived).

The common monetary unit is the Athenian *drachma*, which is equivalent in value to six *obols*. The superordinate units are the *mina*, worth 100 drachmas, and the *talent*, equaling 6000 drachmas. We know that a decent house in a suburb of Athens in the mid-fifth century BC would set the buyer back 500 to 1000 drachmas (or five to ten minas); a gallon of olive oil, more than three drachmas; a good pair of shoes, about 10 drachmas; a healthy slave, 300 to 500. Still, for various reasons, expressing the value of a drachma in today's currency is not as straightforward as finding modern equivalents for, say, distance. According to an oft-cited rule of thumb, the wage for the average laborer in classical Athens was one or two drachmas a day. A talent, therefore, works out to the equivalent of almost twenty years of work, or in modern terms something like a million dollars.

As for the calendar, the reader will notice there are no absolute dates given for the events depicted here. This is due to the simple fact that no universal system existed until relatively recent times (and arguably, does not exist even today, given that the Chinese, Muslim, and Jewish calendars are still in use). Instead, years were designated either by counting the years since some important event, or on the basis of who held important magistracies at that time (in Athens, years were named for the so-called "eponymous" archons). For instance, Thucydides places the war with Samos "in the sixth year of the truce [with Sparta]." More conventionally, the Athenians would have dated the events presented here to the terms of the archons of Timocles and Morychides, 441-39 BC.

PROLOGUE

"Oh yes, my life is marvelously fair."
—Electra, *Electra*, l. 390

Seen from a godly vantage, the Athenian war fleet moved over the sea with a peculiar, spring-like action. Like the head of a caterpillar, the knot of vessels with experienced crews shot ahead, pulling hard as the body of the fleet stretched out behind. Zigging and zagging, the green-handed rearguard was left behind in the westward mist. The oarsmen were lucky to row virtually submerged in wood and the flesh of their companions, with their seats facing astern. It was a rare recruit who would not be discouraged to see the veteran ships race so far ahead that their rigging sank into the blue.

The sole advantage of arriving last was the fact that the pull-outs were already illuminated by watch-fires. The latecomers would then have the obvious target of the beached triremes, lined up like stranded whales on the sand, to motivate them. It was an unlucky ship that failed to arrive by dark, when the offshore breezes rose and the task of laying up for the night became infinitely more difficult and dangerous.

The ships rowed only in daylight, managing seven or eight miles an hour with a good crew and a following wind. Their limited range obliged the eastbound fleets to island-hop to Asia. After weathering the promontory at Sounion, the fleet caterpillared its way to the broad sandy beaches on the western shore of Keos. If going on to the Hellespont and the Black Sea, it touched in turn at Andros, Chios, and Lesbos; if making for Ionia proper, it cut through the heart of the Cyclades to the north coast of Ikaria, where foraging parties were sure to rush ahead to secure a supply of the local apricots to supplement the night's rations.

From Ikaria it was an easy run to the large, wealthy island of Samos—a place where, until recently, the Athenians could expect a warm welcome and miles of empty shoreline to dry their hulls. But this time there would be no welcome. Instead of sailing east into Persian-controlled waters, the Athenians were bound for Samos herself, with the intention of humbling fellow Greeks.

On a spring voyage, the oarsmen knew an island was near when the sea's color, freshened by the flow of stream water from the highlands, changed from a sky-reflecting blue to gray slate. Towers of vapor could be seen rising from the mountains of Naxos and Andros before the summits rose into view. It was not unknown for these plumes to blaze with sunset as the islands, drenched in shadow, floated in their turn above clouds of opalescent green, like sunken constellations. It was said by some that the glow in the water was made by tiny creatures that swarmed there. Others insisted it was the gleam of torches in Hades, as the miserable shades, seeking respite from an eternity in twilight, marched in procession in honor of the Lord of the Dead.

On this particular evening a fleet of sixty triremes was safe for the night on Keos. Another four had yet to reach shore as the sun washed its lower limb in the sea. The laggards, which were crewed mostly by poor citizens with no experience afloat, churned the blackening waves with triple-banks of oars, their bronze-clad rams plowing the swells. A pair of painted eyes on the bows fixed an impassive stare at the beach; behind, the superstructure ascended in a proud, erect curve, like some defiant gesture at departing Helios.

On the slowest-running ship of this, the lagging flotilla in the fleet, the deck pitched and twisted as the unstable, narrow-beamed warship settled in the hollows between the crests. To this motion was added the intermittent lurch of the hull as the ship was propelled forward by its oars. A lookout shouted ahead; the officer of the deck slowed the cadence as the ship approached the flotsam of some lost transport. Closer, they entered a stretch of water with horse carcasses scattered like wet, woolen blisters on the sea. Lifting their blades over the gas-swollen bags, the top oarsmen looked down on the drowned things as they floated, legs splayed in a slick becalmed with blood, each attended by writhing schools of silvery maggots. Novice rowers flinched in their benches as the ship's beak split equine flesh. A putrid cloud rose, sending the marines scurrying to douse the torches, and turning even the most seaworthy stomachs inside out.

Watching this from the deck, just ahead of the steering oars, from a chair that was really no more than a puny shelf, was Sophocles son of Sophilos, general of the fleet and erstwhile civilian. And in green-faced Sophocles there was not a scrap of food, for he had vomited his breakfast into the sea hours ago, and only a single thought: *how, by some perversity of the Fates, have I come to be here, on my way to war?*

Chapter I

NOTHING TO DO WITH DIONYSUS

"He who stands clear of trouble should beware of dangers; and when a man lives at ease, then it is that he should look most closely to his life, lest ruin come on it by stealth."

—Philoctetes, *Philoctetes*, l. 500

1.

A few days before the City Dionysia, the archons held a much-anticipated competition. The *proagon* was staged under the peaked roof of Pericles' new concert hall. The thousands gathered there, under the eighty stone columns with their capitals clad in theatrical attributes, and woodwork cut from the masts of wrecked Persian ships, sweltering in their winter cloaks as the air stank of lampsmoke and tar still drying on the crossbeams. With the weather fair that early March, the mass of citizens overflowed out the doors, around the Odeon, and down the slope like a linen-drab stain.

Athenians came because the contest decided the order in which the tragedies would be staged at Dionysus' festival. Yet few of the spectators, indoors or out, had a decent view of the performance. The stage was built too low, as if begrudging any distinction from the wide, flat expanse of the orchestra in the nearby Theater. The citizen fortunate enough to be a head taller than his neighbor still had to contend with that forest of columns, which doomed nearly every seat in the house to an obstructed view.

This competition was designed to be heard instead of seen. The three tragedians chosen for the season, matched with their state-sponsored choruses, would each present a foretaste of the songs from their plays. When an entrant's turn came, he would get a few moments to impress the throng with his virtuosity. Self-appointed loudmouths would go about telling the people to shut up—swatting them if necessary—until they attained a silence long enough for the first few verses to waft through the hall and out the doors. Athenians, who attended many hours of drama every year, could tell in a few moments if the rest was worth hearing. Fine coming-attractions were politely attended and received applause; poor ones were drowned out by chatter and the cries of concessionaires selling cheap fans, water, fruit, or flatbread peppered with road-dust.

First to lead his chorus to the stage that day was Aristarchus of Tegea. His troupe entered through the side door and processed to the stage in a reverent silence. The poet and his fifteen choristers came garlanded with ivy, dressed in long, pleated stage-chitons, but without masks and without the chitons bustled for dancing. There were a few groans from the crowd as they assembled. In a dozen years, Aristarchus had entered tetralogies for seven Festivals, yet had never placed higher than second. Though the judges never favored him, the name-archon for the year, Timocles, had once again honored Aristarchus with a place among the final three. Timocles sat with the other magistrates in their wooden chairs beneath the stage, his arms crossed, his downcast, lidded eyes revealing nothing. The poet presented himself to the people and sang the usual invocation:

"Aid us, our dear lord Dionysus, as we consecrate this offering, that it may please you, and shed your divine favor upon this city of the Athenians, which above all others honors you by consecrating these fruits at your festival, the greatest in all the lands of the Greeks."

Aristarchus turned to his chorus. The self-styled soldiers of Dionysus in the crowd squelched all chatter, and Timocles unfolded his arms.

Though the poet had not named his play or described its subject, everyone recognized what followed as a tragedy set on the shores of Ilion. The chorus sang of the fair matron of Menelaus' house, borne from Laconian purple over plum-wine seas to Alexandros' scented bower. They sang of Priam's turrets piercing the heavens above Sigeum, as the tenth-part of the cargoes of a hundred nations passed in tribute beneath his walls. They sang of Troy's blooming manhood, playing at youthful games as the tide of death swept toward them from the prows of the easting Achaeans. And though they were forbidden to dance during the *proagon*, the choristers moved in time to the verses, the crimps of their gowns swaying, the sweat-smeared Aristarchus laboring before them, pumping his arms, as if inflating some kind of iambic bellows. The crowd gave their attention to the poet who had chiseled this ode from the mass of his inert talent, allowing him to evoke, like the sweet memory of a dream, that distant beach, that patch of ground waiting for the ashes of great, broken Achilles—but only for a moment. When the Tegean turned back to face the people, he found they had returned to their roasted walnuts.

It was, on the whole, a typical performance for Aristarchus. The chorus, furnished him by the state, had done its level best with the mere competence of his verse. The producer assigned to him, an aristocrat named Theodorus, seemed duly committed to spending a patriotic abundance of his money on scenery and costumes. He even had a fine protagonist in Hegelochus, who had distinguished himself last year in the role of Darius in Achaeus' *Persians*. Yet all this splendid support just inspired everyone to dread the final production even more; it was, after all, doomed to nothing more than a second-place finish. Athenians never had much time for worthy runners-up.

The glumness vanished when the crowd saw the next troupe mount the stage. A wave of relief swept through the Odeon—a spontaneous, collective exhalation—as a tall, familiar figure led his chorus before the people. The shudder of anticipation swept through the doors, into the crowd listening outside, and seemed to radiate into the city. The trees in the temple groves nodded, unfolding limbs laden with spring buds. In Dionysus' sacred grotto under the Acropolis, the priests saw the lamps gutter, then burn with fresh vigor, and with that sign knew that a really good show was at hand, and that the god was beckoning them to run down the slope to glimpse the new work by Dexion, the city's pride.

2.

Sophocles of Colonus, son of Sophilos, father of Iophon, was a handsome man of fifty-five. Renowned since youth for his beauty, he had been kindly handled by age: his physique, which had graced the choral dances so often when he was a boy, had retained the balanced proportions of a champion pentathlete. His head was neither too squat like Socrates', nor too high-crowned like Pericles', but sat square on his tanned shoulders. The features on it were sculptural in their balance, with eyes finely spaced but not too far, lips appealingly plump but not sensuous, nose ascending straight and true from the untrammeled plain of his brow. Those who had not seen him since his last proagon noted that his beard was grayer, more deeply piled, and the lines on his face were deeper. Yet these badges of maturity only seemed to frame the ideality of what remained. When his fellow citizens passed him in the street, they would stare and point, and say "There goes Dexion, inspired by the gods and beautiful to look upon."

Though he was nothing other than a man, his fame had given him an almost feminine comfort with being leered at. Over the years he had learned how to turn these instances into opportunities: as people watched, they would grow so immersed in their admiration they wouldn't notice Sophocles scrutinizing them back. In this way he learned much about the character of his city's people. One of the pleasures of his plays was the economical ways he captured these qualities, communicating them in his choice of words and the small gestures of his actors, so that other Greeks in the audience, visiting from other cities, were sometimes at a loss to understand the hoots of recognition from the Athenians.

Years before he had been frequently seen on the orchestra. From boyhood he was noted for his skill with the lyre, and was heavily sought by other poets as an accompanist for their choral songs. It was young Sophocles who played the harp for the premiere performances of all three plays in Aeschylus' *Oresteia*. When he began to write his own tragedies, he took the protagonist's role himself. His performances came to be as finely wrought as his verse, so that again he was courted by other tragedians. For this versatility of his talent—writing, acting and musicianship—he soon earned the epithet of "Dexion," the Entertainer.

He pursued this hyphenated career as long he was able— until the day he was acting the title role in Neophron's *Medea*, and at a particularly fraught moment, when the heroine was obliged to confront the bodies of the children she had murdered, his voice broke. With fifty lines left to speak, he was obliged to continue in a whisper. The audience was so transported by the show that they leaned forward in a body to hear Medea's barely-audible rant. The producer, Cimon son of Miltiades, won the ivy crown for his work; Sophocles, despite his mishap, also won the prize for his acting. Neophron, however, was forced to take second place among the tragedians. For failing his patron, Sophocles never forgave himself—and never trusted his voice on stage again.

And so he confined himself to writing, and did so with such success that the appearance of a new program by Dexion was something of a civic event. When he took the stage and commenced the invocation, there was no need to call for silence—curiosity stilled every tongue in the room. The chorus behind him was dressed much like Aristarchus', but with a special touch typical of their master: all of them, in addition to the wreaths and chitons, were wearing the special kid-skin bootlets of the type Sophocles had designed himself. Once, when pressed, he explained that they were supposed to prevent slips during the dances. "When," his rivals asked, "had a chorister ever slipped on the dusty floor of the orchestra?" "Never," agreed the people, who ordinarily resisted any innovation. Yet, so good did the fancy things look on the feet of the dancers, for Sophocles alone they swallowed the conceit, and accepted the boots.

The troupe began the first song with voices so subdued that they were imperceptible beyond the first few rows of spectators. The people shushed each other, their hisses rising and falling away like one of the rare oceanic waves that broke on Sounion when the great Earth-husband, enthroned in the deep, tossed his weed-shrouded shoulders. When they settled at last, and the chorus rose, the audience heard them sing:

He set out against our land because of the strife-filled claims of Polyneices,
and like a screaming eagle he flew over into our land, covered by his snow-white wing,
with a mass of weapons and crested helmets.
He paused above our dwellings; he gaped around our sevenfold portals with spears thirsting for blood;
but he left before his jaws were ever glutted with our gore, or before the Fire-god's pine-fed flame had seized our crown of towers.
So fierce was the crash of battle swelling about his back, a match too hard to win for the rival of the dragon.
For Zeus detests above all the boasts of a proud tongue—

They elegized like this for some time as the audience stood rapt, watching if they could, just listening if the columns blocked their view, with snacks unchewed in their mouths and their faces suffused with pleasure. For an ode of Dexion was nothing if not pleasant—neither too austere, like the poets of the generation that had served at Marathon, nor too precious, like the mellifluous droolings of the young. Better than anyone, he respected the people's preference for dances over songs, and songs over dialog, even as he produced expositional verse as clever as the city literati could ever wish.

Yet if there was one criticism—and among the Athenians there was always at least one—it was that Dexion was perhaps too smooth, too easy to take. Some still compared him unfavorably to Aeschylus, whose verses serried and bristled like phalanxes, and whose productions were like forced marches through bramble-fields. While Sophocles was something of a trimmer, all too aware of striking a fair balance, the old master was never anyone but himself. In his severity, Aeschylus seemed primitive, yet also much closer to the source of what once made the tragedies consecrated acts, not excuses for someone to exhibit his cleverness.

But these were the carpings of scolds. When the song was over the people applauded freely. When the poet stepped forward, a fetching sheen of humility on his face, to announce the subjects of his plays, an immodest woman cried out that she would love Sophocles anywhere. Her ejaculation was followed by wolf-whistles from all over the Odeon, from men and women.

"The people will be dignified," announced Timocles, who waited for order, then turned to Sophocles. "Continue."

"The theme of the program," said the poet, "is the wages the gods mete to the unjust. The first play has seven odes and seven episodes, and is called the *Agamemnon*. The second has ten odes and nine episodes, and is called the *Danaids*, and the third, with eight odes and eight episodes, is the *Antigone*. There will also be a satyr play, the *Harvesters*, with six odes and six episodes. The producer will be the metic, Chaerephilus of Chalcedon, and the protagonist for all the plays, Tlepolemus."

It came as a surprise to no one that the competition ended

with Dexion's victory. The last entrant of the day was a newcomer, a youth named Thespis, who produced the kind of metrical fireworks that impressed the sophisticates, but fell flat with the people. The archons gathered, and after a brief conference produced their verdict: Aristarchus would present first, then Thespis, and then, in the plum spot, Dexion. The people registered their approval by pelting the stage with blossoms if they had them, cheeses and uncracked nuts if they didn't, followed by garbage, like fruit rinds and baked long bones with the tasty marrow sucked out, until the proceedings devolved into the usual riot. The archons loosed the Scythian flatfoots on the crowd, who cleared the Odeon by bludgeoning anyone in reach. When it was over, Sophocles was left on the stage with Timocles, looking down on the wooden floor smeared with urine, rose petals, discarded shells, and broken teeth.

"Smooth event this year," appraised the archon as he swung his cloak over his shoulders. "Good luck, Dexion."

3.

Sophocles made a practice of visiting the Theatre in the early morning before his work was presented. This entailed getting up shortly after midnight and coming into town when it was still dark, before the caretakers arrived to make final preparations for the day's productions. He was, in fact, rising with the farmers in the valley around the city, who would likewise roll off their pallets in the deep gloom to turn out the family cow, or milk their goats, or tweeze the pests from the corrugations of their olive trees. In those days, with the nightly breeze blowing steady across the thyme-scented slopes of Hymmetus, it was still possible to hear activity on the farms outside the city. All the animal cluckings and brayings and clanking of iron tools against the stony soil reminded him of a life he had given up long before, when he left his father's armory shop as a young man. Truth be told, it was a life to which he, like most lettered craftsmen, would be loathe to return. Yet it always gave him a pinch of sentimental pleasure to know it was still there.

With spring not far advanced, his trek was through cold, deserted streets. It was the one moment of the day when Athens could be mistaken for a clean city. There would be no smoke in the air yet, and the hardpan of the streets was trackless and freshly wetted. The gutters would be clean for the moment, for the chamberpots of the citizens were yet undumped out the windows. Between the shutters, matronly shadows could be glimpsed collecting wood for breakfast fires. If he saw anyone on the street at that hour, it would be some hard-working storekeep shipping fish or winejars to his stall, or else—like some frail bird rarely seen—a freeborn girl with a wine jug, only permitted out on the streets when they were deserted of men.

The theatre was a wooden, semi-circular grandstand, nestled under the open sky in the southeast shoulder of the Acropolis. Above it, flying from temporary masts, snapped the banners of the ten tribes into which Attica was divided. Higher still flitted the swallows that made their homes in the cracks and ledges of the sacred rock. For two generations nothing was above the birds but the rampart started by Cimon out of the fire-stained blocks of the old sanctuary of Athena. Now, just peeking over the bastion, still controversial in its smug, self-celebratory bigness, stretched the roofline of the yet-unfinished Parthenon.

Inside the theatre, the painted stage scenery was already attached to the pavilion façade behind the orchestra: in this case, it was meant to evoke the Royal Palace of the Thebans. Dexion would look at it from various positions around the stage—front and center, from the stone seats reserved for the city magistrates; from the most distant upper tier, on the wooden benches where the women sat and, more often than not, chatted through the performance; from down on the orchestra, beside the altar of Dionysus, where he would play his harp for the choruses and fret over everything else in the production that failed to comport with his hopes.

No play was ever mounted twice for the Great Dionysia, but the festival itself never changed. Dionysus Eleuthereus, son of Zeus, also known as Bacchos the Twice-born, drinking buddy of Silenus, patron of theater and madness, inspirer of sweet indolence and frenzied violence, had always called forth the most committed of Athenian carousers. The celebrants began to drink during the procession on the festival's first day. After the seals on last autumn's wine jars were cracked, the city watched through blurry eyes as the god, plaster face painted and uncut phallus festooned with ribbons, was borne aloft through the streets. He hit the road in his divine barge, but for good measure, as if ready to preclude any delay, he also had wings and a riding crop. The procession ended at the theatre, where the god was delivered to his altar in the center of the orchestra, and whence, on the first full day of festival performances, he would enjoy an unrivaled view of the year's dithyrambs.

Ten fifty-man choruses—one for each tribe—would compete to mount the best songs and dances in honor of the god. Dexion had participated in his share of dithyrambs as a young man. Ungirdled, with skin oiled and goatskin around his shoulders, he danced in his first prize-winning chorus twenty-five years earlier, during the archonship of Phaidon. It was his first crack at performing as the troupe-leader, charged with introducing all the familiar stories about Dionysus—his rescue as a babe, plucked from his mother's burnt corpse after she dared cast her gaze on the Thunderer; his emergence from his long childhood at Mount Nysa; his triumphant procession through India and Persia in an ivy-clad car pulled by panthers, spreading the blessings of the grape along the way. In every sense, Dexion's career began with the god, for tragedy itself was said to have sprung from the dithyrambs, with the troupe-leaders having long ago evolved into protagonists, and the choral subjects straying farther and farther from the strict worship of Dionysus. As recently as Aeschylus' time one could still hear old men complaining that the new plays had nothing to do with the god. But Dionysus himself, ever amused, ever erect and ready to fly, seemed content to take the best seat in the house.

The second day was devoted to the year's comedies, with the honored poets staging one play each. The crowd would file into the theatre as the sun rose, bearing blankets for their shoulders and pillows for the rumps that would remain planted on those wooden benches, with only brief pee breaks, for the eight hours necessary to see all five plays. For this entertainment, respectable citizens were expected to pay two obols each for a seat—less than half a day's wages. Yet Dionysus would be displeased to see half the city barred from his levee. The city Treasury therefore paid the admission fees of hundreds of the city's worst reprobates, scoundrels, and layabouts. These tended to cluster in the theater's upper reaches, where they honored the god of inebriation out of small wineskins and earthenware cups. When bored, they pounded the benches with their heels; when amused, they guffawed the loudest, while at all times they shouted down impromptu reviews of the rich and the powerful in the seats below.

The atmosphere at the end of the second day was more raucous than ever, with everyone giddy and exhausted after hearing sixty-five hundred lines of verse and sixty or seventy choruses, and the comic poets competing to influence the judges by stirring up the crowd, and the low-class spectators more than ready to oblige by flinging those earthenware cups, until the Scythians were inevitably called in to secure the formalities of the prize-vote. If the judges' decision was unpopular, an undeserving winner would be lucky to escape Dionysus's sanctuary with his ivy crown unmussed and his prize purse unpicked.

And so the people trudged to the festival's third day—the opening day of the tragedies—at daybreak, with most of them not having slept for forty-eight hours. The poet saddled with presenting his trilogy first (this year, the hapless Aristarchus) would have only half an audience for the initial four or five odes of his first play. All the officials were obliged to be there, but it was a rare judge who cast his first-place vote for a program few citizens had seen in full.

By the start of the fourth day, consigned this year to Thespis' tongue-tanglers, the earnest playgoers would have arrived in force, with the less-earnest either nodded off in their seats or slunk off to bed. The sobering influence of the tragedies themselves had its effect on the proceedings, which became ever more serious as the day wore on. In Dexion's experience, the optimal moment came with the premiere of the opening play on festival day five. It was at this juncture, when the prospect of competition between the poets was felt most keenly, and the people came to the theater fresh after a good night's rest, and his chorus and players were in their best voice, and the dust of the city had not yet risen to obscure the magnificence of the setting, that he had reserved to present his *Antigone*.

The poet slumped on his bench as his heart sank. The sun would rise soon, casting its light indifferently on triumph or disaster. The quiet before a festival performance always depressed him, for the actors had learned their lines, the choruses had been drilled, the costumes had been stitched, and there was nothing more he could do. Anyone spying on Sophocles on the morning before a performance would have seen him sitting there with his lips silently moving, but not to his own iambs. The lines, instead, would be the ancient prayers of his fathers, and his audience Dionysus, Aesclepius, or any other god who might take pity on him.

4.

Pericles never lingered at parties for the start of the drinking. Lysicles son of Neanthes therefore gave his review of the year's tragedies while the food was still on the table.

"Truly magnificent . . . a pity it had to end . . ." he remarked, waving a peacock egg for emphasis. "No one can remember an occasion when the giving of the prize was so foregone."

"And what do you know about drama, Lysicles?" said Menippus son of Myronides, Pericles' advisor in things military. "You are a dealer in sheep."

"Even for a tragedy, *Antigone* is such a tedious story," said Aspasia, who had come to the hall in a chiton so delicately woven, and so expensive, that she dared not eat in it. Imported from the finest clothier in Miletus, the gown shone from certain angles like spun silver, while from others it was semi-transparent. On her head she wore an olive wreath circlet made of beaten gold, and around her right arm a golden serpent with ruby eyes and a carnelian tongue. By the twinkle in the eyes of her male guests she could see the impression this ensemble made. Pericles, who had withdrawn to the farthest corner of his couch, seemed irked by the show of her wealth—if not of her roseate, yet-unsuckled teats.

"You insist on embarrassing yourself with this vulgarity," the great man would tell her later, though the puckering of his high-domed brow proved it was the he who was embarrassed. "How will I defend myself from the demagogues, when you go around like a tramp?"

"But I am *your* tramp, great Pericles!" she replied without shame. "And how else shall I present myself in this uncivilized place? Here, even the wives of the thetes pretend they have money, yet I am expected to dress like a pigseller's daughter?"

And noble Pericles, son of Xanthippus, blood descendant of Cleisthenes the Lawgiver, first citizen of Athens and architect of an empire that spanned the Aegean, would make no response except to cover his face. This was partly because he was not the sort to debase himself with petty arguments, but also because he had already learned not to match wits with Aspasia, who had a lively tongue and little dignity to lose.

"In Sophocles' hands the story was not dreary, but the finest sort of agony," continued Lysicles. "For it may have been called *Antigone*, but it really had two heroes—the princess Antigone, daughter of Oedipus, and Oedipus' successor as King of Thebes, Creon. Both were given their due. Everyone was so moved by the plight of each that the audience fell into a dispute with itself after the last chorus, arguing over which character was more admirable. The archons had to delay the next play."

Menippus spat in a fold of his tunic. "Yes, I can attest to that: the whole day was set back. The satyr play didn't end until after sundown. I was numb by the end—you could have stuck a cavalry lance in my ass and I wouldn't have felt it."

"How can the play have two heroes?" interjected ten year-old Alcibiades, his tender young mouth stuffed with roast dormouse. "That is not the correct form for tragedy."

Aspasia reached out to straighten the boy's unruly bangs. Pericles' ward was really coming into fine form—she would soon have to appoint a slave to instruct him in what a handsome young man should know about women. "Don't talk with your mouth full, dear," she said. "And finish your wine."

"I don't like wine."

"Silly child, don't the pine nuts make you thirsty?"

"I prefer water."

She sighed. "Are we doomed to raise a boy with unbalanced humors? Pericles, tell him."

"The poet opens the story right after the war between the spawn of Oedipus," Lysicles went on. "Polyneices, the younger son, has come to Thebes to wrest the throne from his brother, Eteocles. Both were cursed by Oedipus for their disrespect after his secret was revealed; both therefore fall in the siege. Creon, the new king, chooses to honor the eldest with a state funeral, but decrees that the corpse of Polyneices must rot in the dust. Antigone, Oedipus' daughter, will have nothing of that—she tells her sister Ismene so right from the start. . . . "

"It was interesting to watch the people argue over that fable. . . ." mused Pericles, positioned some distance away. Though his body dented the cushions like that of any other mortal, there was a precision about his repose that made everyone else look as if they were slouching. It was a grace Alcibiades was determined to imitate exactly, as was Menippus, though the latter was so naturally twitchy he could manage it only when he was a little drunk.

"You'd expect the monied ones, the knights and the five-hundred-bushel men, to sympathize with Creon—the power of the state—but they seemed divided amongst themselves, with some for the king, others for Antigone—as were the thetes—"

"Try some of this," Aspasia told Alcibiades, holding a fingertip dipped in wine to the boy's lips. "It's the sweet vintage you like—"

"No!"

"So the first chance she gets she's out on the battlefield, giving the body a ritual dusting. When Creon hears of it of course he's beside himself. They can barely dissuade him from killing the messenger, who's a splendid portrait by the way, an exact reflection of your typical Athenian bureaucrat, caring only that he doesn't get prosecuted! Creon orders him back out to the battlefield, to find out who defied his orders—or else!"

"Did you happen to attend the comedies this year, my dear?" Aspasia asked Pericles with a mischievous lilt in her voice. The great man ignored her, but Menippus whooped at the question, spilling the barley stuffing from the sow's womb that was on its way to his mouth.

"Oh, not a good year for that! There was a devastating piece by Cratinus this time, set on an unknown island where the people's heads literally swell up when they receive praise. The producer sprung for masks with inflatable bladders. There was a line in there by a whore that everyone just loved, that just *killed*, that went:

Some girls open up for a well-hung man
But what city can resist Mr. Big Brain-pan . . . ?

Aspasia gave her party laugh. "The slaves are talking about

another coup, where two guardsmen on top of a wall are watching a horse and rider approach the city from a distance—"

"—and from the size of the heads," cried Menippus, "they can't tell if it's the horse or High-head who wears the saddle!"

"That's enough," warned Pericles, turning anywhere for rescue. "Lysicles, tell us more about Dexion's play."

"Forget the dreary mythifying, and tell us about the dances!" Aspasia commanded.

Lysicles rolled his eyes in delectation as he downed a cup of water.

"When has Dexion disappointed us on that score?" he resumed. "As usual, his chorus was the sharpest-looking on the stage. When he wants them to wear white chitons, they are the whitest; when black, they are like dancing shadows. And those darling little boots! Of course, Chaerephilus won the producer's prize. Dexion himself played the harp for the odes. I'll say this for him: I've been to as many festivals as I have years as a man, and I have never seen plays that seem so much like the work of one mind. He was in control of everything— you could see him watching the choristers like a drillmaster, conducting them with his eyes. Through eight odes they never fell out of synchrony, except when he wanted them to. He makes the work of everyone else seem half-baked."

"Do you hear that, my dear?" Aspasia addressed Pericles. "Our Dexion has the makings of a drillmaster!"

"If Polyneices was a traitor, why do the gods make Creon suffer?" asked Alcibiades.

"You may answer that question yourself," replied Pericles in his didactic mode, "if you think about another: is it within the power of a mortal king to define who may be buried, and who may not?"

"That is up to the gods."

"Then you know Creon's error: by decreeing that the dead be exposed, and the living buried, he sought to enlarge the authority of men, and in so doing, he despised the gods."

Aspasia exchanged glances with Menippus and Lysicles as

the irony seemed to congeal in the air above them: Pericles, a
man of almost lordly arrogance, whose disdain for pietist
niceties was almost legend, was instructing the boy on the
virtues of mortal discretion. But none of them spoke. After an
afternoon of testing, even the patience of Pericles had its limits.

When the wine appeared their host made his usual excuses.
Alcibiades was packed off to bed, and Menippus and
Lysicles—with the discreet help of Aspasia—did their best to
make it to a fifth jar of Chian red. But without the foil of chilly
Pericles the fun soon went out of drinking. By the time the full
moon had cleared the mountains the party had broken up, with
Menippus on his way back to his home on Muses Hill, and
Lysicles lurching from house to house, pounding on the doors
of bewildered citizens, demanding entrée to the taverns he
insisted were inside.

Aspasia was snuffing the lamps in the drinking parlor when
Pericles appeared again. She had learned to recognize the
expression he wore, the kind that betokened an idea was slowly
and relentlessly hatching. For although his mind was not as
quick as her's, she knew that none was more thorough, sifting
every conceivable pro and con. When he turned up like this he
was ready to speak.

"An interesting idea you had, about making Dexion a
soldier."

"I wasn't serious."

"Though I imagine he'd prefer to be something more
dignified than a drillmaster," he went on, as if not hearing her.
"A general perhaps. What is his tribe?"

"I don't know."

He turned to leave, but seemed to be frozen when his eyes
swept over her expensive dress.

"Did you buy that in the market, or was it a gift?"

"Would I accept any gifts, after the way you have pestered
me about that?"

"Then what are you prepared to give up?"

"Of all the niggardly tightfisted pinchpenny meanies!"

"I will not have it said I have used my position to enrich myself," he declaimed, as if explaining to a child one of life's eternal verities. "What about that new litter . . . why would anyone need more than one litter?"

She looked down for something to throw at him. But as the slaves had already cleared the tables, all she could find was a single olive. She launched it, hitting Pericles in the center of his vertically-plumb forehead. Since it was one of last year's olives, pickled and pulpy with brine, it hit with a splat, leaving a brown spot.

"You will sell the litter or sell the dress," he said. He then walked out without wiping his brow, for Pericles, of all people, was precisely the kind of man who, over some fine point of home economics, would never wipe away the residue when a soft, briny, year-old olive struck his forehead.

5.

Sophocles was born in the suburb of Colonus, and still lived there. He had bought his little house with the pooled resources of his father's inheritance, Nais' dowry, and the modest income he made ghost-writing speeches for the courts. Prize-winnings for his plays came too infrequently, and were too uncertain, to count as steady income. Indeed, it was not so long ago that the first-place prize for drama was a wreath, a goat, and a pat on the back. For these reasons—and despite his fame—Sophocles' modest pile could never be mistaken for the house of a rich man.

In the warm months he rose early to do his writing in the garden, under the shade of the little plane tree. There, enveloped in the scents of mint and oregano, he would wait for inspiration, reciting the verses as they came into his mind as his slave, Bulos, set them down on a tablet of soft lead. Some days he would cover an entire sheet and send Bulos to fetch another; others, the slave would sit waiting for hours, tapping the cornel wood stylus against the frame.

When his inspiration was particularly dry, his daughter Photia would come out with a pitcher of herbed wine. She turned sixteen that year, looking more and more like his memory of her mother. Crossing the yard she was the figure of a marriageable girl, anklets tinkling, black hair tucked in a kitchen-bun, holding the pitcher aloft as she stepped with careful grace in fancy sandals. But when she looked at the tablet, tracing the waxy etchings with a finger, she became as wondering as a child regarding some mystery of adulthood. Sophocles had indeed made his name with words. He was no different from his neighbors, though, in raising an illiterate daughter.

Colonus was far enough from the center of town to be free of the noise and stench, but close enough for him to stroll to the marketplace several times a day. When the sun had climbed some distance above the construction cranes on the Acropolis, Dexion would leave his garden and go into town. There he would make the rounds at the usual market stalls—the wine merchant, the fish-monger, the bookseller with his racks full of imported scrolls—and send his purchases home with Bulos, because he was loathe to see his wife's expression when she discovered how he had spent the household money.

Sophocles himself would linger at the market for several more hours, never seeking attention but very much aware of his status as a local celebrity. Often he would encounter younger poets in the stoa, who would address him outright if they were bold, or simply orbit around him if they were not, eavesdropping from a distance.

He had met the young Euripides this way. The long-nosed, large-eyed youth had attached himself to his idol's shadow, staring with such plaintive ardor that Sophocles at last felt obliged to bring him in out of the cold. The young man plied him with questions, but not the ones Sophocles would have expected: what did the great Dexion wear when he composed his award-winners? What sort of stylus did he favor? What sacrifices to Dionysus did he make before a performance?

Never did the boy ask his views on the role of the gods in mortal life, nor about the proper sort of hero for a tragedy, nor even about the technicalities of his choreography or meter. And when that bizarre exchange was finished, Sophocles didn't see his admirer again until four years later, when, on the boy's first attempt, his work placed a respectable second behind a tetralogy by Neophron.

The entire incident made Sophocles suspicious that he had been the victim of some sort of witchcraft—that some fraction of his talent had been spirited away while Euripides had distracted him. For Dexion, despite the adulation that followed him in his public life, was always sure that his most recent festival victory was his last one. Was he not saddled with the kind of good fortune that attracted malevolence? What man so honored was not secretly despised? See it behind that genial grin of the tavernkeep, the stinging spirit of Nemesis; see it in the eyes of the Dipylon whores, cockteasing from behind the orthogonals, and in the stare of the old woman who sweeps the ashes from Loxias' shrine. Against these attacks he was obliged to wear a little bronze phallus by a chain around his neck, and never to pass an overturned beetle in the street without flipping it upright. Yet what precaution was ever enough against the determined spite of one's own countrymen?

And so, despite the pleasantness of such afternoons, he would return to his house in a dark mood. Photia would seek to soothe him with a plate of savories. Bulos, meanwhile, would read back the lines he had dictated that morning, and Dexion would spit in disgust, and order most of them scratched out. Nais would then come forth from her quarters, her hands and forearms broiled red, the pouch of her chiton wet with the steam of her laundering pots. In his wife's eyes there would be a look that was faintly opprobrious, mouth twisted in bemusement at the many ways grown men found to waste their time.

"Did you see our son in the market?"

And he would answer, "Not in the stoa, no."

"Oh, the stoa," she would say, nodding her head in such a way that she communicated her meaning: scribbling verses was work barely worthy of a man, but idling in the stoa was a rank betrayal of their marital compact. Looking at Nais, he could see the opportunity was there to despise her—the afternoon sunshine, after all, was harsh on skin that had long since puckered and sagged, and what had been the lustrous sheen of her black hair had cracked, like the façade of an unkempt fountain showing its grout. She was a handsome woman in the literal sense, in that there was now a mannish dignity about her. To penetrate her now seemed as incongruous as buggering some tough old Lacedaemonian drillmaster.

For all her husband's acclaim, Nais had never been to the theater. "My Dionysus grows in the fields," she would say. "He doesn't prance on the orchestra!" His career as a poet she accepted as any other wife might some faintly embarrassing foible of her husband, like chasing pretty boys. This lack of awe was as precious to Dexion as public admiration was unnerving. For this alone, he would continue to love her in that way, inscrutable to many, that men of legendary attractiveness loved women who were less beautiful than they.

"You might look for him when you are out, instead of indulging your hobbies," she said, and then waited, ready to leap down his throat if he dared deny his fatherly neglect.

"I saw his friends near the crossroads altar this morning," reported Photia, "though I didn't see him."

"You should see nothing on those errands, girl, but the ground in front of you."

"The good father speaks!" Nais mocked. "Now if he could guide his son half as well!"

This sparring over young Iophon lately dominated their conversation, now that the boy's disappointing nature had fully revealed itself. Sophocles' answer was always the same: a cluck of the tongue, a toss of the head, and the excuse, "He is a man now. What would you have me do about it?"

He would nap in the men's quarters during the hottest part

of the day. When the doves resumed cooing in the eaves, and the distant pounding of hammers resumed for the evening in the foundries in the Ceramicus, he would rise, re-drape his tunic around his aging frame, and head back to the market. For despite his ambivalence about his fame, despite the hangers on and his fear of demon envy, he was a good Athenian, and could not conceive of spending less than half his time at the stoa every day. To be seen there, to converse and be talked about, to honor the wise and confound the fools—this was the proper job of a citizen.

Nais was waiting for him outside the door.

"Someone to see you."

"Who?" he asked, surprised.

"He says he's Menippus, son of Myronides."

"Pericles' man? What does he want?"

"Who knows?" she shrugged, then added in a dry tone, "But you might ask if he knows where your son is."

Menippus, who was dressed as a civilian that day, was waiting for him in the garden. Bulos—Zeus strike him—had left one of the composition tablets on the stump, and his visitor was reading the verses there with a faint grin on his face.

"Those lines are rejected," said Sophocles as he approached. Menippus looked up, fixing a pair of hungry eyes on his host.

"Yes, but to glimpse the discarded lines of Dexion—is that not a greater joy than to hear the finished work of others?"

The poet answered by collecting the tablet and clasping it, face hidden, against his chest.

"I was at the theater last month," Menippus resumed, allowing the eagerness of his expression to signal what had happened there. "I saw your *Antigone*, sir. You may count me among your admirers."

Sophocles frowned. "Is that what you've come to tell me?"

Menippus snorted with amusement, thinking *Behold the temperamental artisan! He was not so diffident after his play, when he rose for his dozenth curtain call.*

"My business has to do with your leadership during the

Festival," he said, "which was noted by certain others. Dexion, your city has a proposition for you."

Chapter II

A TASTE OF RUE

"But now lend yourself to me for one brief, shameless day, and then, through all your days to come, be called the most righteous of mankind."
—-Odysseus, *Philoctetes*, l. 84-5

1.

When Menippus conveyed Pericles' offer to make him a general, it was not the first time Dexion had been called to public service. He had held a magistracy two years before, having been endorsed by the name-archon Lysanias to serve as Treasurer of the Greeks. That job had come with substantial duties: along with nine colleagues, he was responsible for the collection of dues from Athens' partners in the Delian League, transport of the funds to the sanctuary, and their dispersal to the appropriate subcommittees, contractors, generals, and temple-hierarchs.

This honor left him less opportunity for his real work than he preferred. Too much of his time was spent in meetings with either bored-looking aristocrats or *nouveaux riches* dazzled by their reflected importance. He was staggered by the many temptations the post presented him to enrich himself. For these reasons he was glad when his term of office was over.

After the board of review audited his performance he was certified to have served his city well. On stepping down he was rewarded with a fine brass wine-pitcher and a pat on the back.

But to be a Treasurer of the Greeks was, in essence, to do nothing more than collect money and spend it, which were things every householder did. It required no special expertise. On what grounds did Pericles believe he would make a competent military leader?

"Dexion, you underestimate yourself," said Menippus. "For who has led men more often than you, in circumstances where the whole city was watching?"

"Surely you don't mean to compare—"

"There's nothing to it!" declared the other, making a motion as if flicking lint from his shoulder. "Or shall I say, it is nothing a capable man like yourself can't learn very quickly."

They went on like this, with the poet voicing skepticism and Menippus dismissing every objection, until close on sundown. Menippus made what he thought was a series of decisive arguments: if Dexion agreed to serve, he would be only one of ten generals for the year. There was no chance he would be left alone to make a single tactical decision. In any case, there would be little risk of testing his military skill during the upcoming year of his service: the Persians, still smarting from defeat off Cyprus at the hands of Cimon, were content to glower defensively from Asia. The Delian allies, moreover, were offering no inconvenient resistance to Athens' protection. In the expert opinion of those in the know, the most that would be demanded of General Sophocles would be to accept the adulation of his peers, to supervise one of the annual shakedown cruises for new vessels, and to sport one of those nifty red overcloaks on his daily turns around the market.

"I thank you for bringing me this offer," he said to Menippus at last, "but I regret I cannot accept."

As he rewrapped his cloak to depart, Menippus stared at him with eyes full of mirth. He found the pattern of Sophocles' protestations suggestive: even the poets of Athens knew better than to accept any suggestion that the generalship was a sinecure. Everyone understood that the job had political implications. This told Menippus what Sophocles was only beginning to accept in his heart: he would indeed rise to Pericles' endorsement, and stand for general of his tribe.

And why not? Appearances of modesty to the contrary, Sophocles' soul was as fiercely competitive as any other Athenian's. To become general of his city was a singular honor—one Pericles himself had never surpassed—and would certainly place him on a higher plane of renown than Aeschylus or any other poet likely to follow him.

"That is disappointing. Will you promise your fellow citizens, at least, that you will reconsider?"

"Perhaps," said Sophocles, as he shut the garden gate and retreated indoors. He was ambivalent, bereft of words, and also feeling somehow unmanned by his indecision. Perhaps Nais would know what to do.

He found her spinning goat's wool in the women's quarters. This was a task she always hated, and so took special pains to represent it as her sacrifice. When he began to explain the purpose of Menippus' visit, she showed her impatience, cocking her lips at the abiding foolishness of men and their politics. The news that Pericles wanted him as a general did give her pause, however.

"Couldn't lord high Pericles be bothered to recruit you himself?"

"Aeschylus fought at Marathon."

"He went as a soldier, not pretending to be a general."

"Is that all you have to say about it?"

"Pericles needs allies against the demagogues," she said. "If you are eager to have your name used that way, you don't need my blessing."

"I don't need your blessing under any circumstances!" he snapped. "And there are other advantages." Then he stomped away, still dubious about the job but sure such an exceptional offer was worth more than a casual dismissal from the likes of her.

He next saw Menippus in the market, carrying a mullet wrapped in burlap. Though he intended to let his refusal stand, his legs somehow stopped on their own accord, and he was obliged to make pleasantries.

"Truly a fine fellow," he said, meaning the fish. "Where did you find him?"

"At the seller by the courthouse," said Menippus, angling it let Sophocles admire its slick, filmy visage. "And so unblemished! So many look like boxers these days, beaten to a mash."

"Yes, you will eat grandly this evening."

There was an awkward moment as Menippus wondered if he should raise the obvious issue, and Sophocles, half-wishing he would, could not force himself to make his escape.

"And so, have you reconsidered that particular matter?"

"I have, and I must say again that I decline."

Menippus shrugged. "Well, I can see the man is serious," he said to the mullet. "You will have to help me overcome my disappointment."

"That, I trust he can."

"Yet, I see no reason to inform our other friend of this news," said Menippus, searching Dexion's face.

The poet turned away, knowing the "other friend" was Pericles himself. He departed with a wave of his hand, saying, "That is your decision."

On his way back to his writing tablet he encountered someone else he had not expected to see. Against the steps of the Royal Stoa, surrounded by a gang of companions, reclined his son, Iophon. The boy was looking fixedly in his direction when Sophocles spotted him, but showed no sign that he was about to hail his father. Instead, Sophocles approached him.

"There you are! Are you hoping to learn something of the law by sitting on those steps?"

"So that's him, is it?" asked one of the other boys, pointing with his chin.

"Yes, that is my father," said Iophon, shaking his head in

affirmation as the young men, all pre-ephebes on the threshold of their military training, stared at Sophocles with frank admiration. It was not a look he was used to receiving from Iophon's acquaintances.

His son took almost entirely after his mother, from his wide, mobile lips and broad face to the soapy black locks that curled around his head. Adopting the depressing unanimity of every youthful generation, he also wore his chiton with one pale shoulder bare, like some strange species of effete workman. He was not a beautiful boy, Dexion had to grant, nor a particularly clever one. Yet on the few occasions he showed himself in the market, he did appear to be popular among his peers.

These qualities were things his father had to deduce, like a fisherman guessing the habits of some rarely-seen species. He had, in fact, lost Iophon years before to the brotherhood of the gymnasium. It was there, in the aromatic oils and dust and flirtations of the daily workouts, that the small, wondering boy he once cherished had slipped away. In the final break, the boy came to profess, loudly and often, that the public theater was terribly dull, and that he now preferred the new custom of private literary parties that were, by design, always held in proximity to wine. The quality of his father's fame underwhelmed him.

Yet here he was, showing his old man off to his friends. The poet would not have been more surprised by a month of full moons.

"Where is your red cloak?" a bud-lipped boy asked of him. When Sophocles frowned with incomprehension, the boy became impatient. "Your general's overcloak. You're supposed to wear one, you know!"

"He's probably having one custom-made," suggested Iophon. "My father is known far and wide for the quality of his costumes."

"Never mind the cloak. What about his armor?" inquired another boy.

"My grandfather was the best armorer in Colonus."

"Don't forget the transverse crest!"

"Maybe he'll buy you a panoply, too, Iophon."

"Not likely. He'll want me to go through that training nonsense," replied Iophon.

"You will do your training like everyone else," Sophocles said with some irritation, fixing Iophon with the end of his index finger. "And you will show your face at home tonight, boy! Your mother has forgotten what you look like."

The other snapped to his feet and, without a hint of puerile mockery, saluted. "Yes, general!"

Sophocles stalked back to Colonus cursing that fool Menippus, who had clearly been bandying Pericles' offer around the stoa. It should not have been a surprise: merely publicizing such an offer would earn Pericles nearly as much public credit as actually having Sophocles accept it. These were deep waters he was swimming in, he realized—full of slippery, repulsive creatures.

Yet beneath his disgust there persisted a glow of paternal happiness. Iophon had not looked at him with such pride since he was a very small boy; it was unprecedented that he would show the slightest awareness of the details of his father's reputation, or of his family's legacy. As patriarch, these were things he had every right to expect, but, like a penurious man, had learned to live without them. Having tasted them again, he was only aware that he wanted more.

When he reached home he shouted for Bulos. The slave was busy at the far end of the house, sweeping the floor. Sophocles called again, threatening to administer a beating. Bulos appeared in the doorway, out of breath, making no effort to hide his annoyance.

"Yes, master?"

"Fetch my small tablet."

The slave returned with a stylus and the board he used for domestic messages. Sophocles snatched them away and, in the middle of inscribing it, glanced up at Bulos.

"Put on your cloak," he said. "You're going out."

Moments later Bulos was on the road out of town, on his way to the house of Pericles and Aspasia in Cholargus. He would have to cross the River Cephisus on the way, and since it was spring, he was now obliged to make the crossing up to his armpits in icy water. At that price, he reasoned, it was only fair for him to get a peek at the message he was carrying.

Waiting until he was out of sight of home, he pulled the lead from the fold in his cloak. On it his master had written just a few words:

Sophocles says he will do it.

2.

On a hill west of the Acropolis, in the natural amphitheater facing the shore, the Assembly of the Athenians gathered to hear the city's business. Dexion was seated with the other generals-elect behind the rostrum, staring into the wall of citizens that spread above.

He was used to being on stage, but here he was bare-faced, without a mask or persona to conceal himself. And there were so many faces confronting him that morning; some ingrained with despair and some livened by wealth, beautiful ones and ones disfigured by disease, ones that spoke volumes and others like closed scrolls, and eyes like lodestones attracting or repulsing, each reflecting passions that mystified and appalled him. All were on display under the morning sun, like the contents of a library blown across the slope. The stories behind every set of features screamed to be read. Where the impact of a bigger crowd on a politician was merely additive—the more the better—to a poet like him the effect was exponential, rising in its power, until it became an immensity both awesome and exhausting.

The elections for generals were held in the tribal gatherings, but were subject to veto by the city Assembly. By the session's end, just as the citizen-legislators were getting hungry and bored, the magistrates commenced ratification of the generals-elect. As usual, there was little reaction to the names of the more obscure figures—Androdikes of Cydathenaeum, Glaucon of Kerameikos, Xenophon of Melite, Lampides of Piraeus, Cleitophon of Thorae, et al.—though there was some murmuring when the name of a young philosopher, Socrates, was read. (The crowd settled when the nominee's affiliation was specified as Anagyrous, not Alopece, the deme of the sophist.)

This marked the fourth straight year the tribe Acamantis had elected Pericles general. A rumble of opposition rolled from among the aristocrats, which made the archons lift their eyes. But although they waited for sentiment to crystallize one way or the other, and some of the general's allies began to applaud, neither faction managed to produce more than a brief stir. Someone shouted out his derogatory nickname—"old Squidhead," from the prodigious height of his head—to which a defender replied with his honorific, "the Olympian."

Pericles' election was allowed to stand.

Sophocles' nomination was greeted by a deafening roar. It went on with the ratification of the last candidate, as the general-designates were presented to the assembly as a group. With Sophocles in the very center, and Pericles inserting himself to his immediate right, the crowd cheered on with unmixed enthusiasm—no catcalls this time about Pericles' grandiose public spending, his personal ambition, or the hubris of empire. For the imperial apologists, it was a very good day.

The generals knelt before the presiding priest and received on their brows a daub of blood from a consecrated pig. Now Sophocles blushed like a bride bereft of her veil. He didn't hear the prayers uttered at session's close, and he allowed himself to be led out without paying much attention to who was tugging his arm. As the poet emerged on the street opposite the Areopagus, he realized it was Menippus who was escorting him, and that he was being led toward His Dolichocephalic

Splendor.

Pericles had already donned his cloak of office. It made an impressive display on his tall form, though the impression was somewhat undone as the smear of pig blood, dripping down his high forehead like a string of flung paint rolling down a wall.

He was jocular by Periclean standards, smiling through his red-tinged beard, manhandling Sophocles with a mighty forearm clasp and a drum solo on his back. "My dear sweet friend, you have been too long absent from my table!" he declared as he draped a sinewy arm around Dexion's shoulders. This was a physicality Pericles showed only rarely, but deployed well. Sophocles opened his mouth, choked, then let the tears of his acceptance wet his eyes. Pericles and Menippus looked at each other like proud parents watching their son instinctively reach for the spear.

"I'd say that went well," said Menippus.

"More than well! Not since the Persians came have the people been so united about anything."

"Then I have done my part," said Dexion, who was suddenly missing his composing spot under the little plane tree.

Pericles squeezed him harder. "But how is your dear Nais . . . and that wonderful boy, Iophon? He is almost old enough to take the vow, is he not?"

He stayed at the poet's side throughout the requisite observances. The generals, like fresh ephebes, were obliged to go as a group to the north face of the Acropolis, to the sanctuary of Aglauros, goddess of new soldiers, and there, at the altar, to collectively extend their arms over the blood-crusted marble. From there they mounted the Acropolis and, after wending their way around the stockpiles of wood and stone for the ongoing reconstruction, paid homage to Athena the Guardian in her temporary shack.

The goddess' crack-fraught image was hewn with a blunt blade from some ancient trunk of cornel-wood. Centuries of succor had reduced her to a gnarled lump, her arms and legs merely suggested, her face an embryonic swelling. It was said she was not fashioned by human hands, but had dropped straight from the sky, whence she would ultimately return. Sophocles stood by for the sacrifice and did his part to replenish the oil for the eternal flame. But in the end the attention of his fellow initiates, who glanced at him when they thought he was not watching, rekindled his self-consciousness. He was glad when the ceremony was over and he could escape, losing himself among heaps of marble accumulated for the new Propylaea.

He was looking out at the market through the columns of the old entrance, but hardly saw it. Instead, he was contemplating a new play. The story would be a prequel to *Antigone*, set in the time after the fall of Oedipus, but before the *Seven Against Thebes*. Last time, he had tried to convince his audience of Antigone's courage in the face of outrageous, institutional impiety, and by all accounts he had succeeded well enough. He never entirely believed this story himself—it stank of unfinished business, its success proof only of how far a skilled liar might go in the theater. His first-place prize was, in his eyes, nothing more than a loan which future work must redeem.

The new play would be called *Polyneices and Antigone*. The subject would be the forbidden love of the sister for her brother, and the tragedy the fate of Polyneices after he is fooled into an act of physical incest. When the hero recognizes the outrage of what he has allowed to be done, he knows the Furies will destroy him, but goes forth to his end without reservation or complaint. Antigone, meanwhile, broils in her shame, and by the end of the play lacks only the means by which she will end her misery. Creon becomes her instrument.

Standing above the city, the cloak of his new responsibility around his shoulders, the tragedian felt uncomfortably close to his themes. To know one's mistake—to accept one's transgression and embrace the inevitable—was all very well to write about, but weighed like a heavy stone on the heart of the living.

In her shack, Athena the Guardian stood earless in the lampsmoke. Gaunt an eternally stern, biding her time until her return to the blue, she seemed to repel his prayers like the light from her polished face.

3.

There was a persistent rumor in Athens about Dexion and Pericles that went like this: a quarter century before, when Aeschylus ruled the stage and Pericles was just one of many contending politicians, the archons broke with tradition regarding the judging of plays at the Great Dionysia. Pericles' main rival, Cimon, had just returned from a splendid victory by land and sea over the Persians in Pamphylia. As a special honor for him and the other returning commanders, the special jury of theatrical judges was dispensed with, and the generals given the ballot.

The result was a rare defeat for old Aeschylus. Cimon's jury placed him second that year behind the novice Sophocles, and though there was no evidence of collusion, it was widely assumed that the result signaled Cimon's partiality for Dexion. Given that Cimon had cultivated a grudge ever since Pericles' father, Xanthippos, had prosecuted Cimon's father, it was further assumed that the young poet was in Cimon's camp, and therefore opposed to Pericles.

But Sophocles was in political hock to nobody, and had always been on friendly terms with the Olympian. This was especially true early in their respective careers, before Pericles had, for purposes of cultivating his mystique, taken up the practice of bestowing his social graces sparingly, like some precious unguent. Back then Sophocles was already noted for his musicianship, and Pericles was an enthusiastic follower of the musico-social theories of Damon of Oa. Pericles and Sophocles would be seen together at symposia, discussing the edifying effect of a good tragic *emelia* or Cretan *iporchima* as they shared the pillowy hips of some Asiatic couch ornament, or admired some sharp-kneed lad. Dexion had, on one occasion, praised to him the looks of a particularly lovely boy, likening his smooth white haunches to a fawn's. To this Pericles replied, "Careful, Dexion, for although I don't say you're wrong, a politician must learn to keep both hands and eyes clean!"

After the death of Cimon, Pericles had less occasion to mix with mere poets. They did spend a spring day together during the archon-year of Philiskos, after Sophocles was heard to ask, in public, why his friend was turning the most sacred places of the Athenians into construction sites. Pericles responded by turning up personally at his door in Colonus.

"Come with me, my friend," he said, "if you want to know how Athens will look after we are dead."

And so he took Sophocles on a tour of their future city. Picking their way around the scorched and venerable stones of the old Athena temple, burned by the Persians, he paced out for him the footprint of the new Parthenon, which would be either the most grand or the most bombastic in Greece. From there they traversed the sites projected for the new sanctuary of Erechtheus, and the enclosure for Athena's sacred olive tree, and the towering new Propylaea that, vowed Pericles, would frame the splendor of the secular city from above.

"Surely you mean the opposite, that the gate will glorify the temples from below," corrected Sophocles.

"I mean both," replied the other, entirely serious.

The sun was bending toward the gulf when the presentation finally ended. As they descended the path back into town, Sophocles found himself impressed by the breadth of Pericles' vision, but also subtly unnerved by it.

"It scarcely seems given to mortals to plan with such confidence," he said.

To which Pericles laughed, saying, "Let us claim the confidence first, and try to merit it later!"

"Who will pay for it all? The allies?"

"Of course."

"But why should they pay for our temples?"

"Why shouldn't they?" he asked. "When you hire a contractor, Dexion, do you care what he does with the money? Do
you care if he spends it wisely, on his family, or wastes it on
wine and flute girls? Of course not, as long as he performs the
service you hired him for. The same principle applies here.
Athens will defend the Greeks, and in exchange for that
burden she wishes only to inspire them—to become what has
until now existed only in dreams. And who will say which
purpose will serve them best in the end? The Greeks pay for
security, and they get a vision of their greatness. It seems like a
bargain to me!"

However lofty Pericles' purposes seemed that day, Athens
had a way of leveling mortal pride. While he and Dexion were
descending they passed a stranger coming the other way. The
man was clad in sooty rags, his person suffused by the stench
of human dung, his arms and face so encrusted with grime his
features were barely discernible. Yet as this creature approached he seemed to recognize Pericles; pausing, he glared as
if personally swindled by him.

He began to rebuke the general in a loud voice, "How dare
you show your face in the house of the gods, Pericles! You,
who would enshrine your own ambition at the temples of our
ancestors! What need have we for barbarian enemies, when we
have your tyranny to fear? Come now, defend yourself in the
sight of ordinary citizens! Or are you too good to face a free-
born Athenian?"

He went on like this, shouting at Pericles' back as they
reached the market, following so closely that they could feel his
spittle on their necks. The other people in the street had
varying reactions to the disturbance: a few were amused, glad
that the Olympian was being held to account in such a public
way, while others seemed embarrassed by it. Most took it in
stride—as did Pericles himself, who continued to chat with
Sophocles in a calm, conversational tone. Although he was not
the target of the man's anger, it was Sophocles who was most
rattled by it, becoming at last unable to converse at all.

"It is not unusual," Pericles confided, "and the poor fellow must have his reasons."

"What an example for us all, Pericles!" the filthy Fury went on, "You, who foreswore the mother of your sons so you could live with a whore! How do you dare lecture any of us, with your record!"

Coming at last to the Areopagus hill, Pericles bid Dexion a good afternoon, and then went off to the Council House with his nemesis still in tow, shouting, "You think yourself glorious, don't you? But what does a self-important bastard like you know about glory? *What did you ever do for Athens, Pericles?*"

Sophocles learned the sequel to this incident the next day. The derelict went on haranguing Pericles until the sun went down, ranting and insulting him up and down the streets of the city. By this time they had gone a long distance from where they had met, and having arrived at Pericles' townhouse, the man was left torchless and alone in the gutter. It was then that Old Squid-head showed his quality: just as his tormentor was about to face his retreat through a maze of deserted, unlit streets, Pericles sent a slave with a lantern to escort him to his hovel. At this kindness the man was struck dumb—either because he had lost his voice abusing Pericles, or in wonder at a leader who, in the end, seemed to think only of the safety of others.

4.

The evening after Sophocles's election he was invited to the great man's house for dinner. All the other new generals were there, along with Aspasia, who was the only one in the hall without official rank but the best strategist of them all. And what a singular performance she achieved! At the same time, she ran the staff, played the couch ornament, and conducted the kind of conversational midwifery that made each guest feel as if his hesitant musings were the most interesting things ever uttered. She was poised on the couch opposite his, her face leaded and burning, dipping with languid wrist into the relishes, saying nothing at all to Sophocles with her crimson mouth but everything with her eyes. It seemed his taste for beautiful tramps was no secret to her. She shot him looks that seemed to share a private joke between them, as if her silence was evidence of some secret crush, and that her arts were no match for his. And yet he almost believed it was an accident when, as the dinner dishes were cleared away, he caught a glimpse of aureole under the top of her chiton. Dexion, flushing like a schoolboy, shifted on the cushions. Brazen Aspasia, who noticed such things, waited for him to regroup, and gave him a wink.

Now what is this? Sophocles asked himself, not unintrigued. Damnable weakness! For he suspected, with all the foreboding of the doleful womanizer, that he had enough depravity left in him to seek an answer to his question.

"You must come visit us sometime," said her precisely moving lips, "with that new play you are writing. Even Pericles will drop his work for that honor."

Since his election it was exactly as Menippus had promised: little was demanded of Dexion but to strut around the market draped in red, receiving the salutes of the ephebes and favors from the merchants. He would come home at night with a self-satisfied glow on his face that Nais would immediately commence to mock—until he presented her with a four-foot eel that a fishmonger had shoved into his hands for nothing. At this she was struck speechless, holding the fish before her, stiff-armed, as if it would wriggle out of her grasp.

"By the gods, how do you expect me to cook something so big?" she asked, managing at last to fashion something like a complaint.

Her aplomb did nothing to help him face the reality that he was now a powerful public servant. Instead, his cloak of office still felt like nothing more than a costume. Nor was he inclined to invest in a new panoply of arms and armor—what would be the point, he reasoned, when the shield and spear he used as an ephebe were still perfectly good? He searched through the mess in the back storeroom of his house to dig them out. After thirty-five winters of mildew and the wet, the spear shaft had warped into a bow, and the shield had become misshapen from being compressed between the wall and an old whetstone. Trying to loft the shield with his left arm, he discovered the leather carrying-straps were nibbled to nothing by mice, and that his middle-aged wrist could no longer slip through the armhole.

No armor was necessary at the dedication ceremony for the year's new triremes. As he walked the road to Piraeus, he was appalled to find he merited an entourage. This included some respectable citizens, who took the transit of a general through their neighborhoods as an opportunity to make a gift of sage advice to the state. To these Dexion thought it best to nod, and agree that yes, the proper routing of gutter-water was indeed a matter of national importance, to be referred immediately to the attention of the archons. His escort also included a number of citizens of lesser means, who made neither suggestions nor demands but seemed content just to move in the proximity of power. Among them, Sophocles was pleased to glimpse his son, who watched from the margins of the crowd with a look of distracted enjoyment on his face, as if he was absorbed in a fine show. It was a look the boy had never worn at one of his father's plays.

Down at the shore the day had dawned with pitiless severity, the heat soaring, the few forlorn clouds in the sky hanging as if uncertain which way to cross the blue. The navy's new ships were already launched. They were, in fact, little more than empty shells, without crews, cordage, or arms, their oarlocks plugged with leather. Unballasted, the hulls rode high in the water, their newly-pitched planks shining in the sun like the down of newborn birds. After the blessing they would be hoisted ashore again and stored for months in the arsenal to await the appointment of a private contractor to pay for their complete fitting-out. Under such circumstances Dexion thought the ceremony somewhat premature—like announcing the subject of a play without a chorus or a protagonist.

He watched the proceedings from the generals' box without really seeing it; he was rarely much at ease in the harbor town, where the very air was redolent of barbarity. With the growth of the Athenian navy had lately come a burgeoning of the city's trade. The combined odors of commerce in the Middle Sea now clashed and competed from ramshackle stalls—cypress logs from Crete, Phoenician dates, Hellespontine mackerel, Cyrenian rosin, Arabian asphalt. On his way to the quay, he detected the slight mildew of animal skins loaded for freight, and of Carthaginian blankets, and Gaulish woolens, and Lycian rugs. When the breeze shifted, there was the perfume of frankincense from Tripolitan Syria, and Somalian myrrh, but also from the fringes the pall of human dung, which even the most diligent slave dealer could not cleanse from his wares.

Far away the priests intoned and spilled offerings into the water from silver bowls; from some bronze torchier a flame kindled in Poseidon's temple consumed the bundled bones and sheaves of fat dedicated to the god. The poet, gazing over the water to the southwest, thought he saw a glint of sunshine from the sanctuary of Athena on Aegina. He was engrossed in looking for it again when a commotion cut through his reverie.

It seemed at first as if the port was under attack. Young men and boys were running from the city, dispersing into every court and backstreet where people went about their daily business. As they swept toward the shore, a disconsonant buzz rose in their wake, as the citizens of Athens received whatever news had arrived with loud, public dismay.

The closest of the self-appointed messengers was a small boy, no older than nine or ten, whose thin, naked body was sunbaked as deep black as the newly-pitched ships. The boy had managed to out-run his competitors by squeezing between the legs of anyone in his way. But when he saw Pericles himself sitting there, backed up by the full council of generals in all their official finery, he pulled up short. Then he stood mute as the Olympian rose to his feet.

"Well then, out with it!" said Pericles. "Or must we pay to hear what you've been telling everyone else for free?"

He tossed an obol in the dust. Retrieving it, the boy cracked a mercenary grin.

"Damaged ships put in last night at Anaphlystos. They were attacked by the Samians."

5.

"I would tell you about the people of Samos," Aspasia was saying to him, "but you would not believe me."

It was one of her peculiar habits, to talk about politics in bed. Dexion had not found it distracting in the beginning, when the newness of his position made him senseless to anything but his immediate pleasure. She had, in fact, counted on this carelessness to draw him in, as if dropping a line of breadcrumbs between the twin edifices of her built-up shoes. As he flitted up the scented path, past the tinkling silver anklets on her parted legs, he was not poet enough to think of verses sweeter than what he found at its end. And when he hesitated there, she pushed two fingers—shamelessly, fingers of her right hand—into that tender juncture, the gold of her antique ring, a Phrygian signet, cold and thrilling against the summit. She pleasured herself before his eyes, until he was as stupid-seeming as any other man, and she was amused just at that moment to ask, "Have you ever smelled the scent of pines on the streets of Priene? The great Cyrus walked those roads, and knew them worth possessing. If someone must rule it, what city deserves the honor more than Miletus, I ask you?"

"I can think of none other," said he.

She continued to expound, providing historical context as he climbed up on her. "The war over Priene started last year, before Diphilos surrendered the archonship. Samos struck first, smuggling in their troops in converted mer-chantmen. They had driven the Milesian garrison from Mount Mycale before word of the attack—*Ouch. Don't be in such a hurry, my love*—before word of the attack crossed the Meander. But what Samian has ever conducted his business in honorable fashion? They are a race of swaggering, cowardly braggarts, impressed by nothing but force—*Yes, move a little side to side, that's the way*—it is a certainty they will despoil the place before they give it up."

"And your view has nothing to do with the fact that you were born Milesian?" he asked.

"What an oaf you are, to impugn the motives of a woman who accommodates your cock!"

"I stand ashamed, then."

"As well you should! And mark my words: the Samians are better cheats and liars than warriors. The Assembly knew it well when it voted to intervene on the side of Miletus. Ask anyone who went with our fleet to settle the matter last year—against Athenian steel, the ringleaders showed their true nature, running away to exile in Sardis. Pericles found the rest of Samos—the common people—as hungry for self-government as children. And he gave them what they wanted, so the island would be pacified and the aggression of their nobles would never again trouble Ionia."

"Until now."

"Until now," she repeated, a bit rueful. "You must know that no one expected the exiles to return. When Pericles left, the democracy was established on a firm footing. There was no question of a reverse. If we have made any mistake, it is underestimating Persia's hatred of the democrats. Don't doubt it, my love. It is the satrap who is behind this rebellion. Pericles told you the truth as he knew it when he promised there would be no war."

He made no reply until, with a tightening in his extremities, he signaled he was reaching the end. Aspasia, who was expert in noting these signs, pushed him out and held him as he climaxed in her hand. For several moments they stared at each other, until Sophocles asked the question that was long on his mind.

"Shall I assume, then, that you've invited me here on the Olympian's behalf?"

Aspasia smiled, regarding with learned detachment the contents of her palm.

"Poet or slave, it is always the same," she said, and then looked up at him with eyes half-lidded with reproach. "Assume what you want. Only know that I have peons for such work, if that was all it was."

"And is that the work to which you will return, while *he* is away?"

She smiled. "You have such contempt for me, Dexion! It makes you most ordinary, I think. But if you must know, I will spend that time with my writing tablet."

"Writing tablet? Why?" Sophocles asked, testing her. It was one of the worst-kept secrets in Athens that Pericles and Aspasia collaborated on his speeches.

"There will be a funeral oration. Men will die in this war, of course— Relax Dexion, not you! This is an important campaign, and Pericles must have his speech just right."

Walking back to Colonus, he went torchless, his general's cloak balled under his arm. To be sure, he'd had more than his share of women and boys in his time, and against that experience Aspasia's skills were no more than above average. But there was something else about the woman, he thought, that conveyed an official quality both impersonal and edifying. It was as if he had lifted Athena's golden chiton to glimpse the goddess' ivory ass in the Parthenon, or been lent the state barge for some private tour of the harborside stews. Was it how she spoke with that unique mid-Aegean accent, somewhere between Athenian precision and Ionian swank? Was it those little sculptor's tits? Or was it the way she smelled of the oily stuff they used to perfume the cult statues?

His lust. Golden Sophocles in his youth had no trouble attracting admirers, and with experience he'd learned to make his looks serve his purposes. As time passed, though, he was slow in noticing the change in how they all saw him: at some point as those soft contours eroded to crags and his beard grew, they all began to look at him differently, as a thing of distinction but not as an object of desire. Yet the gods had fashioned him with no appreciation for his mortality. When he watched the boys in the ballfields, or the arms of the girls lofting their baskets, or clambered into the beds of uptown courtesans, he was still a boy of twenty. A mature gentleman of fifty-five, he still pursued them all like a feckless virgin, eager for experience he had already gained over and over. All the while he was increasingly aware of how foolish he must seem, losing himself in those snatches that never changed, never yielded fresh secrets. He swore each time was the last. And yet when flatterers like Aspasia crooked their liveried fingers, he complied with shaking knees.

He puzzled over this perversity all the way home. He was glad of the distraction, for in the morning he would embark for Samos. If the winds were right, he would board ship for the war he was promised would never happen, but now accepted as his obligation. In this sense, the consolation of Aspasia's bed was unnecessary. He had been prepared to suffer his fate the moment he swore his oath before the Assembly.

Then it occurred to him—Aspasia was spotless. For all he had seen of her, she had not a blemish, not a birthmark, not a scarlet freckle from too many turns in the sun. The thought chilled him; it seemed Pericles' woman was statuesque in more ways than her bust or her smell. He shuddered as he reached his house, and quaked as he pulled off his clothes, unable to control the quivering of his limbs until he reached his bed and, finding Nais there, wrapped his body, still fragrant with adultery, around his wife's soft frame.

She awoke with a start a few minutes later. Heart pounding, he lay frozen, waiting for her to sniff out his shame. But instead she pushed her tear-streaked face close to his, and surprised him with a kiss—a wet, affectionate nuzzle that was more adolescent than wifely.

He stared at her. "What is it?" he asked, and waited for an answer until he suspected she was still asleep. He planted his lips on her forehead.

"You trouble me," Nais said suddenly.

"That isn't what I want."

"You trouble me, but what will I do if you don't come back?"

"I will come back."

Watching the gleam of her eyes in the half-moonlight, he felt a surge of relief—that she had not accused him of whoring again—and self-loathing—that he had been whoring again. But instead of saying anything more, he saw her lids close, and her head turn as she threw off the coverlet. For the second time that night, a woman offered him her back, pressing herself against him as he, pleasantly aroused, left behind all fear at last.

Chapter III

THE HIPPOCAMP SEES HIS SHADOW

"No, let me see fear, too, established, where fear is fitting; let us not think that we can act on our desires without paying the price in pain."
—Menelaus, *Ajax*, l. 1080

1.

The staging beach at Keos appeared at last from out of the shadows. If Sophocles had the stomach for it, he would have risen to his feet to see it better, but the motion of the hull made him reluctant to stand. Instead, he waited until the watch fires appeared over the swells. Turning to the helmsman, he fretted, "Do you see the pull-out? I don't see the pull-out."

"I see it," said the other, pointing with his chin at two small signal-fires north of the sailors' camp. This was the spot where, after generations of experience, the Athenians had learned that the beach shelved most gently to shore. Between the markers, another ship was being pushed by her crew, their efforts supplemented by a large windlass mounted far up the beach— perhaps the very same windlass he had seen when, as a young man, he had sailed to Delos to dance the *geranos* in honor of Aphrodite.

The helmsman leaned against his steering oar, making a

kind of clicking sound with his lips that had annoyed Sophocles ever since they rounded Sounion.

"With this breeze, we still have a long wait," the man said, and resumed his constant, infernal shucking.

"Great Hera's tits, stop making that sound!" Sophocles finally shouted in exasperation.

The sound of his voice above the wind and wash of the sea drew curious glances from the archers at the ship's bow. The old bosun, who had spent the entire journey on the catwalk between the ranks of oarsmen, stuck out his head just above the level of the topdeck.

"Everything alright, sir?" he asked.

"It is now," the poet replied. At long last, after his outburst, the helmsman's lips went silent. It was the first order Dexion had made as a field general.

After they landed he lurched and weaved around the beach as if he was still afloat. He was acutely conscious of his own helplessness as he leaned ankle-deep in the surf, waiting for the oarsmen to file off and Bulos to debark with his personal baggage. When the slave appeared they shared not a word— only a single glance, through eyes rimmed with puke-green, that betokened their mutual misery. With no apologies, Sophocles added his shield and day-pack to the burdens on Bulos' back. He was in no condition to take pity on slaves.

There were sixty triremes on the beach but only a handful of figures to tend them. Once free of the confines of their benches, Athenian oarsmen liked to retire well out of sight of water—in this case, on the plain over a little rise of scrub and jumbled rocks.

Mounting the hill, Sophocles beheld an enormous camp with hundreds of fires and some twelve thousand Athenians gathered around them. Since they were camped on a friendly shore, their mood was relaxed; there were oarsmen dancing to the flutes, feasting, or drinking wine from their canteens, and some trying to do all three at once. Walking on, he saw archers bent over their dice games, and still others lounging half-covered with blankets, bobbing female heads concealed at their laps. All of these needs were cheerfully fulfilled by enterprising Keotes, who had long appreciated the commercial possibilities of Athenian naval operations. A small flotilla could easily deliver as many customers to their doorstep as lived on the entire island; Pericles' huge war-fleet more than quadrupled the island's population. To supply them, the natives had erected a permanent market—a wooden arcade with a well and space for stores, and an adjoining tower from which to keep eager watch for the arrival of their customers.

Dorus, Menippus' aide-de-camp, found Dexion's party as they scouted a place to collapse for the night.

"You can't camp here," he whistled through a set of gappy teeth. "You're a general!"

"As a general, I claim the authority to sleep where I please."

Dorus glowered, eyebrows kinked. "You must come with me anyway . . . you are late, and the Supreme Commander has called for a council."

"Would the Supreme Commander object if I piss first?"

"Hmm—perhaps the general would not mind walking backwards, and pissing as he goes—?"

As Dorus led them on a circuitous path through the camp and toward Pericles' tent, Sophocles' other priority—aside from the condition of his bladder—asserted itself.

"Can you tell me where I might find my son?"

"Didn't he arrive with you?" Dorus asked over his shoulder.

"If he had, would I have asked?"

The slave paused, reached into his cloak for his tablet.

"What ship did your son sail on?"

"The *Rhamnous*."

Dorus slid his index finger over the leaded surface, moving his lips slightly as he scanned the list of ships.

"The *Rhamnous* came in some time before you did. The crew has debarked."

"Can you tell me where?"

Turning up his hands in a hopeless gesture, the slave indicated the city-sized encampment around them.

The rest of the generals were gathered in a semi-circle on the far side of Pericles' tent, away from the eyes and ears of the *hoi polloi*. When Sophocles arrived he was greeted with a diffident silence. This was rare for him, and hurtful, yet hardly unexpected. The assembled brass was a far more select group than the mob in the Assembly that had confirmed him, filled with ambitious men who thought of Sophocles not as a national treasure, but a dangerous competitor. He could see it in the eyes of Xenophon of Melittos, the petty resentment; the glance of Cleistophon of Thoraeus actually chilled him.

His colleagues were seated on a rude bench made from the blackened keel of an old wreck. As their wide bottoms had taken up all the available space, and no one moved aside for him, Dexion was forced to squat with Bulos on the ground.

"Now that we're *all* here," said Menippus, with a faintly reproving look toward the latecomers, "we will proceed with our business this evening."

He was standing before them all with Pericles looking over his shoulder. It was typical of the Olympian to leave the speaking to Menippus, supplanting his mouthpiece only when the occasion demanded. In this instance, with no audience to impress with his finery, the Supreme Commander appeared in a plain cloak. Around him were arrayed his usual satellites: Lysicles the ex-sheepdealer, Evangelus his bookkeeper, Lampon his tame soothsayer. The latter had been reassigned from Italy, from the colony at Thurii, to accompany his master—evidence, if any more was needed, of how seriously the Olympian took the Samian campaign.

It was the first time Sophocles had seen Pericles since his afternoon with Aspasia. The moment presented him with typical ambivalence: guilt for the sake of the man he had cuckolded, yet with a hint of cheap superiority. Neither, he knew, were justified; Pericles had not married Aspasia, and in all likelihood had acceded to—even conceived—her infidelity. He pondered the question as he stared at Pericles. For all the understanding he had gained of his fellow men in all his years, he could see nothing beyond the crust of bland nobility on that face.

"Regarding the task ahead of us, gentlemen, we should neither ignore the dangers, nor exaggerate them," Menippus declared. "In these matters we believe there is no substitute for the kind of plain-speaking that is hardly heard in the Assembly anymore, but can only be welcomed by mature ears. As all of us here are men of experience, we therefore offer you everything we know, so that you may approach your duties with no illusions. We believe the truth will give you enough to think about.

"First, the difficulties. As you all know, we intervened last year in the war between Samos and Miletus to put an end to a situation that might encourage Persian meddling in Ionia. Our arrival came as a complete surprise to the enemy. Our forces were able to sail to the island unopposed, virtually into the harbor at Samos Town. With the help of the gods, we routed the oligarchs, and freed the Samian people to rule themselves. As a guarantee on the good behavior of those who remained, we liberated one hundred members of the local aristocracy, and removed them to Lemnos, where we believed they would remain in our power.

"The current situation is not as we left it. It appears that certain exiles found support for their schemes in Asia. The satrap of Sardis, a pantlegged gelding named Pissuthnes, had a hand in slipping the counter-revolutionaries back into Samos. He lent ships for them to retrieve the hostages from Lemnos, and also took custody of the garrison we left in the city. We must presume that those brave Athenians are even now suffering all manner of torments at the barbarian's hand.

"Every hour brings us closer to a reckoning with Pissuthnes—that is a certainty. But for the moment we must accept that the Samian tyrants are back in power, and that they are aware that we Athenians keep our oaths. They know we are coming. They will try to stop us. It is also a certainty.

"The enemy's ships, their *samaenas*, are easy to spot. You can recognize them when they approach by their wide beam—half again as wide as ours. Also, from the side, you'll see that their rams project somewhat above the water, like this." Menippus presented a hand edge-on, palm down, with his fingers flexed slightly upward. "We think they find some advantage to this— we don't know what that is. The wide beam, though, makes the samaena a stable platform. It's a better sailor in rough seas than a trireme. Bear this in mind when and if you have a choice of whether to offer battle. The higher the sea, the more advantage you give away to the enemy. As for exactly where they intend to fight—" He turned to a map of the Aegean pinned to the side of Pericles' tent. "—we can only expect they know our routes as well as any of these islanders. They might decide to meet us in the Cyclades, or *here*, off Ikaros, or even Patmos, *here*. Or they may be content to keep their crews fresh and wait for us to come to them. That strategy has been used against us for years—waiting in port and hoping Athenians wear them- selves out rowing to the battlefield. I say let them continue to hope!"

The generals laughed, and Menippus looked pleased with himself, until Pericles cleared his throat and refolded his arms. Menippus became serious again.

"The Samians have probably begged Pissuthnes for ships. The only fleets in the King's service that are worth anything are Phoenician, and so we must expect their reinforcements to come up from the south and east, possibly from the Carian ports. In what numbers they will come is impossible to say. For this reason, we will be sending twelve ships to round up our allies in Lesbos and Chios, and four more to keep watch for the Phoenicians. Callisthenes will be leading the ships going south."

At this acknowledgment, Callisthenes gave a curt nod, as if receiving this assignment conferred on him some air of valor. Dexion supposed, in fact, that intercepting the Phoenicians in all those stades of open water was an unlikely prospect, and all the distinction really meant was that brave Callisthenes would miss the battle with the Samians.

"So much, as I said, for the difficulties. Now to our advantages, which I think you'll find much more compelling. First, upon our conquest of the island last year the Samians did not fight us at sea, with the happy result that their entire fleet was captured in port. In addition to the giving of hostages, the settlement specified the reduction of the Samian navy to just ten ships. Assuming that the oligarchs have had only a few months in power, they simply haven't had enough time to build many more. We should therefore outnumber the opposition by at least four to one on the water.

"As for the land, from the size of the force we have gathered—larger than any ever sent against an island—you can see that we can land more than ten thousand men, which is equal to the entire free population of Samos Town, including the women and children. The town is walled, to be sure. But their old tyrant Polycrates seems to have spent more treasure on temples and aqueducts than on fortifications. The city walls should give us no particular trouble.

"More important than fleets and fortifications are the hearts of the men who use them. On this count as well, our friends, the Samians, have not covered themselves with glory. When the Greeks of Asia fought the forces of the Great King the first time, at Lade, the Samians betrayed their allies, the Milesians, in the thick of the battle. At Salamis, the Samians fought for Xerxes. At Mycale, they were counted among the King's vassals, but were thought so unreliable that they were disarmed before the fight. Keep these events in your minds when you meet our adversaries. They will tell you all you need to know about the character of those who oppose us."

Menippus looked to his patron, who made no move to come forward. Instead, the Olympian spoke from deep inside his own beard, where not even his lips seemed to move.

"Menippus has been most thorough. I have only one thing to add," Pericles began in a tone that was low and deliberate, as if he were sharing a secret. "To my knowledge, none of you have served with me at your current rank, and so you cannot be familiar with the manner in which I prefer to handle crises like this.

"It may surprise you all that I am the same age as our friend Sophocles. How handsome he looks sitting there, and how haggard I have become! The reason is not hard to guess: though he would deny it, it is because he has spent the last twenty years around pretty chorus boys, while I have spent far too much time at this business of war.

"Believe me, then, when I tell you this: it is an honor, but not a pleasure, to deliver funeral speeches to grieving widows. Yes, our cause is just. If not for the perfidy of those we face, what need would the Athenians have for a navy? What democracy has ever started a war? Yet when a city has lost its young men to battle, whether in defense or in aggression, it is as if Mother Earth has revoked the promise of spring. Judging from the way things have gone since Plataea, it seems that the Greeks will miss a few springs yet, and we all have a few orations yet to give.

"In my view, the inconstancy of men like the Samians is not worth the life of a single loyal Athenian. It is true that we go to war to defeat the enemy. But it does not follow that we must sacrifice more lives than we need to accomplish our goal. I like to think I make a pact with every man who answers the call to fight with me: give me your best effort, place your fate in my hands, and I will do my best to assure you come home alive. Insofar as it is up to me, you might as well count yourselves immortal, for all the likelihood that I will send you to your deaths!

"As my colleagues in this campaign, I expect the same of you. And so if any of you think of yourselves as a latter-day Achilles, if you are another Tolmides lighting out for Boeotia on a prayer and too few troops, I say thank you for your enthusiasm, but your services are no longer needed."

On this matter Pericles was not satisfied by unanimous

verbal agreement. In addition, he sent Lampon forward to exact a formal oath from every man present, in the names of Helios, Ge, and Poseidon, and Athena Polias—but not blood-thirsty Enyalios, who would see them all slain—that he would respect the scruples of the Supreme Commander.

2.

For the final run to Samian waters they gave Sophocles a new flagship—a trim, fast sailer with a good crew, called the *Helena*. Poristes, the captain, was in peacetime only a squid fisherman. In times of war, however, he was much sought-after by contractors loathe to see their benefactions end up broken and scattered on distant beaches. Poristes had yet to lose a ship under his command, though he had lost an ear—burned away in battle, along with much of the skin from left side of his face. Sophocles could not resist staring at these wounds as the captain presented himself: the scars that seemed to shimmer and drip down his cheek like fresh plaster, and the nerve-damaged mouth that trailed downward from the sturdy arc of his smile.

"Pleased to have you aboard. *Very* pleased indeed," he was telling Dexion, who wondered in turn if he was being made fun of, or if Poristes was rehearsing for a run at public office. And he went on, "For the man who wrote *that* play, a special honor: we have renamed the ship for you. She is now called the *Antigone*."

At this favor he barely restrained a groan of embarrassment. For in what way could anyone think this a good idea, to name a ship of war for a self-righteous scofflaw, a denier of the very prerogatives of state power? It seemed as foolish as hiring a nursemaid named Medea. Had the man even seen the play?

But he had one good reason to be courteous to Poristes: the captain had agreed to take his son aboard as a passenger. Only with much difficulty had Sophocles found Iophon in the camp at Keos. The boy was sitting amongst a party of true rustic lowlife—the fourth or fifth sons of dirt-poor Oropian goat-herds with nothing to lose but their lives and the shit under their fingernails. Upon seeing that Iophon was from Athens, and better yet the son of a famous poet, they plied the boy with wine and flattery. When Bulos brought him back, the boy was deep in devotion to Dionysus.

"Do you think I brought you along to embarrass yourself and your family?" asked Sophocles. "Did I not tell you to find me as soon as you landed?"

To which Iophon drew his legs straight under him, saluted unsteadily, and lost his balance. He was unconscious before he hit the ground.

Across the width of the Aegean the Athenians saw little evidence of their enemies. Off the south coast of Ikaros a ship with a peculiar, wedge-shaped profile was glimpsed by a patrol. Two ships gave chase, but lost her in a squall. Callisthenes likewise failed to report any contact with the Phoenicians.

This quiet filled the expedition with apprehension; word spread of a huge Persian-Samian fleet hoping to ambush them from under the shadow of Mycale. Pericles, though personally impervious to rumors, had to take this one into his calculations: an order went out that the fleet would not make directly for Samos, but to rendezvous instead on the north shore of the island of Tragia.

This was an oblong potsherd of an island, no more than fifty stades at its widest, midway between Samos and Leros. No one could remember the last time an Athenian fleet had touched there. Some said it was uninhabited, or inhabited only seasonally by fishermen. Others insisted it was either a nest for pirates or, more worryingly, the spawning ground for a race of giant birds that plucked men from the decks of their ships and dropped them directly into the maws of their monstrous spawn.

What was sure was that Tragia had no large beaches, and so would force the fleet to disperse through its many tiny, unknown coves. The island's sole advantage, it seemed, was its lack of a tall central peak, behind which an enemy fleet might hide. From there, with a favorable wind, the crossing to Samos Town would take only a few hours.

The suspense ended as the *Antigone* approached within sight of Tragia. Dexion's flotilla was, as usual, bringing up the rear, although under the guidance of Poristes, his four ships had succeeded in keeping in contact with each other. The sun had already sunk into the Aegean. What was left of daylight was filtered weakly through a bruise-colored overcast that seemed to swell downward, as if the sea was trapped under a water-logged tent. Worse, the wind had risen until it blew hard from the west, whipping up eight-foot swells piled up as thick as phalanxes on the water. As the hull began to pitch Sophocles hung on by his bloodless knuckles. When the *Antigone* bottomed out, suspended by its bow and stern over the troughs, he could look over the port rail and watch the blades of all three oarbanks churn high and dry in the air.

"Bury her nose in the waves!" Poristes shouted to the helmsman, who was wrestling with the steering oars. Battered and groaning, the ship turned with agonizing slowness, until her beak was pointing south of Mycale, toward the island of Lade. Peering between the peaks of water, Sophocles could see the green shadow of Tragia in the distance, and beneath that, intermittently between the swells, a vast, confused mass of wooden hulls, sprits and masts.

He blinked, wiping the sea-spray from his eyes. He looked again—the spectacle was still there, spread now over a wide stretch of water. Columns of smoke ascended in raking fashion toward the clouds, and beneath them, tiny tongues of flame.

"The gods have blessed us!" Poristes cried over the blast of wind. "We have met the Samians."

3.

The sea settled just as the *Antigone* came abreast of the north coast of Tragia. Dexion could now take in the scene in its entirety.

From the northeast flew the enemy samaenas, a dozen strong and formed up in a wedge. Their profiles, like great metal-tipped plows carving the sea, were hulking and murderous; the triremes, by comparison, seemed thin, waspish. Over the unsettled water the broad-beamed Samians moved with absolute steadiness, none of their precious momentum wasted sideward. Even to an eye as inexpert as Dexion's, their ships' superiority in a high sea was obvious. The enemy had picked the perfect conditions for an attack.

In their path the Athenians were strewn in various states of disarray. Some of their ships were already immobilized, oars snapped by the enemy rams, their hulls peppered by flaming arrows as the Samians passed. The triremes ahead were struggling to turn away from the attackers, but were rocking dangerously on their keels, their oars finding poor purchase in the swirling water. Further beyond, Dexion could see tiny figures—his countrymen—struggling to refloat several vessels that had already been beached for the night. If these got into the action at all, it would be too late, after the attackers had smashed the rest of the fleet.

As he watched, a samaena crushed a stalled trireme broadside. The ram, which was sharp and long like a leather-maker's punch, disappeared into the body of the Athenian. The sound of the collision followed later—a thunderous, fibrous *crack*, like the rending of a misshapen tree. This was followed by the screams, thinned by distance, of a hundred terrified oarsmen as their ship was torn in half.

As all the world seemed to pause and watch, the Samian backed water to extricate her ram. From the vast cleft the weapon withdrew cleanly, and like a jar suddenly uncorked, the stricken Athenian disgorged its contents. The bobbing heads of live and dead oarsmen spread over the sea, surrounding the trireme as it settled to its topdeck. With most crewmen capable of no more than the most rudimentary dog-paddle—Sophocles himself could not swim at all—few of the men in the water would survive.

Without drastic action, a similar fate awaited the rest of the Athenian fleet. When Dexion thought about it later, the gap between this realization and his next action was frighteningly short: turning to Poristes, he issued a command that surprised them both as soon as it left his mouth.

"We must attack. Give the orders you must."

Poristes gave a half-step forward, cocking his surviving ear as if he had misheard.

"Don't make me repeat myself!" warned the poet.

"Attack broadside to the sea? We're as likely to wreck ourselves."

"So be it."

With an outburst of archaic mariners' curses, Poristes turned to his bosun. The pipers quickened the cadence, and the steersman, with a dubious expression, dragged his starboard oar to bring them about, on a course to pursue the Samians. Looking astern, Dexion watched as the other three ships in his squadron followed the *Antigone*'s lead, forming themselves up in a staggered line off her port quarter. Offense became the Athenian character: from a place seemingly beneath the sea, hundreds of hidden oarsmen asserted their presence, chanting "*ryppapai, ryppapai.*" It was an enthusiasm borne of ignorance, for most of the oarsmen could not see the danger awaiting them. Yet the song thrilled Dexion as much as any ovation he had received in the theater.

"Is it a battle, father?"

Sophocles found Iophon standing behind him.

"I told you to stay below."

"You couldn't have been serious," the boy calmly replied. "How am I supposed to see anything from down there?"

"You will see what I want you to see."

"Then why did you bring me, if not to face war?"

"By Zeus, obey me!" Sophocles cried.

Iophon didn't move.

Though Dexion's triremes made ugly progress—rolling on their beam-ends, sliding down the windward faces of the swells—they made an instant impression on their adversaries. The swagger abruptly went out of their maneuvers. They sped up, tightened their line; they chose not to ram an Athenian that was immobilized in their path, passing her by as her oars flailed. The vaunted samaenas, it appeared, were steady but slow.

The poet was filled with the confidence of a predator in sight of his kill. As he clung to his shelf, riding the rocking *Antigone* through the troughs and up the lee side of the swells, his intense focus on the targets ahead banished all anxiety. Poristes shouted that the ship would swamp. Sophocles barely heard him, feeling instead as if some god was lifting his ship by the outriggers, yanking her onward to some predisposed glory. The sight of the four gleaming rams forming a line off his right shoulder came as a powerful thrill.

Unnerved by the unexpected attack, the Samians paused. The light was draining from the west with an unnatural slowness, as if the day was reluctant to end. In that flat, tenacious twilight, a new factor appeared: a squadron of six triremes beating its way out from the shore, coming at the Samians from the other direction.

With the possibility of envelopment, the Samian warships broke formation. The Athenians, having much experience in such things, spread their line to trap the stragglers. As divine Hesperus, the first star of the night, gleamed on their spray-drenched rams, they assured their first capture: a samaena, turning this way and that, slowed to a drift as her captain realized he would not escape.

Coming closer, Dexion watched the enemy crew ship their oars. Time seemed to slow as the Samians abandoned their benches and poured out on the topdeck, each one bearing a spear or short sword.

"They're spoiling for a fight this time," observed Poristes, surprised.

"Then let them learn the consequences!" Iophon exclaimed. And he began to dance a little martial jig, cutting the air with a dagger he had secreted aboard in his tunic. His father, aghast, caught the boy's arm and snatched the knife from his hand.

"And who will save me from your mother if you hurt yourself?"

The archers and marines on the oncoming triremes rose to meet the Samians. One of the hulls in Dexion's squadron, the *Doros*, was the first to make contact. With a scream of abrading wood, the two vessels struck and their crews had at each other. A strange, unbidden thought occurred to Dexion: the sound of men fighting with blades was reminiscent of his father's armory, except the beat of metal on metal in the shop was less regular in time. It was a commotion he had learned to go to sleep by as a child—a sound not unlike battle.

Another trireme crashed into the Samian from the other side; the Athenians assaulted the defenders just as they had beaten back the attack from the *Doros*. They would have driven back the second wave, too, if a third trireme had not joined the fight, and a fourth. The Samian oarsmen were now trapped between multiple parties of invaders. Many of the latter had hoplite armor, and long infantry spears, and so could wear down the Ionians with impunity. The mass of live defenders began to dwindle.

With the conclusion foregone, Poristes murmured something to the bosun. The *Antigone* slowed, keeping a distance between herself and the knot of snarled vessels.

"Aren't we going to fight?" demanded Iophon.

"Poristes, get him below!"

Two archers appeared to drag the boy below as he kicked and cursed everyone in reach. Embarrassed at the scene, Sophocles buried his head; it took several moments before he realized he was still holding Iophon's knife. With a contemptuous flourish worthy of his acting days, he cast the dagger into the sea.

"That boy," said Poristes with a shake of his head, "was

born to trouble his fathers."

4.

In its reality, the battle was a complex and terrifying spasm of chaos. The story spun around it, on the other hand, was the picture of simplicity: in a surprise attack at dusk, the Samians attempted to inflict enough damage on the Athenians to discourage an invasion, but had been repulsed. In the telling the number of enemy ships had somehow increased from a mere twelve to an armada of seventy. The Athenian fleet suffered four ships damaged and two destroyed, against one Samian ship lost to fire and one captured. Pericles' fleet would hardly be slowed down by these losses. The rump navy of the Samians, however, was reputed to be finished as an offensive force. The talk around the Athenian camp was that the samaenas would never again venture out of port. The dispatch about the battle sent back to the Assembly was two lines long:

> Met Samian fleet near Tragia. Enemy was set to flight before nightfall.

A trophy was erected the next day on the promontory of the island closest to the action. It was a spare, spindly thing. Constructed out of a few Samian oars recovered from the captured wreck and a few helmets, it looked like the skeleton of some horrid creature that had expired on those deserted rocks. To Sophocles, it was hard to tell if it was a monument to victory, or starvation.

The story went that the battle had hung in the balance until Dexion saved them all with his decisive action. The intervention of his squadron from behind the Samians, though the sea was running against him, was hailed as a tactical masterstroke. As he came into the generals' camp on Tragia, wine cups and pats on the back were proffered from every direction.

"Quite a *show* you staged for us today!" declared Xenophon.

"Your best *production* ever, if you ask me!" The man was positively bursting with pleasure at his own wit.

"Get him his crown! Get him an ivy crown!" demanded Cleistophon.

"We've tried! There's not a sprig of ivy on this whole blasted rock!"

"We should at least give him his prize goat . . ."

"It makes me sick just to watch you cross the current, Dexion," said Lampides of Piraeus. "What possessed you to try it?"

All went silent to wait for his answer. Under the circumstances, with the generals making such a fuss over what was nothing more than a snap decision, he was tempted to throw away his reply. But the sight of all those expectant faces, each desperate to bask in some glimmer of reflected glory, aroused the showman in him.

"It was Dionysus, my usual patron," he declared. "To whom else can an actor attribute his good timing?"

Pericles, his pride contained behind pursed lips, stepped out from behind his colleagues and put his arm around the hero.

"Our friend Dexion understands what is at stake in this war," he said.

After applying a kiss to Sophocles' forehead, and giving a squeeze that rounded his shoulders, the Supreme Commander disappeared into his tent. The tribute to the victory went on through the night, with the prize for Dexion's "drama" delivered in the form of a dozen fatted goats that feasted all the generals and their staffs. Pericles, for his part, did not come out to celebrate. It was not his practice to make a spectacle of his good fortune.

And then there was the worrisome omen hidden inside their triumph—one that gave Sophocles brief pause, but etched deep creases up the height of Pericles' brow. The Athenians had used stories of Samos' poor performance in the Persian wars, and the ease of their last invasion, to convince themselves that this enemy would buckle at the first reverse. But at

Tragia the Samians had taken the initiative against a numerically superior force. When they were surprised, they resisted like Greeks; when they were forced to retreat, they did it in good order. This would be no quick intervention, but a campaign full of hard fighting. Despite Pericles' best hopes, there was no chance he would bring all the Athenians home.

5.

He had grown to hate Antigone because she refused to let him go. All of his characters spoke to him for a time; their voices became clearer in his head as the writing progressed, rising sometimes to a shout as the festival approached. But in every case they began to quiet after the premiere, until the time came when they became mere characters on a scroll, abstractions as surely dead as the petty spirits of doorways and crossroads once feared by his grandfathers.

But not this girl—this outlaw princess. She was not his best-drawn creation, or his favorite, but she was the most vociferous, costing him months of sleep, refusing to retire to a decorous literary grave. Lately her words seemed to come to him from the beach, where her namesake was parked. *O Sophocles, your mask is slipping*, she would say. *O Sophocles, your little boots won't save you from slipping up this time!* The bristling desolation of Tragia seemed to amplify her voice, which always resembled that of some woman in his life. Sometimes she sounded like his wife, sometimes Photia, sometimes Aspasia; occasionally he had to ransack his memory to recall which relative or lover she conjured. On the night after the victory she was unmistakably Nais, and she kept him awake to within an hour of daylight.

Frustrated, he rolled off the cushions and stepped over the snoring Bulos. Standing on the sand, he watched the dawn claw with rosy fingertips to rise above the mainland peaks. He strode down to the water; the hulls in his squadron were drawn up together, beam on beam, lean shadows in the gloom. To a less tortured eye they would seem indistinguishable, but Dexion could easily pick out the *Antigone* by her painted eyes. Instead of dish-like circles with balls set in the center, like those of some dumb beast, the flagship had almond, seductress eyes, with kohl-like rings and pupils set forward, as if permanently fixed on her next victim. They seemed to follow Dexion as he approached.

ANTIGONE: So here is the hero, blessed of Enyalios and Eris, and the well-robed one whom his countrymen call Athena Parthenos, the well-armed maiden. Greetings and felicity to you!

DEXION: How you disappoint your creator, princess of Thebes, who did not make cunning your sin! You know well you have no need to greet me, for you have followed me without mercy, like the Furies Tisiphone, Allecto, and Megaera, and banished from me all power of sleep. Keep your pleasantries, and permit me only the felicity of your silence!

ANTIGONE: O gallant warrior, can it be that your mighty helm has met with Samian club? Do you account yourself dreaming even now? For it has never been in my power to cost you sleep. For that affliction, you must blame only one man: Sophocles son of Sophilos.

DEXION: Yes, a dream this must be, because your words are a riddle I cannot solve—or that have no solution.

ANTIGONE: Pitiable man, who is a riddle to himself!

DEXION: Be not coy with your invocations, tormentor! Of this Athena Parthenos I care little, as I care little for gods unknown to my fathers. They burned the fat for

Athena Polias, the true goddess of our city, protectress
of field and hearth. To her the fighters at Marathon bent
knee, not some patroness of speculators and oarsmen!
For her we go to war to defend the Athenians.

ANTIGONE: Take care when you insult oarsmen,
Dexion, when you address a ship! And what is this about
defending the Athenians? Can it be that a figment like
myself can understand what we are all doing here better
than you, a general of the Athenians?

DEXION: The nature of this latest deceit escapes me,
for it is obvious that we sail to fulfill our oaths.

ANTIGONE: What oath did you fulfill when you bent
knee for the whore Aspasia, great Dexion?

The poet was distracted by the sound of loose oars dropped
in a heap on the dirt. Turning, he saw the officers of most of
the ships gathering from every corner of the cove, bringing
spare equipment with them. This was to be the last opportunity
for the crews to trade for replacements before the run to
Samos that day.

Poristes was also there for the morning sailor's market. He
was standing over a pile of oars so ancient they must have
stroked the waters off Salamis in the days of Themistocles.
From the way he was staring he had clearly heard the general
talking to his ship.

"It's not unusual to hear them speak," Poristes said before
Sophocles could deepen his shame with some feeble excuse.

"You can know a ship for years and hear nothing. And
then, just when they get a new name, you can hear them in
your dreams just as if they're whispering in your ear. It can be
as simple as that—they won't speak to you until you call them
by their right name," said the captain.

Chapter IV

SHIELDBREAKER

"But disobedience is the worst of evils. This it is that ruins cities; this makes homes desolate; by this the ranks of allies are broken into headlong rout. But of the lives whose course is fair the greater part owes safety to obedience."

—Creon, *Antigone*, l. 670-5

1.

The island of Samos presented a undulating outline just twenty miles long and ten broad at its widest point. Verdant and high-shouldered, it was famed for its fertility and its location as the Greek bridge to the East. The Strait of Mycale, which separated the island from Asia, was by ancient reckoning no more than ten stades wide.

To Hellenes with an ear for nautical Phoenician, the name of the high-peaked island sounded something like "lofty." Through the ages the place had also been known as Parthenia, Imbrasia, Anthemis, Dryousa, Doryssa, Phyllas, and Melamphylos. It was said that its first inhabitants were the Pelasgians who arrived before the age of metals. They came to mine the green clay that was peculiar to the place and held to be unmatched as a salve for wounds and a bleaching agent in the production of fine wool. Phoenicians, Leleges, Carians, and Achaeans followed, finding the valleys and slopes of Samos hospitable to the olive and the grape. Golden-shod Hera was born on Samos, on the banks of the river Imbrasos, in the shade of the purple-blossomed chaste tree. The goddess herself had since decamped for other quarters, but the Ionian Greeks honored her birthplace by erecting the temple that, by Dexion's time, was unmatched in its splendor.

Local bards sang of Ageos, the island's first king and a shipmate of Jason on the *Argo*. They never sang of Polycrates son of Aeaces, the tyrant of a century before who truly put Samos on the map. This was curious, for Polycrates was in many ways the most remarkable Greek of his time—an educated man, a patron of artists and poets, a redoubtable general, and a tireless builder. Polycrates' era began when he and his brothers Pantagnotus and Syloson, along with a gang of sympathetic merchants, took control of Samos Town when the rest of the people were out of the city. When the Samians returned from worship at Hera's sanctuary they faced a *fait accompli*—yet another in a long line of tyrants in possession of their city. They resigned themselves to the brothers' rule.

Polycrates soon found a pretext to eliminate Pantagnotus and drive Syloson into exile. For the next twenty years the tyrant went from triumph to triumph. Building on his island's wealth, he built a navy of one hundred blunt-nosed penteconters—the ancestors of big, modern samaenas—and swept the Aegean of all rivals. He conquered Rhodes, humbled Lesbos and Miletus. He made an alliance of equals with Pharoah Amasis, making Egypt dependent on Samos for her naval power. He took control of Rhenea, the small island adjoining sacred Delos, and made a spectacle of giving it to Apollo by stretching a chain across the strait to the god's sanctuary. From the Ionian coast to the Greek mainland, Samos was mistress of the sea, where not even the pirates dared to operate without Polycrates' leave.

At home, the tyrant undertook a building program that

dwarfed anything that preceded it. On Samos Town he bestowed a new circuit of high walls, spanning nearly forty stades, that made it almost invulnerable from the land. Her harbor was protected from the sea by a stupendous breakwater, the biggest yet seen, that rose one hundred feet from the sea floor and stretched more than two stades in length. The temple of Hera was renovated and enlarged, its massive roof raised atop more than a hundred columns each sixty feet tall.

Polycrates then turned to securing the capital's water supply against siege. Under the direction of Eupalinus the Megarian, his engineers dug a tunnel that stretched more than six stades from the springs of Agiades to a place inside the walls. How Eupalinus contrived to start the construction at both ends and have his workers meet in the center, deep in the limestone heart of Mount Ambelos, was vaguely understood to involve abstruse mathematics—which is to say, some kind of sorcery. In any case, Samos Town got its aqueduct, and Polycrates the glory of commissioning a wonder comparable to the monuments of old Egypt.

Having decorated the landscape with his works, Polycrates set about adorning his drinking couches. From Ionia and Italy came the lyric poets Ibycus and Anacreon, from Crotona the physician Democedes, from Megara the architect Eupalinus, from Samos itself the mathematician Pythagoras. Long before the floruit of Athenian genius, Polycrates the Samian hosted the most sophisticated table-talk in Greece. His example was not lost on later leaders like Pericles.

Polycrates' success soon began to attract other, less admiring sorts of attention. Pharoah Amasis, who was jealous of his good fortune, devised an ingenious scheme to rob Polycrates of his happiness. Under the pretense of friendship, he wrote a letter to the tyrant extolling his achievements, and expressing only hope that his reign continue to be blessed. However, Pharaoh argued that to perpetuate his good fortune he should anticipate the bad that would come. "It is not given for any man to enjoy nothing but endless prosperity," he advised. "I therefore beg you to protect yourself, dear friend, by taking it upon yourself to throw away whatever you value most. Indeed, you must not just throw it away, but put this thing forever beyond the reach of anyone. Only in that way can you forestall the Fates, who must otherwise deal you a reverse."

As Polycrates was a tyrant, and tyrants survive by anticipating challenges, he found Pharaoh's reasoning sound. But what to give up? Briefly, he considered having his infant daughter thrown from the high walls. Upon reflection, though, he had to concede that the girl was far from what he valued most. Should he raze the Temple of Hera, which of all his works he was most proud? He thought not, for it made no sense to appease the Fates by angering the goddess.

At last his plans settled on a particular signet ring—one of pure gold set with Scythian emerald—that he had worn since the day he had seized power. Being a superstitious man, Polycrates became anxious at the very thought of removing the ring from his person. Yet was this anxiety driven by nothing other than fear of losing his position—a disaster sacrifice of the ring might forever preclude? Amasis' letter convinced him this was so. With the same ruthlessness that had enabled him to kill one brother and exile the other, he strode out on the breakwater he had built, tore the ring from his finger, and threw it into the sea. He then withdrew to his palace to await what the Fates had in store for him.

When the rafters holding up his roof didn't collapse on him, and his island was not swallowed up by the sea, Polycrates began to recover his confidence. Nothing happened that made him suffer the least bit of trouble; the Samians, if anything, seemed to love him even more for his sacrifice. "So this was the hidden wisdom of Amasis' advice," he thought. "Because of what I have done, the people love me, and so will not plot against me." After a few days he became absorbed in the usual business of state. After a week, he forgot all about the ring.

Having been installed with the help of the wealthy merchants, Polycrates particularly valued the devotion of the humble people. He was therefore pleased when a fisherman came one day to his door with a gift—a swordfish so large it took three men to carry it into Polycrates' presence. Placing it on the floor broadside to the tyrant—showing it to be more than ten feet long—the fisherman bowed, kissed Polycrates' ringless finger, and said "I caught this marvel this morning off Mycale. And even as it was dying by my feet, I knew I could not sell such a prodigy in the market, but must give it to my king, for it is the only fish I have seen worthy of him."

Happy Polycrates replied, "Of the fish it may be as you say. But it is more important to me to have worthy subjects than worthy fish. Therefore rise, good fellow, and join me at table!"

As tyrant and subject set about sharing a meal, the cooks opened the fish's belly and made an astonishing discovery: there, perfect and whole as the day he cast it away, was Polycrates' signet ring. When the servants restored it to him, and explained the circumstances of its return, Polycrates wept with joy, his prior attachment to the ring now rekindled in his mind. "Now I am sure I am most favored by the gods!" he declared. For it seemed to him that even his efforts to deprive himself met with nothing but profit. And he called his scribe to write a letter to Amasis to share his good news.

Pharoah read the letter with a great deal of fear. "The gods must be preparing this Polycrates for some especially grim end!" he exclaimed. Not wishing to share the Samian's doom, Amasis sent a formal embassy to Polycrates to break their alliance. Yet so assured was Polycrates in his continued prosperity, the abrogation of the treaty caused him not a moment's concern. "If my friend thinks it best to go his own way, I will not deny him," he said, and turned his attention to the plans, presented by Eupalinus, to carve a giant image of the tyrant's face into Mount Ambelos.

2.

Pericles had the Athenians land at two locations on Samos.

Hoping to overawe the enemy, he ordered half his fleet ashore southeast of the capital, a few stades from Hera's sanctuary, and the other half at a beach to the west, just off the Asian straits. The men were then quick-marched to the town from two directions.

The morning was perfect for Pericles' show, with the sky an untrammeled blue, and onshore breezes to cool his men as they strode the land in their polished armor, shining in the sun like enameled figurines. The Samians, however, seemed underwhelmed: no alarm was sounded as the hoplites appeared, and no one was sent out to oppose them. Instead, the Athenians were faced with a locked gate, high walls, and guards staring back with withering disdain.

"This had to be expected," Poristes told Dexion. His squadron had landed at the western beach, and general and captain walked together to the town in ruts the troops had left in the strand. "Polycrates didn't give them that wall and aqueduct for nothing."

Dexion made no answer but watched the rest of the Athenians—the corps of oarsmen, almost eight thousand strong—as they trudged in from the beaches. Most were making for the siege camp the surveyors were laying out inland, just out of bowshot from the Samian walls.

From the sea, all approaches were blocked by the great mole. The blue-gray ring of Polycrates' fortifications protected the town on its three landward sides, including the southern flank of Mount Ambelos. The walls were forty feet tall and in excellent repair. The spectacle depressed Sophocles. He had somehow hoped the Samians would make the gloomy denouement of a siege unnecessary. After his tactical masterstroke at Tragia he expected some god to be winched down to make a sudden, orderly end to the tragedy. Was there anything worse than a play that wore out its welcome?

The next day messengers were sent to the enemy to offer terms. They were lenient: in exchange for surrender, the Samians were required to expel the oligarchs, restore the democracy, release their Athenian prisoners, and raze their walls. Having fulfilled these conditions, they would continue to serve as full and independent members of the Aegean League.

The Samian commander took the embassy inside, listened patiently to its offer, and sent it back with an insolent reply: Samos would only excuse the invaders from their land if the Athenians returned all prisoners, paid restitution for damage done to Samian ships and farms, and dedicated an apology at the Sanctuary of Hera. This commander, who was called Callinus, reportedly cut a modest figure—bald-headed with skin broiled brown like a slave, clad in a simple tunic and commoner's sword hanging from a baldric.

"Does he fancy himself a philosopher?" scoffed Menippus.

"I believe he does," replied the messenger, dead serious.

A council of generals was convened that evening. This time Dexion's colleagues competed to offer their seats to him; the hero, fearing a reputation for hubris, declined and sat on a stool some distance away.

Once again Menippus led the discussion, with Pericles standing behind and to the side, with Dorus and the other servants. The atmosphere was different from the meeting on Keos: there was no swagger in Menippus' manner this time, nor any whooping or carousing by the generals. The surprise attack at Tragia, and the Samians' determination to force a siege, had tempered them all.

"The following of you will each be responsible for a part of the wall—Lampides and Glaucon, the western side; Xenophon and Cleon, the east; Androcides, Socrates, and Dexion, the longer stretch to the north."

And as simply as that, Sophocles found himself counted among the 'real' generals of the campaign. It was not unlike the time when he learned he stood second only to Aeschylus in the pantheon of Athenian dramatists. No one ever informed him when he attained this honor, or asked him whether he thought he deserved it. It was just a universal fact that came from nowhere, as natural as the sea was salt. Such honors made him nervous.

Menippus went on, "Cleisthenes has special responsibility for the fortress at the northwest corner, on the mountain. Glaucon's squadron will patrol the sea beyond the breakwater."

"And the rest?" asked Xenophon.

"There is still the matter of the Phoenicians. When Callisthenes returns with his four hulls, we will send a larger fleet to stop them."

Silence. Uncertainty over the wisdom of further splitting the army hung in the air like smoke from a guttering lamp. Pericles, sensing the mood, intervened.

"We should have more than enough forces left to cover the siege lines. When the enemy understands that nothing will enter or leave the city, and that no one will relieve them, they will surrender. A favorable end is inevitable as long as we stick to the plan."

Whether out of the confidence he had earned or a sudden fit of madness, Dexion could not restrain an urge to speak up.

"With that famous aqueduct, they won't suffer for water."

Pericles, who took pride in never being surprised, looked to Menippus. The latter stared at Sophocles like a somewhat frustrated tutor.

"I will take care of that myself. They've hidden the end of the tunnel well, but we'll find it. Have we forgotten anything else, Dexion?"

There was a chuckle from the back of the group.

Sophocles, annoyed, persisted. "The Ionians knew we were coming, so they must have laid in stores to wait us out. And have we ever faced walls like these? Spears and bare hands won't be of much use against them. If we can't breach the walls, how will we ever force the issue?"

Pericles was already on his way to his tent. Menippus, who was folding the cover over his tablet, made no other answer but to say, "Proceed to your positions."

By the next day the Athenians had erected a ring of strong-points around the perimeter of the city, joined by a rude causeway by which reinforcements could be rushed to wherever they were needed. In preparation for the attack, the Samians had stripped away every tree and stone big enough to provide cover, everything bigger than a sprig of grass, within a hundred yards of the wall. When the Athenians strayed within range, the Samians shot arrows at them. This gave the besiegers an excellent idea of the effective range of their archers.

Dexion's zone was at the northeast corner; from his day-tent he could see the Polycratic walls march north from the blue floor of the Aegean, make a ninety-degree turn to the west, and mount the slope of Ambelos toward the fortress on its crown. The Athenian strongpoints were mirrored by a series of towers built into the walls, a bow-shot apart, topped with guardhouses. To Dexion the entire setting seemed like some fruitless dispute hewn in stone, with each Athenian thesis confronted, point for point, by its Ionian rejoinder. As he knew from years spent hearing such arguments in the marketplace, no side ever truly convinced the other.

At midday he beheld a strange sight coming up the road from the shore. A red-haired man, well-dressed in a clean tunic and shoes but otherwise clearly a slave, was pushing a cart up the slope. Inside the cart was another man clothed not nearly so well—more or less in plain sackcloth—with black and gray-flecked hair and beard rampant as if never cut in his life. Even his eyebrows were exuberant, hanging down a finger's width below his eyes. But strangest of all was the fact that he was but half a man—in the cart there was nothing below his torso but a blanket to cushion his limbless form.

"Stop," the cripple commanded the slave. He was staring at Dexion through his personal thicket, evaluating him beneath a hard, steady glare.

"You are Sophocles son of Sophilos, the poet?" he asked, in a tone verging on the accusatory.

Dexion shifted. "I am."

"Artemon, son of Aristeus," replied the other. "You will read my poems sometime, yes?"

To such an unexpected request Dexion hardly knew what to say. Poristes saved him by interjecting, "Can that be your job in this campaign, sir? To produce verses?"

Artemon scowled and turned his appraising eye to the ground held by Dexion's forces. With a quick glance at the walls opposite, a quick mental calculation of distances and angles, he barked at his slave:

"Mark this place as suitable." Then, to Dexion, he said, "I will be back."

When he had been rolled to the next strongpoint, out of earshot, Sophocles turned to Poristes.

"Suitable?"

"He must mean a *gastraphetes*—a shieldbreaker."

Dexion had never heard of such a thing. But as the sun settled into the crook of Ambelos he saw a crew of workmen approach, leading a tethered ox. Behind them was a wagon laden with strangely-shaped wooden objects—a great oaken pedestal; a winch like the ones used to beach the ships; a bow the length of a man, its surface clad in opalescent animal horn. When they reached the spot Artemon had designated they dumped the components and retreated back to the shore. Assembling the shieldbreaker, it appeared, required yet another crew of specialists.

The commotion attracted the attention of Iophon, who had otherwise avoided his father's presence.

"By the gods, is this one of Artemon's engines?" the boy gushed.

"Yes."

"Did you *meet* him?"

"What there was of him."

"What there was of him? Artemon of Gela is the most famous man in the world! Didn't you recognize his face?"

"Should I have?" Sophocles retorted.

The other shook his head sadly. "Father, there's been a picture of him in the Painted Stoa for the last ten years. He is a hero of the wars in Sicily. Don't you know anything?"

"No, I suppose I know nothing."

"He was wounded in a battle against the Carthaginians. One of his machines broke as it was sprung—three other men were killed, and he lost both legs. But Artemon was so coolheaded he supervised his own amputation, right there on the field. He refused to give up, and the Greeks won the battle. Is there anyone who has not heard this story?"

"I confess, I haven't."

Iophon laid a hand on the great composite bow, his face suffused with wonderment.

"We'll make short work of the Samians with this," he declared.

3.

Pericles' Athenians were not the first mainland Greeks to invade Samos. In the days of Polycrates, another army sailed into the straits, and invested the place for forty days. It was the greatest danger the tyrant ever faced to his rule. But like the episode of the discarded ring, what started out as a calamity ended in vindication, and Polycrates' reputation of bottomless good fortune became not just a curious rumor, but legendary.

The war began when the tyrant attempted to strengthen his position by expelling from the city anyone with any wealth, ability, or fortune. Putting the outcasts and their families on ships, he sent them to the Great King, inviting him to do what he wished with them. What he had not counted on, though, was his victims' resourcefulness: the exiles, perfectly able to see what fate was in store for them, attacked their captors and took over the ships. They then sailed to the city they thought most able to help them take their revenge.

The Spartans received them with the hospitality they usually reserved for strangers—that is, begrudgingly. There was at that time a heightened fear of revolt by their Greek-speaking slaves, the Messenian helots. The Samian exiles—all aristocrats—were not seen as natural allies of the Messenians, to be sure. But the rulers of Lacedaemon were always nervous when foreigners were on hand to see their inherent weakness.

Bound by honor to hear the appeal of those seeking refuge with them, the ephors sat through three hours of eloquent testimony by the most honey-tongued of the exiles. The Spartans replied, "That was a long speech. The first half we have forgotten, and the second makes no sense to us." This was an answer the Samians should have expected, for the Lacedaemonians were always suspicious of the ornate speech of Asian Greeks. Trying again, the emissaries reduced their story to three sentences. When this, too, met only with incomprehension, the emissary had a bow and arrows brought before the magistrates, pointed at them, and said, "Our quiver needs arrows."

Conferring, the ephors seemed to come to some agreement.

"If you had said, 'Need arrows,' it would have been enough," they said. "But we will help you."

Unlike the cautious, casualty-adverse Spartans of Dexion's time, these were bonafide, old-time Lacedaemonians, as eager to excel in battle as most other men would be to tuck into a fine meal. Once delivered to Samos by their Corinthian allies, the army of the Spartan king Anaxandrides attacked Polycrates' walls with reckless valor, climbing the battlements where they could, hoisting siege ladders where they couldn't. Their helot retainers were put to chipping away the limestone with hunks of diorite fetched from Egypt; both master and slave died by the hundreds under Samian arrows.

At last the Spartans gained control of one of the towers. There they stood, meeting the Samian counterattacks with those murderous short swords, breathing the names of their forebears into the faces of the defenders as they pulled them into their deadly embrace. The Samians began to despair. Protected on their island, there was nothing in their experience of war to prepare them for this stubborn, unreasoning savagery. They attacked the Spartans with spears. They attacked with swords and clubs. They resorted to throwing stones and flaming logs, knowing full well that if they let the Spartans hold the tower, their city would fall. Through it all, the Lacedaemonians beat them to every extremity, until it seemed that it was their territory they were defending, and not just one of thirty-one identical towers in a city wall they had never even seen before. It was an education the Samians never forgot.

The Spartans were finally beaten not so much by force of arms as by spectacle. Polycrates, who had saved himself for an instance like this, appeared on the walls in a panoply of shining silver, his helmet topped with falcon plumes, his shoulders draped, like Herakles', in a lion's skin. He also chose this occasion to don the Girdle of Amasis—a corselet of the whitest linen, adorned with fantastical beasts embroidered in gold and threads of that priceless rarity, Indian cotton. It was called the Girdle of Amasis because it was a gift of the Pharoah to the Lacedaemonians—until the Samians seized it at sea and dedicated it to Great Hera. That Polycrates would display this theft so brazenly, before the very people from whom he had stolen it, stunned the Spartans. And while they were stunned, they stopped fighting.

In that instant the Samians pressed their attack. Polycrates himself rushed to the forefront, his sword flashing, as the Spartans hesitated over whether they should risk damaging the Girdle by fighting back. In the end there were just two Spartans left in the tower: Archias and Lycopas. These two made a hopeless stand with a joy that could only be described as incandescent. As they held off twenty times their number, to fight them was to be in the presence of divinity, and to strike them down, a sacrament.

The Lacedaemonians abandoned their siege. In Sparta, the war was not forgotten (for the Spartans never forget anything), but never spoken of. In Samos, to his credit, Polycrates foreswore his right to erect a victory trophy, choosing instead to bury Archias and Lycopas as heroes of the state. The Athenians, for their part, derived their own lessons from the failure of Sparta's human waves to break the walls of Samos.

4.

As an actor, Sophocles had never felt comfortable in costume. Though in principle it was no different from other sartorial contrivances, such as the soothsayer's hood or the horsehair crest of the military officer, the actor's costume had one big disadvantage: it was meant to be worn only once, for the staging of the play for which it was made. If it had its quirks— if it draped awkwardly over the shoulder, or impeded dancing on this foot or that—the actor simply had to adjust to them on the fly. In his career, Sophocles had seen his share of balky chitons, belts that refused to cinch, masks that drooped no matter how tightly clasped. These had caused him so much trouble over the years that he fantasized about having his actors perform naked, like athletes in the Games.

And so he was surprised in this, his first honest job, to become so at ease in his cloak and panoply. Indeed, he found them changing the way he carried himself. He came to enjoy the swirl of the cape, punctuating his orders as he turned on his heel; the weight of the helmet on his head and the greaves on his shins made him feel not only invulnerable, but somehow more substantial. Though he wore these things because he was a general, in a real sense he was a general because he wore the panoply. A costume could be an asset, he discovered, if the actor had occasion to learn its care and advantages and thus, over time, to let the clothes remake the man.

Comfortable at last in the role of general, he permitted himself military opinions. The first of these was that he hated Artemon's Shieldbreaker.

The engine was completed a few days after it was delivered. About the height of a man and somewhat more in length, it was composed of an oblong wooden frame with a pair of massive bow arms mounted at the front. Sinew bow-cables ran from the ends of the arms to a rear-mounted winch. The bolt was loaded in a groove in the frame, and the mechanism cocked by cranking back the bow-arms; when triggered, the bolt was snapped forward by the sinew cables, much like an arrow from the strings of a conventional bow.

It was like a bow, that is, except that it shot a six-foot, iron-tipped bolt more than two hundred yards. Testing it, the Shieldbreaker's crew put a shot into the Samian walls that buried itself a foot deep in the limestone. Aiming high, they shot another so far over the walls they could not hear it land. Such a weapon would not be stopped by the roof or walls of a typical Greek house; civilians in any room or floor would be vulnerable as the monstrosity ripped through joist, reed, furniture, or flesh. Dexion heard one of the engineers boast that, during the wars in Sicily, he saw a "lucky shot" pierce the belly of a pregnant woman and propel her fetus fifty yards, impaling it in a wall.

That was a lucky shot indeed, for the Shieldbreaker's power was matched only by its inaccuracy. This, Artemon explained, had something to do with the mounting of the bow arms, which vibrated as the machine was discharged. For this reason the engine was useless as a tactical weapon—it could not be used to pick defenders off a wall, or to deliver a flame to a particular roof. Its only purpose as far as Dexion could see was to deliver sudden, random death.

"I would not call it perfected," mused the genius from his cart, "but a thing only in its infancy. But what a force it will be when a leader comes who will invest the proper resources!"

Dexion had further questions about the weapon, but Artemon preferred to talk about poetry.

"You are the true prodigy in this camp, but there are those of us who flatter ourselves that we have some talent."

The engineer produced a scroll from the loose folds of his sackcloth. His intention, it seemed, was for Sophocles to read it, though he never put his desire into words.

"You must excuse the scribblings of someone with other matters on his mind," Artemon said, fidgeting like half a schoolboy. "I only wish I had the time to apply myself as I know you would—"

Out of the corner of his eye, Sophocles saw that Iophon had come out to stare at Artemon. On his face was the same wondering gaze he had worn when he first beheld the Shieldbreaker. That his son saw Artemon now, with the hero soliciting Dexion's opinion of his poetry, was the kind of good timing a father couldn't buy. Sophocles took the scroll.

Under the circumstances, with the engineer exposing himself in this way, Sophocles felt a pity for him as strong as the disgust he had for the man's handiwork. He glanced down. Alas, the verses were standard-issue doggerel—an ode to Hephaestus, gummed with self-pity; an elegy to lost love in limping trochees. It was the kind of thing produced by a thousand amateur poetasters in every fishstall and warehouse in Athens.

"It shows talent," he said, handing the scroll back.

"Really? You patronize me," replied Artemon, the unkempt length of his eyebrows giving his face a sudden, unwonted femininity. Sophocles kept his mask steady on his face.

"No, I'm not. I think you should apply yourself more to it, and perhaps not so much to this." With a tilt of his head, he indicated the Shieldbreaker.

Artemon laughed. "Perhaps. But I don't think I'd be happy striving always to live up to the likes of you. In this other art, I am the master!"

After a month, it still seemed as if they were besieging a city only in theory. The Samians had withdrawn their extramural population inside the walls before the Athenians had arrived; aside from the guards in the towers, and the occasional baying of an unseen goat, Dexion might have believed that he had invaded an empty country. But when Pericles sent troops or surveyors anywhere near the walls, ranks of archers would spring up, driving the intruders back.

A dozen shieldbreakers were erected in a ring around the

city. The crews were instructed to shoot into the town at all times of day, with the timing of their attacks kept patternless to maximize their terror. When the machines were triggered, the bolts soared over the walls, arced downward, and fell unseen into whatever lay below. Most of the time the Athenians heard nothing more; on occasion, there was the faint echo of screams or yells. They never heard a missile strike anything solid.

Soon after, someone hit on the idea of shooting into the town at night. This kind of attack was impossible to anticipate or avoid. The engines made little noise when they were sprung—just a *snap* and a *whoosh*—and the bolts flew in complete silence. The Samians only learned of them after they struck, perhaps landing harmlessly in the street, or penetrating roofs and perforating civilians in their beds.

Now Sophocles was in no way naive. He knew his Homer and the other poets of battle; he understood that the craft of war called forth repellent acts from men. As a poet, though, he was cursed by Loxias with certain compulsions. One of these was to make up the stories that lay behind those faint screams at the far end of the bolt's arc. He was cursed to give a name to the pregnant woman in Sicily, forced before she died to watch her baby murdered before he was born. He could not avoid seeing a young man much like himself, full of fright and boyhood bluster, excited to help defend his city at last, pinned like some soulless insect to the ground. He would imagine Iophon as a small boy, split in half in his cradle by assailants who would never see the consequences of their acts.

In the tent he shared with his son, he made the mistake of sharing his doubts. Iophon stared at him with pity in his eyes.

"Father, you brought me here to see the face of war. I think maybe you thought I would run away from it, like a child. But I see it is you who needs the education!"

"So this looks like war to you, this cowardly slaughter from a distance? Is this why we still read of divine Achilles, and Hector breaker-of-horses, who had the courage to face those who would kill them?"

"I remember Hector running in fear from Achilles," the boy replied. "And I think anyone who carries a shield for Samos deserves to die, until we say they don't. The fault for their deaths lies with those who decided to make war on the Athenians in the first place."

"Spoken like Menippus himself! You seem almost grown up, boy, but you have not yet learned to use your own judgment."

In a way that was surprisingly apt for a thespian's son, Iophon struck his brow in mock bewilderment. "Could this be the same father who told me not to question those who know better?"

When Sophocles didn't answer, the boy rose and presented himself with arms open, like Haemon beseeching his father to spare Antigone. Had he seen the play after all?

"Father, I can see that we agree on very little anymore. You indulged me when I asked to come and watch you fight the war, and for that I thank you. But why should we allow ourselves to cause each other pain with these ceaseless arguments? I think we both know there's a better way."

"What do you suggest?"

"Menippus says I am welcome to join his staff. I can collect my things right now and go to him."

Sophocles considered the prospect. He obviously would not allow it, but putting his reasons in rational order would have been a challenge. All he had were images and feelings associated with them—Nais and the fear of failing in his responsibility to her; a boy within the city, much like Iophon, getting the Shieldbreaker treatment; Menippus' cocky face and his revulsion therein.

"The answer is no," he said.

"Father, you seem set in your decision, so I won't try to convince you. But please promise me that you will reconsider it once the logic of my request becomes evident?"

The boy had clearly spent too much time disputing in the stoa.

"I will make that promise—if you agree to show me the respect a son owes his father."

"Of course."

Dexion rose to leave, but ended up with his feet tangled in the hem of his general's cloak. Struggling in a half-crouch to free himself, with Iophon watching half amused and half embarrassed, the poet finally tore the cloak from his shoulders, hurled it to the ground, and stomped away.

5.

Dexion proceeded directly to Pericles. The Supreme Commander had a tent not much larger than any of his colleagues, but set up in a central place in the hills above the city. There he established a presence like the one he had in Athens: he was available at all times for official business, meeting with anyone irrespective of rank, but otherwise standing aloof, never joining the other generals for drinking parties or hunting.

When Sophocles called out, he was admitted by the voice of the Supreme Commander himself. Splitting the flap, Dexion saw the bookkeeper, Evangelus, scribbling at a desk in the anteroom. The slave glanced up, showing not a flicker of recognition except a slight arching of his brow.

Pericles greeted him in a plain linen shift, his arms extended, a smile on his face. "Dexion, I'm glad you've come!" he declared. "We've had some excellent news: forty more ships stand tonight on Tragia, and will join us tomorrow. That shall double our force! That will make an impression on the Samians, I'd think."

Distracted by what he wanted to say, Sophocles agreed without really hearing him. Glancing around the tent, he got a rare look at the Olympian in repose—his bed turned into a daycouch, covered with open scrolls; a stingy meal of figs and white cheese, half-eaten on a tray; his armor arranged neatly on a stand. There was also a little folding desk beside the couch, and on it a small painted portrait of a woman. He didn't need to look closely to recognize the face of Aspasia.

A flush of guilt slowed his tongue again. Pericles, regarding him, kept up the air of bonhomie.

"So I hope you are finding the time to compose your next work. It was *Antigone and Polyneices*, was it not?"

"*Polyneices and Antigone*. And I'm sorry to say I haven't had much time for writing."

"A pity! Do I need to remind you, old friend, that what you do in the theater is as important to Athens as what we accomplish on this island? For that reason alone, for detaining the great Dexion, the Samians commit a crime against all the Greeks! Is there anything we can do to restore your inspiration? Would you like some of your duties reassigned?"

"No."

There was a brief pause, in which Sophocles could hear the scratch of Evangelus' stylus next door. Pericles bowed his head as he belted his shift—the sight of that naked pate, so rarely liberated from a cap or helmet in public, was perversely fascinating, like a glimpse of the breast of another man's wife. As it was, it wasn't so unusual after all—high-crowned to be sure, and smooth. What was most strange about it was that it was polished to a high sheen, like the floor of a temple.

"I wanted to talk to you about something else—those engines of Artemon's."

Pericles' eyes lit up.

"Yes! Aren't they fascinating? We were very fortunate to engage his services—almost as fortunate as we were in getting you!"

Sophocles couldn't hide his discomfort. He began to speak, stopped, started again.

"The trouble is—I don't think they're doing any good. They won't knock down the walls, and the way they are being used is—provocative. All they can do is make the Samians more defiant."

"So what you are telling me," Pericles said, "is that you think the engines are being used incorrectly. Is that true?"

Dexion had heard him use this tactic in the Assembly—confronting dissenters by first repeating their words back to them. At best his opponent's argument would seem more ridiculous on repetition; at worst it bought Pericles time to compose one of his elegant replies.

"Not incorrectly. I just don't see the point of using them when we might pursue other options."

"Other options?"

Pericles sat down on his couch, his smile steady on his face.

"We might try something . . . more direct."

"Dexion, we have been friends for quite a few years. Regardless of what you may have heard about me, I am always happy to learn better ways of doing things. So when you say, 'try something different,' I'm intrigued."

"Wouldn't it be better—" Sophocles began.

"What I won't do, though," the other interrupted, "is take needless risks. What we all need to accept is that this is not the kind of war our fathers would have approved. We are not two armies here for an afternoon, in search of a piece of level ground to settle our differences. The Ionians have repudiated the honorable course by hiding behind their walls. I tell you, in fact, that they are dogs, every last one. Ask the Milesians who washed up naked on the beach at Lade after the Samians betrayed them! Ask the Great King, who feared the same at Mycale! Collectively, they are not worth the life of a single Athenian shieldman."

"If this Artemon is as clever as you say, maybe he can devise some advantage for us. I have heard of turtled battering rams, for instance."

Pericles' smile faded as he spoke; talk of "turtled battering rams" seemed to strike him as not only naive, but tasteless.

"Such devices might help break a weaker city. But Polycrates built better than that," he replied. His tone was still genial, but with a didactic edge. "If you have any other suggestions that will put us inside the city without resulting in many dead Athenians, I would be glad to hear of it."

As an artist in words, Dexion had few peers in his city. But as a debater he was no better than average for an Athenian—still less so when it came to military matters, in which he had little confidence.

"No, far be it for me to suggest that."

Pericles rose, put an arm around the poet. "If I had to predict, I would say all of us will feel as you do sometime in this campaign. You only feel it first because you are the best of us. That you have been put in this position, dear friend, I am deeply sorry. I think you must know that by now—"

Sophocles felt a disgusted languor come over him. Was Pericles admitting he connived in the poet's dalliance with Aspasia?

"—but I insist that you may best serve Athens by finishing your play. Don't let yourself be distracted by matters that are beneath you. And if we are all fortunate, you will present *Antigone and Polyneices* for us at the Dionysia next year!"

The poet left knowing that he had been out-argued before he had even opened his mouth. The thought cast a cloud over him; had he been a fool, pretending to be a general while all the real decisions were out of his hands? Nais had said it—if he wanted to follow Aeschylus' military success he should have picked up a shield and served in the line. Perhaps Sophocles, best acquainted of all of the tragic consequences of hubris, was guilty of pride after all.

And yet . . . who were his colleagues in the generalship, that they deserved the honor better than him? What great battles had Lampides, Callisthenes or Xenophon won? Who were Cleitophon and Glaucon but well-connected nobodies, having accomplished not a fraction of what Dexion had for Athens? Why should the likes of them reap the honors, while poets like himself wring their hands and wonder if they were worthy?

On his way back to his tent he passed the remains of a Samian village. Like all the settlements in the vicinity of the walls, it had been abandoned and burned before the Athenians arrived. But there was suddenly new life between the charred debris: having cobbled together useable plows out of sabotaged equipment, the Athenians were tilling the fields for sowing. To reap any crops they planted there would take months; Pericles, it appeared, was preparing for a very long wait.

Dexion made one detour on the way back, to the makeshift armory east of his camp. The line-weapons of the hoplites in his squadron were kept there: eighty dogwood spears, propped against a rude wooden stand with butt-spikes planted in the ground. The two guards on duty roused from their bored stupor, startled by the arrival of their general. But this was no surprise inspection. Instead, Dexion strode to the nearest spear and, with grave deliberateness, grasped the iron tip with his right hand.

It was the closest piece of metal he could find. Pericles had probably been sincere in flattering the poet and his worth to the city, but no prudent man would risk taking such an outburst of praise without taking precautions.

6.

When he missed his wife, the feeling was as precious to him as artistic inspiration. Nais hadn't made such sentiments easy in recent years. Often she seemed actively to discourage it, telling him not to write her any "lover's twaddle" when he went on trips, or making little answer to the short testaments of matrimonial passion he did indulge. She professed to have no need for the physical act anymore. Yet there it was, as reliable as the apple blossoms in spring, whenever he crossed the borders of Attica—the aching absence of her, like the turning of a note in a song he recalled once broke his heart, but could no longer hear in his head.

He met her long after he had achieved fame for his dancing and his harp-playing, and his stylus was just beginning to outshine Aeschylus'. He wasn't "Dexion" yet, but he was the toast of both sexes. Servants of famous courtesans would approach him after performances, offering locks of hair clipped from undisclosed places, while five-hundred-bushel men came with propositions, dangling pretty slaves as bait. Elite athletes came offering commissions for odes celebrating exploits they hadn't yet achieved.

What, then, was a young man of sizeable appetites to do, with a city full of temptations and nothing more than a blank tablet waiting by his bedside? He took the best offers. He drank his share of the wine. Then he went home, feeling vaguely let down, and faced down his blank tablet anyway.

On the fateful day he was going to the market along one of the back lanes of Colonus. He'd used these alleys since his boyhood to deliver messages to his father's clients. In recent times their narrow confines and darkness, with the pavement invisible from the overhanging balconies above, helped him avoid the curious eyes of his public. He knew them better than any other place in the city. Yet as he approached one of the less appealing houses on the already unsavory street, he collided with a door that was suddenly thrust into the thoroughfare.

"Don't you knock first?" he complained, rubbing his nose. He saw no offender standing there, but felt something pass between his legs: the door had been pushed aside by a small, speckled sow. Looking after her, the poet saw her kinked tail waggle as she passed in headlong flight.

"Don't just stand there!" a deep-pitched female voice said from within. "Catch him!"

"Madam, if you think this is somehow my fault—" he began, but was brought up short as a singular vision stepped into the light.

Her voice notwithstanding, this was no 'madam' but a young woman: a thin figure with gangling extremities and shocks of midnight straying from the linen wrap that covered her head. In one of her oversized hands she held a butcher's cleaver; the blood from previous efforts soaked both arms up to the creases of her elbows. Other colors—a bilious black, intestinal green—daubed the pillow of material around her waist where she had gathered up her tunic for work. This, in turn, exposed knees that were positively boyish in their chapped, scrapped, and soiled perfection.

The girl was not beautiful in any way that could be fixed on the marriage or sex markets. Her blood-spattered vitality lent her an allure as elemental as Kore's, while the intelligence that flashed in her eyes gave her all the mannish intensity of the young Athena. When she opened her mouth, her voice was like a blacksmith's after a workday of breathing smoke.

Within a moment of glimpsing her, he knew he must have her.

"Young woman," he said after gathering himself to orchestra height, "do you know to whom you are speaking?"

"I am speaking to the man who is letting my father's dinner get away," she replied.

Though it pricked his pride, he was glad of her ignorance of him. Few Athenian bachelors, even those who staged plays, respected women who frequented the theatre. His pride smarted worse when she leaned toward him with a flirty gleam in her eye, grasped the handle, and closed the door in his face.

A few minutes later he knocked again. She opened up quickly, as if she had been waiting for him. Mirth brushed the edges of her lips as she looked down at the sow in his arms; frightened by its capture, the porker let loose a stream of loose stool against Sophocles' bare leg.

"Your father may have his dinner back," said the poet, "if he agrees to speak with me about his daughter."

One thick eyebrow shot up. "Then you might as well know my name is Nais. His other daughter is married."

He started to follow her inside, until she turned again.

"What are you doing?"

Sophocles glanced at his soiled leg. "Yes, I suppose I should come back when I'm more presentable."

"Not too bright are you?" she smiled. "I mean get rid of that pig—you caught the wrong one."

Chapter V

THE SANCTUARY

"Now he is true no more to the promptings of his inbred nature, but dwells with alien thoughts."
—Chorus, *Ajax*, l. 614

1.

ANTIGONE: So you come to me again, dear maker, when your comrades are either asleep, or stand the watch before the walls of your enemies. It must be a powerful disquiet that drives you from your tent of honor, here to this beach, to speak with a mere girl.

DEXION: A mere girl you may be, but it is manly freight that you bear.

ANTIGONE: See me lying here, O adept of the Muses, and tell me that I weigh more upon the earth than I should. Is my waist not slim? Do my eyes not shine with youth's steady fire? Are my loins clad for motherhood, or are they as unswelled as they appear, wetted by the goddess of sea-foam? Mount me, and will I not transport you?

DEXION: It is well for you to toy with words as you toy with me.

ANTIGONE: Subtle is the curse of the goddess Envy, that she may convince the most fortunate that they are miserable! For when have you known a day of trouble in your life, Dexion? You are the most esteemed of poets in your city. You are heaped with honors, and great men tell their wives to give their backs to you. And yet here you are, sickly with womanish doubt! How else must Athens show her esteem for you?

DEXION: Too true—I made a mistake coming here. For when have I come to women for consolation, and received anything but scorn?

ANTIGONE: A field sown with nothing yields nothing.

DEXION: So you are girlish after all, because you speak nonsense.

ANTIGONE: Is it nonsense, O master, to recite the indisciminate roll of the whores you have slept with, instead of making more sons for Athens? Phyrne of Piraeus, Nysa the Ethiopian, Arete the One-Eye, Aspasia of Miletus, the cooze with the tattooed eyelids behind the grave of Sikelos, that Thracian you did on a bet, Tlepolemus the actor—

DEXION: What of it? Who pines for his wife after twenty years of marriage? Indict me for whoring, and you indict half the men of Athens!

ANTIGONE: Not half the men of Athens—only the men of Athens who mope about, pining for their women to console them.

DEXION: I pray the gods you will soon be made silent.

ANTIGONE: So much the worse for you, to whom I speak the truth!

2.

As Pericles predicted, reinforcements arrived the next morning. Thirty more triremes were beached, and ten transports laden with heavy troops and supplies. This swelled the besieging contingent on the island beyond fifteen thousand—more than any army fielded by Athens in some time. The newcomers were dispersed among the units of the eight generals surrounding the city. If the gods looked down on the scene, they would have been hard pressed to say which was more menacing— Polycrates' wall, solid and frowning, or Pericles' siege line, encircling the city like a coiled dragon, bristling and restless as it spewed forth its haze of campfires.

Not all the Samians were inside the city. As Athenian scouts explored the island, they found scores of small farms and villages functioning as if the war was happening across the sea. Fishing boats departed the north coast villages every morning, their masters perched high on their raked gunnels. Overnight huts, built of thatch and protected by the paint-daubed skulls of wild animals, were found in the forest. In the high pastures, tiny figures were glimpsed tending their flocks; when the wind was right, Dexion could lie in his tent and listen to the tinkling of goat bells. Pericles saw these common folk as allies of the Athenians, naturally opposed to the rich oligarchs of the city, and so ordered his troops to leave them alone. There would be time enough after the victory to bring their patriarchs down to take their places in the new democracy.

It would take more than a war to force the natives to abandon the great Temple of Hera. The sanctuary lay four miles from the town, at the end of a straight causeway of beaten earth. It was sacred because the wife of Zeus was born there, and in the dry months, with the air sweetened by flowering willows and blossoms growing on the banks of the Imbrasos, it seemed a fitting place to consecrate to the goddess. For most of the year, though, the sanctuary was a stinking, bug-infested swamp, requiring constant upkeep to prevent the buildings and votives from sinking away into the morass. Indeed, the custodians of the Temple were the first of the Samians to approach Pericles, demanding that the Athenians take up the maintenance disrupted by the invasion. This he declined, blaming the Samian oligarchs for any neglect. He did, however, forbid the Athenians to interfere in any way with the business of the sanctuary.

Sophocles visited the temple one day when the temperature soared and he could no longer bear to stare at the city's blank walls. High summer had arrived, with breezeless days that made the world seem to flutter with the heat rising from the pebbly ground. As he approached the sanctuary, he saw what he took to be the mirage of a giant towering over the Sacred Way. Coming closer, he saw that the apparition was real—a massive, archaic figure of a boy in cream-colored marble, his arms locked at his sides, left leg set slightly forward, lips cocked in a mirthless smile. He was five times higher than a man. Beyond him was another fellow of similar proportions, and the image of a woman in a skin-clinging chiton, locks of chiseled hair spread over her shoulders, topped by a bluntly columnar headdress. As he approached the gate to the sanctuary, the votives became so thick on the ground they could not escape their neighbors' shadows. At no other holy place he had visited—the Acropolis mount, Eleusis, the seat of Loxias at Delphi—had he seen so many bombastic, oversized offerings.

The spectacle culminated in the sanctuary. The Temple, on which the Samians had been working for a hundred years, reared like a red-tiled mountain. The degree of its completion depended on the angle from which it was seen: from the open-air altar directly in front, a marble forest of columns loomed, their shafts dressed and gilded with azure and vermilion; from the side, half a dozen columns had yet to be erected, and a section of the roof gaped, half-ribbed. Around the temple stood more expensive dedications: treasuries donated by the rich families of Samos, statues of bronze, a whole samaena hauled from the water and mounted, toy-like, in a great marble cradle.

Between them traipsed the birds from India sacred to Hera. These dragged their tapered tails around until, for whatever reasons moved them, they unfurled them like great, parti-colored sails, studded with hundreds of feathery eyes. The air of purposeful exoticism was completed by a strange fragrance that filled the place—an overflow of sickly sweetness, as if from geraniums the size of palm trees. The effect overall was of conspicuous excess, with everything designed to be the richest, the shiniest, and above all, the biggest.

The Sacred Way was empty of city pilgrims, but the country folk continued to come in from every direction. They bore those modest offerings for the goddess simple people could afford: wives brought rude cakes of nuts and honey; husbands, sheep and fowl; brides, the dolls and baubles of their girlhood. Sophocles sat on a rock near the great altar and watched a peasant try to lead a young bull through the gate. Spooked, the bull dug in its forelegs, jerking its head back as his master whipped its nose.

The poet was engrossed in the struggle until a voice startled him.

"Is this the famous Dexion, here to honor the goddess?"

He turned. A gray-haired man stood there. The mass of his well-fed belly swelled his black chiton; his fingers were dripping with jewels, and his skin shone pale in the sunlight, as if he had spent most of his life indoors, at some counting desk.

"You know who I am?"

"Of course! There are Samians who travel to the Dionysia every year. I myself have gone on two occasions."

Sophocles was facing one of the magistrates of the

sanctuary. Such men were usually scions of the leading aristocratic families—just the sort who would have the time and money to journey to Athens for the festival. He was the first live Ionian Dexion had conversed with since his arrival.

"I have to say that I'm surprised you, a poet, have taken part in this war," the sacristan continued as he fanned himself with his writing tablet. "It is a very impious act. I remember your own words, in *Philoctetes*, 'But of this be mindful when you lay waste the land: show reverence toward the gods. All things are of less account in the sight of our father Zeus. Piety dies not with men; in their life and in their death it is immortal.'"

It grated on the poet's ears to hear his own verses quoted back at him.

"Have you been mistreated?"

The man shrugged. "Not to speak of. But your Pericles acts out of calculation, not fear of the gods."

"Some say it is the Samians who flout the gods by breaking their oath of alliance."

"A promise to a liar is no bond."

"And what would be the value of our oaths, if we may pick and chose which to obey?"

"You Athenians are a phenomenon! You profess to save us from being plundered—then you steal your allies' money from Delos. You tell us you guarantee the freedom of the Greeks, yet you interfere when the Greeks form a government of their choosing."

"Did they form a government? Or have one formed for them?"

"Some wonder why that question is your business."

Greeks arguing over politics was not a new thing in the world. The heat of that afternoon, though, made neither man anxious to waste his breath on immoveable opinions. The magistrate sighed.

"It is, in any case, a sad business between our people. To have the Greeks war against each other, on the very doorstep of the Great King! Darius must be very amused."

The pilgrims had finally gotten their bull through the pylon. As they came closer, Sophocles could see that the animal's face was daubed with blue paint, its horns gilded for sacrifice. The magistrate checked the drape of his chiton as he moved to greet them. He turned to Dexion.

"I hope to sail to Athens again one day to see your next play," he said. "I hope, though I fear everyone connected with this will come to a bad end. A very bad end."

Mounting the steps of the Hera temple's east front, Sophocles passed between the carven bulk of the columns. The great iron doors had been wheeled open for the day. Stepping inside, he first saw nothing as his eyes adjusted to the faint, milky light filtering between the roof beams. There were no torches and only one lamp near the door to the treasury. The great image towered over him like an alabaster waterfall, defined only by undulations of sculpted drapery and flesh, until his gaze rose to the top, and the goddess stared down at him through crystal eyes. Though the air was hot, he shivered.

The glint of gold caught his eye as he turned to go. Pausing, he saw a small table set up in a niche between the columns. He came closer. In the middle of the table lay a square of marble two fingers thick and about a foot on a side; in the center of the square was mounted a ring of solid gold.

As baubles went, it was a crude piece, with no jewels and no carving, thick and finished with all the delicacy of a plough blade. It seemed made to fit a finger at least twice as thick as Sophocles' thumb. The only decoration was some letters inscribed on the inside. As Sophocles cocked his head to read them, the hair rose on the back of his neck:

πολυκρατου

He stood staring at the relic for some time, ignoring sensations of hunger, until he heard the sacristan levering the great doors closed for the day. Now that he had found it, he wanted to fix forever in his mind's eye the sight of Polycrates' famous gold ring.

3.

Several more weeks into the standoff, the swollen Athenian contingent became as grave a threat to itself as to the enemy. Boredom took its toll on Pericles' wise policies. Reports came back of farms pillaged by thugs with Attic accents, and Samian fishing boats learned to run at the very sight of Athenian warships. Discipline problems spread along the line, with fights breaking out over gambling, stolen supplies, lovers' spats and, in the end, nothing much at all. Maneuvers at sea were held to keep the ships and oarsmen in good condition, but the men knew these excursions amounted to make-work and trained without enthusiasm. Backtalk and griping rose. To citizen-soldiers like them, with farms and families at home to worry about, extended foreign campaigns had a definite whiff of betrayal.

Meanwhile, one of the shieldbreakers was put out of commission when its crew, desperate from idleness, tried to launch a sack of human excrement into the town. The weight difference between an arrow and the unconventional load wrecked the action, showering the Athenian camp with shit. Purple with rage, Artemon had the crew flogged, the spectacle of which only increased the men's discontent.

Pericles at first pretended to take no notice of these problems. He had espoused a philosophy, rooted in the teachings of his friend Anaxagoras of Clazomenae, that all chaotic things had an inherent yearning for the refining influence of *thought*. A controlling mind, whether human or divine, could bring order to the complexities of a universe, a city, or an army. In the face of rising disorder, then, Pericles perfected his own self-discipline, trusting in the influence of his good example.

His hand was forced at last when, despite his philosophic rigor, a serious altercation broke out between oarsmen from Athens and a ship's crew from Salamis. The trigger was one of the wrestling matches called by the officers to help the men vent their spare energy. A bit too much was vented when one of the city men did not simply throw a Salaminian, but launched him into a thorn bush. When the ensuing brawl was over, two men were dead.

A council was called, and Menippus made an announcement that surprised no one:

"We've received word from our spies on the mainland. The Phoenician navy has been sighted off Caria. We must decide whether it would be better to fight them at sea, or wait for them here."

The generals looked at each other. Obviously, it would be safer to engage the Phoenicians on the open sea, where the Athenians' superior training would tell, and where Samians could not sally out to reinforce them.

"Agreed. A fleet will be prepared to intercept the Phoenicians—sixty hulls under our colleague Pericles. You will receive assignments for your squadrons later this evening."

Xenophon appeared to swoon in his seat.

"Did you say *sixty* ships?"

Menippus frowned. "Yes. Sending an inadequate force would be worse than sending none at all. Don't you agree?"

"Of course. But that would leave our line thin here. Half of my ships are laid up because certain others are hoarding their cordage—"

"*Others* need not be responsible for your mistakes," snapped Lampides. "You started out with as many supplies as the rest of us."

"Wisely declared, by someone who never got a ship out at Tragia."

"Irrelevant."

"Talk sense to a fool, and he calls you foolish."

Sophocles raised a hand. "You can talk to my quartermaster about cordage," he said. "We have plenty."

Chastened, Xenophon and Lampides fell silent. Dexion's ships were the most damaged of all by the high sea at Tragia.

"The division of the ships is correct," resumed Menippus quietly. "The Samians have nothing left. But if they should come out, you should have more than enough to deal with them."

The next day oarsmen from sixty triremes were called back to their benches. From the walls it might have seemed like the Athenians were withdrawing, as more than half the army pulled up stakes and marched away. By nightfall the sky over the beaches glowed with their campfires.

The full moon that night did not encourage the Greeks to sleep. By the first watch, most were still awake, and witnessed firsthand a troubling phenomenon: the moon was burning.

It didn't seem like an eclipse exactly—the moon was not so much hidden as drenched in a baleful red light. To the wondering eyes of the Greeks, it was as if she had wandered too close to some hidden source of heat, and was smoldering in the sky. The apparition set tongues fluttering the length of the beach; the oarsmen who had been getting their rest were awoken by the uproar. The trierarchs—envisioning sailing into battle against the Phoenicians with spooked, exhausted crews—appealed to Pericles for help.

The Olympian, half-asleep, strode to the water's edge with his chiton knotted clumsily around his midriff. Hundreds gathered in silence behind him. With the surf breaking against his ankles, he stared up at the moon as the sanguinary glow spread completely across her face. Instead of a moon, it now seemed as if there was a gaping wound in the sky.

Pericles spun around and walked back toward his tent.

"What? Have you nothing to say?" someone asked.

"Of course he won't! It's bad news!"

"It's a curse from Hera!"

"Commander, tell us what it means!"

The Olympian paused. "I'll tell you what it means, boy, if you tell me what *this* means."

Pericles unwrapped a portion of his chiton. Stepping near one of the campfires, he held it up so the light shined through it: although the chiton was gray-white, the glow of the flame appeared crimson through the fabric.

"Tell me: do any of you fear this?" asked Pericles.

"No!"

"Then you have nothing to fear from *that*," he declared, indicating the sky with a contemptuous chin-flick.

It was an unprecedented performance for a general. The men, surprised not to receive the usual mystico-astrologic ratiocination, fell into confused debate. This, in turn, made them forget their fear. By the time most of them looked up at the moon again she—and the swagger of the Athenians—was restored to her former self.

4.

Dexion and Poristes sat on a hill looking out over the azure ribbon of the mainland strait. Across the water, seemingly close enough for the Shieldbreaker to plant an arrow in its shoulder, stood the undulating gray body of Mount Mycale. Far to their right, where the straits opened up, the distant sails of Pericles' fleet dissolved in the sultry air. Poristes handed the poet the wineskin they were sharing.

"There was a time these eyes could make out the alpha on those sails, even from here," said the captain. "That is, before a life spent squinting into the wind."

"Or staring at scrolls by lamplight," said Dexion, who was so weary he had to rest the skin in the crook of his elbow to raise it. Poristes had mixed the wine, a Thasian black, with sweet water from the Imbrasos. Its taste was a curious combination of resin, fruit, and mud, like something one would suck direct from the horn of one of the Seleni. He let the skin drop, propelling the wine between his teeth; to his pleasure, a shard of almond that had been lodged between his molars washed free.

"Do they have a chance of finding the Phoenicians?"

"We would have found them, if they were coming," said the

captain, who was still disappointed that the *Antigone* was not selected for the expedition.

"I'm glad you're here." Sophocles put an arm around Poristes, coaxing a bitter smile from his friend's lips. "Anything not to listen to that blasted ship!"

"Waves talk. And rocks, and dolphins, and clouds. And the wind, most of all. Be glad, dear friend, that you don't have to listen to them, too!"

Men bewail their own curses, thought the poet, while all around them swirl untold miseries that are almost always worse. Sophocles' latest misery was his son. While the rest of the camp was arguing over signs in the sky, Iophon had spent the night trying to convince his father to let him sail with Pericles.

"Don't you believe me, dear father, when I tell you my only purpose is to fulfill the one you meant for me—to see war, and become the kind of man who is temperate and wise? Is there something in my face, in my voice, or in the words I speak that tell you I am somehow insincere? Tell me, and I will try to show you otherwise."

"I see no insincerity," Sophocles agreed.

"Then if you see I am in earnest, and if you have heard the lengths Pericles will go to preserve Athenian lives, and you understand that this war is perfect for our purposes—by what logic can you deny me?"

"War is to the purpose of states, not men."

Iophon's mouth fell open. It was beyond his understanding how such perfect proofs could founder on the rocks of parental stubbornness.

"Then you are being unjust!" he cried.

"Look, boy. I took you along for good reason, though not entirely for you to see war. There'll be plenty of time for that later. Getting you away from those layabouts in the stoa was just as important."

Iophon stared back with eyes aflame. And like any Greek patriarch, Dexion would not deign to notice his son's fury. But it hurt him nonetheless.

"It is not your reasoning that I object to," he continued, "but the way you speak of gaining wisdom. This war is no joke, boy. In time, it will give you more than you can handle. Why seek it out? Why tempt the Fates? You'd do better to approach this with forbearance, and a sense of humility. It is the patient man that experience rewards."

"Do you mean the patience to sit and scribble about life, instead of living it?"

What petty meanness! The eruption of it took the poet off-guard and, at the same time, inspired him: he had not thought to give this quality to Haemon, or to any of the other defiant sons in his *oeuvre*. It was an omission he would remedy at his first opportunity.

Iophon watched his question have its effect, then added, "You've always wanted that for me, to follow you. You don't say it, but I know."

"I have counted on no such thing."

"Then I know you better than you know yourself. You might as well learn the truth then: I'll never do what you do. I don't want to. I don't respect it."

Sophocles resented these words, but his anger was drowned in a great tide of sadness that seemed to pour from a hole in his heart. *I know you better than you know yourself*, the boy said. It was almost an echo of what the voice of Antigone had told him, down by the ships.

"Pericles has no need for a petulant boy," the poet declared. "You will stay by me here."

Poristes extended a hand for the wineskin. "Come now friend, don't leave me dry."

Dexion surrendered the wine. As he watched the captain drink, he was so dogged by the image of Iophon's contempt that he reached to take the skin back before Poristes was finished.

"You've found your sea legs, I see," said the captain as he handed it over. "Just remember to leave a little for me!"

Dexion left matters as they stood for another night. After tossing and turning on his pallet, he rose and searched for Iophon. The boy was reclining in the no man's land before the Samian walls. It was almost as if he was tempting an enemy archer to take a chance at clipping him.

"What are you doing! Get up, you fool!"

Iophon, with a motion as slow as flowing honey, poured himself to his feet.

"You will not sail with the fleet," said the poet, "but I've reconsidered your request to billet with Menippus. You may collect your things from the tent and report to him. And may the gods have more patience with you than I do!"

Thrilled, the boy jumped in the air. Then he approached as if to give his father a hug—but at the last second reached out to exchange a manful handshake. Sophocles looked at his hand, grasped it.

"I hope I won't have reason to regret this," he said.

"It will all be over in a week."

Sophocles tried not to watch Iophon go, but couldn't help but peek through the tentflap as he made his way to Menippus' sector. As he receded, there were moments when it became hard to distinguish him from the other young soldiers and slaves walking around. Yet there were others when some small gesture, some tilt of the head or twist of the shoulders, brought the figure of the small boy back to him, running once again after lizards in the garden, or standing on his mother's feet as he sucked on the linen of her skirts.

It was an ambiguity he was used to with Photia. His son's maturity troubled him far more, and he was tempted to send Bulos to drag him back, to gaze at him again and reaffirm his minority. He wrestled with this temptation until Iophon turned behind the bulk of one of Artemon's engines, and did not emerge from the column of shieldmen exercising behind that. He was gone.

5.

Just before dawn the next day, unfamiliar sounds—the clack of iron on wood, followed by a sliding noise, like a ship being towed through the slipway—was heard near the Samian wall. The ground was covered that night in a mist that rose in twisting tendrils like pale mirror-images of tree roots. The Athenian sentries peered through the gloom, speculating openly over what the sound was. Soon more recognizable clues appeared: the glint of setting moonlight on bronze helmets, and the crunch of armor on bodies hurtling forward. The original sound, it seemed, was the heavy maingate of Samos Town being opened for the first time since the invasion. The others were the first warnings of the enemy attack.

Between the alarm and the clash of spears on shields, Dexion only had time for a few hurried breaths. To be killed there, run through by armored men as they simply flattened his tent, was a humiliating prospect. Jumping to his feet, he lifted his shield, fixed his helmet—but couldn't find his sword in the dark. He turned this way and that, trapped between the impulses to get out immediately or find his weapon first. When he finally put his hands on the blade, he could hear the voices of men fighting mere yards from the flap. Some of them were shouting with an Ionian accent.

He emerged to a vision he had previously seen only in spectacles mounted in the Painted Stoa. To the right and to his left, a front of enemy hoplites were surging, pressing forward with their shields. Between them, spearpoints darted out like the tongues of serpents; behind, more men were running, shouting, piling into the scrum. As the dawn sky brightened, the scene was livid with the glow of flames engulfing the Shieldbreaker. The sight of the battle, and the roar of it funneled through the tiny earholes of his helmet, left him momentarily stunned. He stood, sword and shield at his sides.

And then he was in motion. An enemy shieldman had tumbled an Athenian to the ground and was about to finish him with his lizard-sticker. Sophocles was upon him before he could raise his eyes, slashing downward at the shieldman's exposed forearm. The arm came neatly away, still gripping the spearshaft, splattered with blood from the stump. The man released the weapon with his good hand, his face contorted as he tumbled, submerged back into the chaos as if he were drowning at sea. The poet wheeled to his right for a fresh opponent. He didn't give a moment's thought to the prone man whose life he had saved.

A Samian came forward with shield raised. Sophocles swung at him, the blade lodging in the rim. The Samian took his turn, striking Sophocles' shield in the center. The impact of the blow seemed to reverberate back through the man's body, shaking Dexion's loose. This left the blade mere inches from the Samian's neck. Using only his wrist, Sophocles flicked the point at him, applying a three-inch slash that spanned the jugular. The Samian turned to him, his eyes just visible under his visor: their expression told of some tender hurt, as if the poet had disparaged him at a banquet.

He looked down. Another enemy was on his hands and knees, reaching out to retrieve his dropped shield. Sophocles stood over him, measuring the spot in the middle of his back where his cuirass didn't protect him. The Samian froze over the shield, his left hand stilled in the gripcords; the blade passed into his body with a viscous crack, like the butcher's ax into some old, spent milkcow.

It went on like this for as long as the sun took to rise. The Athenians, surprised, took some time to assemble enough men to force the Samians back. The enemies who managed to penetrate the lines stumbled into Sophocles and a few other swordmen. The latter struck them down, then used their fallen bodies to brace their feet for the next wave.

When he finally had a moment to look around, Sophocles saw that he and the Athenian line were standing farther from the tents than they had begun, almost abreast of the ruined shieldbreaker. All up and down the siege line the defenders were turning the Samians to flight.

The enemy sally had failed. It had left its mark, however. Dexion stood in a wide band of earth plowed up by the frantic maneuvers of all those desperate feet. Bodies peppered the churned landscape. As the flies began to mass, tormenting the eyes of the fallen who still lived, Athenians with grim faces did their rounds, using their butt-spikes to pierce the hearts or cave the skulls of the survivors.

It was one of the Athenians who finally paused, smiled, and pointed at the muddy, blood-smeared figure of Sophocles. All his usual self-consciousness, which had vanished in the time he fought, came rushing back to him. He wondered if he had made a fool of himself, pretending to know how to swing a sword.

But it was not his hackwork that became the stuff of camp legend that day. Instead, it was the way he had rushed from bed to battle with everything he needed except his modesty. By the end of the morning, all around the great circuit of the walls, everyone heard the story, had a good laugh, and passed it on.

"Did you hear about our poet general? He went into battle today as naked as Achilles!"

6.

The poet had learned the meaning of awe. Sitting in his tent with hands shaking, he felt as if he had been passed over by some capricious demon. Though it was not uncommon for a man of fifty-five to fight in the line, the sight of so many younger, deader men made his survival seem perverse. Perverse, he thought—or purposed. He found his canteen, poured it over himself. There was a sensation of burning on his brow that seemed to sear away all moisture, draping him in steam. Clearly the gods were sparing him for some greater design.

He came out. Samians from the city were out with draught-horses now, permitted by truce to drag away their dead. Poristes was standing there, watching the reclamation with a doleful expression. Dexion thought he understood the captain's mood.

"Yes, it could have been us," he said.

Poristes turned, nodded toward the water.

"It's not over yet."

Dexion followed his gaze. Out on the straits, the enemy samaenas had reappeared—half a dozen stalking the approaches to the breakwater, with another two far to the south, under the shadow of Mycale. The triremes of the Athenians were nowhere afloat.

The poet turned back to Poristes. The look on the unburnt side of his face was now the same as the disfigured half, grim in its immobility.

"Where did they come from?"

"We invited them out," spat the captain, "when we let Pericles go with all those ships."

"So what does it mean?"

"It means the Ionians own the sea! They can get food in by water, and they can keep our supplies out. We're the ones under siege now."

Poristes was never one to hide his worries. Dexion looked around: the Athenians still surrounded Samos Town, and the shieldbreakers that had survived the attack were already bombarding the city. Who could doubt which side was winning?

Yet events proved the captain right. Before long, Dorus, Menippus' aide, turned up looking for Poristes. When he came out of his tent, the latter was already dressed for the open sea—cloak of oiled leather, sun-hat, felt anti-slip boots.

"How many ships are you sending?" he asked Dorus.

"Two. You, and the *Terror*. You are instructed to stay at sea day and night until you catch up to the fleet. The course they had planned would have taken them west of Tragia, then into the lee of Akrite, probably beaching at Leros last night, and possibly Cos today—"

"Don't tell me my trade, boy!" Poristes scolded the slave. "We were picked because we know where Pericles will be— and we're fast." He turned to Dexion. "Won't be able to accommodate you this time, I'm afraid. Oarsmen and crew only. We'll be flying high in the water."

Sophocles shrugged. He had, in fact, no intention of going back to sea until he absolutely had to.

The departure of the *Antigone* and the *Terror* drew spectators to the beaches from every quarter of the army. A squadron of four samaenas was waiting offshore, rams to landward. To confuse them, the Athenians seemed to prepare half a dozen hulls for launching, though most of them lacked good crews, equipment, or pilots familiar with local waters. At the critical moment only the two ships designated for escape went into the sea. The Samian oars came down, and the contest began.

As the soldiers cheered them on from the beach, the triremes struck out in roughly parallel courses. The samaenas were less than a stade away when the *Antigone* pivoted southeast and the *Terror* southwest, drawing two enemy ships after each. By a narrow margin, the Samians got their noses into the *Terror*'s path, and she was forced to turn due west. This put her on a course toward the beaches near Hera's sanctuary. She continued to push hard, trying to outpace her pursuers, but she soon ran out of water. The samaenas closed, hoping to ram her before she could find a spot to beach. The race ended when a cohort of archers reached the shore and began shooting at the Samians, forcing them to retire.

The *Antigone* had fled into the teeth of the wind. This, it turned out, was a wise choice: all of the ships were slowed somewhat, but the samaenas, with their wider profiles, were affected more. Before long it was clear that Poristes would break free. From a distance the banks of oarblades seemed to flash, dragonfly-like, as the white lines of a bow-wave formed, and his pursuers were left toiling in his wake. The trireme pulled away. The Samians on the city walls groaned; the Athenians on the beach gave a roar so thunderous that it was heard by goatherds on the foothills of Mount Mycale. The enemy oarsmen heard it too as they laid to, shipped their oars, and gave up the chase.

Chapter VI

TUNNELING TO GLORY

"To look on self-wrought woes, when no other has had a hand in them—this lays sharp pangs to the soul."

—Tecmessa, *Ajax*, l. 260

1.

The Athenians could only stand by and see what the Ionians would do with control of the sea. Bringing in provisions would have to be their first goal; with the city water supply still secure and Pericles unwilling to sacrifice men in a frontal assault, the mere importation of enough food would all but win the war. Dexion left his tent every morning expecting to see a procession of grain ships heading out to sea. The return of just a few of them, a dozen perhaps, would make the town self-sufficient for more time than the Athenian army could afford to besiege it.

And yet—unaccountably—he saw no such thing. Instead, in response to some imagined disloyalty, the Ionians sent out ships to punish their own outlying villages. Columns of smoke rose from the north and west of the island; refugees flocked to Hera, herding slaves and livestock along the rut-roads to the Sanctuary.

Menippus, sensing an opportunity, sent troops to help put out the fires. He then sent work parties to clear charred debris and collect building material for the villagers to rebuild their homes. The rural Samians, whose allegiance to their villages always seemed stronger than to the city, accepted this help warily at first—then wholeheartedly. As Ionian and Athenian worked shoulder to shoulder, sharing canteens and jokes, the mood in the back country shifted. Young girls were allowed out on the roads again. Thankful parents trusted the Athenians enough to let their children play in the vicinity of the soldiers. Nothing the Athenians could have done would have been more effective in winning over the villagers than the petty vindictiveness of the Ionians.

This success helped restore the swagger of Menippus and the other generals. Yes, they granted, the Athenian army was cut off from home. But the Samian position was little better.

"Do you think they'll get grain from anyplace close by, with our fleet in the neighborhood?" asked Menippus at council. "Do you think the Chians or the Lesbians would risk it? Do you think they'll get anywhere with the Milesians? No! They'll have to go all the way to Byzantion, or to one of the ports of the Great King. Then they'll have to get back here before Pericles. When it comes down to a race between the fleet and those merchant tubs, I'll count on our boys every time!"

Then Fortune turned and smiled on the Ionians. A few days after the battle, three Athenian supply ships appeared from the west on a routine supply run to the army. As their captains neared shore, they beheld a frantic bout of signaling from the island, warning them to turn around and run for their lives. The merchantmen shortened sail, baffled by all the smoke and flashing from the Athenian camp. By the time three samaenas came out to greet them it was too late. Over a short distance, no fully-laden roundbottom could outrun an oared warship.

Dexion joined the mob of spectators watching the encounter from the top of Mount Ambelos. A sharp-eyed boy from the fleet was brought up to compensate for the tired eyes of the generals.

Shading his eyes, the lookout narrated the dismal events. "One of the ships is running. He's putting up every inch of cloth he's got, including the crew's underwear! The other two are dumping supplies over the side." He paused. "They look like storage jars, not weapons. The Ionians are just about on them. One of them is making for the runner, and making up ground fast. Wait . . . Great Ares' dick, the crews are shooting back! They've gotten out some bows from someplace. Oh, this is really too much, they're not hitting anything. But the Ionians are slowing down . . ."

"The gods bless them," said Glaucon, turning to heaven with palms raised. "They're trying to make it hard on those bastards."

"Some of the jars are floating," said Xenophon, squinting hard through the midday haze.

"Yes, that's true," said the lookout. "The crews are trying to push them away, but the Ionians will pick them up."

"If they're full of grain we're finished," groaned Cleistophon.

"Calm yourself," Xenophon warned. "You'll frighten the youngsters."

"They don't have to be full of grain to float. A jar of wine will float, too, if there's enough air in it."

"And why would a wine jar have air in it?"

"You must be a child," replied Xenophon, "if you don't know how wine jars get empty at sea!"

"I'd hand over a jar myself, if you'd only shut up."

"They've rammed two of the ships now," the lookout resumed. "Their men are coming across. The crew is still shooting at them."

"We ought to sign those men up for the service," Dexion said to Glaucon.

Glaucon leaned forward as if to make a tart reply, thought the better of it, and observed, "These could be ships owned by their captains. They'd rather die than take a total loss."

The struggle was soon over on two of the ships. The third,

which got a short head start in its retreat, was fortunate that the
wind turned around to the east: as its great square sail bellied
out, its backstays straining, it receded faster into the mist as the
samaenas increased their cadence to follow. The sail was soon
a tiny patch, blued with distance. The oarbanks of the warships
stroked the water one more time, then paused, cocked at an
upward angle and glinting with wet. They were letting the
merchantman escape.

A cheer went up from the Athenian shieldmen on the hill.
The hair's-breadth escape of the last ship was a kind of victory,
costing the Samians tons of additional food. It also guaranteed
that no more supplies would be sent from Piraeus for the time
being. It was only a minor piece of good news, however, in
what could only be seen as a dismal week for the Athenians.
Dexion, who over his career had developed a sharp ear for the
subtler characteristics of applause, perceived a desultory quality
in the cheer. This was an audience that wasn't sure it would
enjoy the drama's final act.

2.

Two days later Pericles returned. All sixty hulls of his fleet were
behind him, surging from the west at combat speed, pennants
flying from their mastheads. As they closed, Sophocles thought
he recognized the shamelessly leering eyes of the *Antigone*,
keeping pace beside the Olympian's flagship. Poristes had
succeeded in retrieving Pericles faster than anyone had anticipated.

The Ionians had half a dozen samaenas in the Mycale straits
when the fleet appeared. They at first turned their prows
toward the mass of triremes, as if contemplating some desperate, glorious stand. But they soon thought the better of it,
spinning on their keels to flee inside the breakwater. The
spectacle put Xenophon in a contemptuous lather.

"Cowards!" he spat. "I told you we should never have sent
away so many ships. We practically invited them to disrespect

us!"

Menippus, having been proven wrong, kept his mouth shut.

Pericles didn't wait for his ship to beach but jumped into the surf. He came out with his red cloak soaked purple and clinging to his skinny legs, his helmet pushed back on his head as his eyes swept the beach. If Old Squidhead now believed he had erred in taking away so many ships, his expression didn't betray it. Instead, he looked like a homeowner returning to discover his house was burgled while he was gone.

To have been so careful in his generalship, yet to have to rush back to save his position—this was unprecedented for Pericles. Yet the Athenians saluted him genuinely as he strode past. Though he showed nor inspired much passion, his mere presence, with its confident physicality, still had a steadying effect. He approached Menippus with all his questions in his eyes, and the other scurried alongside trying to answer them.

Pericles approached the Athenian lines, inspecting the kill zone where the Samians had been stopped. The ground there remained as broken and undulating as beach sand. Its color, though, had lightened with exposure to the sun—except for the places were blood had spilled and congealed into a grisly kind of slurry.

"They made it all the way to here?" Pericles asked, a trace of incredulity in his voice.

"More or less. A bit farther in some places."

The Olympian looked up and down the line. Then he pointed at the blackened husk of a Shieldbreaker.

"Why has Artemon not fixed that?"

"He has many others to put right," replied Menippus.

"Let him have all the men he needs for the job."

Pericles then seemed to bury his chin in his chest as he strode on. His eyes swept over Sophocles, but they showed no greeting or recognition as he passed.

Poristes turned up soon after, looking exhausted after having spent the last two nights afloat. His eyes had that un-focused look of someone whose gaze had been glued to the

horizon; his face had been so long exposed to sea spray a
ribbon of dried salt ran from the corners of his eyes to his ears.
The poet, smiling, hailed him.

"By the gods man, you look a fright! So tell me—did you
see anything of the Phoenicians?"

The captain just closed his eyes and shook his head.

With Ionians bottled up again, the jam of Athenian supply
ships on Ikaria was finally released. Two roundbottoms laden
with dry provisions came first, followed by two more with
additional weapons and shieldbreakers. The latter also brought
a cedar box full of scrolls—letters from home, as well as
reading material for soldiers with more elevated tastes in
entertainment. Sophocles got in line to look through the
inventory, half-hoping to see a play of his own included. Sure
enough, he found an edition of the *Antigone*. He stepped aside,
pretending to watch the small waves roll in, then checked the
box again. His play was one of the first titles to be taken away.

He was on his way back to his tent, feeling not a little
pleased with himself, when the ship's clerk shouted after him.

"Dexion, stop! You have letters."

This announcement struck him so unexpectedly that he was
at a loss to imagine who could have written. But of course it
had to be Nais—and her news would have to be serious indeed
for her to go to such trouble. He took the letters—two small
scrolls each wrapped with a leather thong and sealed with
wax—and went back to his tent, closing the flap after him.

He unwrapped one at random. The date at the top was 7th
Pyanepsion, and by the blockish, professional script he could
tell that Nais—whose script was as poor as most Athenian
females'—had not drafted it. It read:

Dear Father,

I have come to the shop of Horus the paperseller to
get this letter written. I have told the scribe to write it

exactly the way I dictate it to him so if I put things wrong it is my fault not his (he wanted this made clear to you). I have bad news so I hope you are sitting down there. Please do.

Mother is sick. It started with a bad stomach so bad she couldn't keep anything down, but worse than the usual for a pregnant woman because it went on all day. When this went on a long time I told her to call a doctor but she said she would not because of the money. After that she let me call Clitus the groom to have a look because he has been around many foaling horses. He looked at her and said, "I don't know, but the cord be in the wrong place, you should see an Aesclepiad." She thanked him and gave him a skin of wine for his trouble, but she never called the doctor. Since then I have cared for her and watched her closely, she is not getting any better.

Father, I am scared. She brings up everything that goes down, including water, and this can't be good for the baby. Will you write to tell mother that she should open her purse and not worry about the cost of a professional? Or else give us leave to close up the house and go to the temple to see what the Healer commands? I've already gone down to the water to find a ship to bring this letter—there are many ships going to Samos these days. The captain of the *Oropus* is leaving the day after the Festival of Apollo if the auspices allow it. So if you reply we should have it within ten days or maybe within a week, in time to do her some good.

I hope you are as well as you can be, so far away. Mother has told me how proud she is of your service to the city though she doesn't want me to repeat it to you, she is as stubborn as a mule. Please give our love to Iophon and tell him we are proud of him too. Also, please don't be mad this is such a long letter because I saved a few obols to buy this paper myself, I bet you didn't think a girl could be so clever! Also, please write back right away before the ship starts back, so we hear your opinion the soonest.

—Your loving daughter, Photia

Sophocles fell back on his cot. Nais, pregnant? On physical grounds it was certainly possible—she was seventeen years his junior. Yet the opportunity puzzled him. Then he remembered the night he came home after spending the afternoon with Aspasia.

He opened the other letter. It was dated two weeks earlier, on the 22nd Boedromion—it had been held up on one of the ships detained on Ikaria. The handwriting this time, and the letter's brevity, were unmistakable.

Husband,
I had not intended to distract you by writing, but I know your vanity would demand you know the news.
You will have a third child. It is too early to tell if it is a son.
I curse you.

—Your WIFE

He folded and rewrapped the letters. Then he closed the tent flap and sat with his head in his hands. What had already been a puzzling situation now filled him with confusion. He would have laughed if a sudden chill had not come over him; the improbability of it all had the signs of a divine joke—or some hidden design. After all, there were no accidents in the world. So what could this news, and the order in which it was revealed, mean?

It occurred to him that he had been given another son to square accounts for the ultimate sacrifice. Was that the purpose he sensed unfolding around him—to give his life to something other than the worship of Dionysus? What other influence than that of bright, heartless Athena could explain his quick

thinking at Tragia, his ready sword during the Ionian sally? Or
was it all orchestrated by the Furies, to punish him for his
presumption to rival the military legacy of Aeschylus? He liked
to imagine the white-armed Virgin favored the work of
Dexion, and weeping Demeter that of Euripides. But the
Furies always liked Aeschylus.

Yet the news of Nais' pregnancy had met his eyes only after
he had learned she was ill. The circumstances of this had to
meaningful. He could have chosen either letter to read first,
and had been led to Photia's. This could portend the opposite
choice, that he must take ship right away and see to his family's
welfare. Pericles could hardly begrudge him leave to go home:
he had already contributed more to the cause than anyone
could ask. His fate, therefore, would be bound up in his ability
to see the wisdom of sacrificing further glory. Or at least that
was how he might have written the tale.

"Bulos!" he cried.

No answer. He stuck his head out of the tent.

"Bulos!"

"Here, master," the slave replied with a weary half-insolence.
He was coming up the path with a water jug balanced on his
shoulder.

"What, only now getting water? What were you doing this
morning?"

"The spring was muddy then."

"I want you to take these letters to Iophon. He's with
Menippus' staff. You will wait while he reads them, and then
bring them back—and stop making that face!"

The slave quashed a scowl.

"It is sometimes hard to find the young master—for reasons that are not our fault."

"Yes, yes. It's never your fault! Just do your best."

3.

Bulos returned two hours later with his head low, a look of

consternation on his face. Sophocles, who was just finishing his reply to Nais, frowned.

"You didn't find him?"

"I tried, master. No one knows where he is."

"Did you ask Menippus?"

"He wouldn't see me."

The poet shook his head as he re-read his letter. Bulos, anxious to visit the latrines, shifted on his feet.

"Tell me what you think of this," Dexion began. "Dear Nais, I am pleased to hear you are with child, but troubled that you see fit to endanger yourself and our son in your time of illness. Please stop being a fool and let Photia fetch the doctor. You may use the owls stashed in *that* place, *the one we discussed*, if you run short of coin. I expect to hear of your recovery in your next letter. You now know your husband's will. Signed, so and so forth."

"A most forceful production, master," replied the slave.

"Don't mock me," Dexion said as he fixed the seal, then reused some of the leather from Photia's letter to wrap his.

"Now take this down to the sanctuary pull-out. It goes out on a ship called the *Oropus*."

4.

If there wasn't already enough on his mind, the poet received a summons that evening to appear at council. As the generals had already met two days before, and nothing out of the ordinary seemed to be happening on the battlefield, the call surprised him. Was it about something he had done—or not done?

They met this time in a grove far from the camp. As he approached, he noticed an extraordinary number of sentries had been posted to keep out eavesdroppers. This, clearly, was no routine gathering. As he took his place among his colleagues, he could feel the apprehension in the air. In any case, Dexion's arrival barely registered on their faces. Whatever this was about, it wasn't about him.

For the first time, Menippus did not lead the discussion. Instead, Cleon of Scambonidas took the floor. Sophocles' impression of this character was that he was trouble incarnate. Though he still a young man, and only the son of a tradesman, he already had the confidence to stand up in the Assembly and pander away with the best of the populists. Nothing about him, not the mulish stolidity of his face, nor the ambition he freely displayed, nor his overwrought podium style, accorded with the poet's ideal of the public man.

He did, at least, have the virtue of brevity when it suited him. When the preliminaries were done—the sacrifice of a piglet that, thought Sophocles, resembled no one more than Cleon himself—he made his case without preamble or circumlocution.

"Gentlemen, I won't waste your time this evening. We all know what happened in recent days that has brought matters to this sad pass. Certain decisions were made recently by the current leadership—demonstrably poor decisions with repercussions that nearly lost this war. I think you'll agree that the Assembly did not send us here to give the Ionians second chances. The People fielded an army to accomplish one of two things: to force our enemies to submit, or to destroy them. I don't think I'm alone in my determination that their will be done.

"Lest it be thought otherwise, I take no pleasure in questioning anyone's competence. Show me some positive consequence of the options taken, and I will be the first to salute them. If the expedition in support of which so many of our ships were diverted had the result of destroying the Phoenician fleet, the cost might have been worth it. If the fleet had merely chased the Great King's navy away, so it never again sets out to interfere in these waters, that too, would have been something. But I think we all know that none of these things were done. I think we can agree that nothing much was accomplished at all—except the near-destruction of the land army.

"Nor should anyone mistake what is being proposed. No one here claims the martial excellence our brother Pericles presumes for himself as Supreme Commander. Instead of the hegemony of one man, we propose something that is much more in keeping with the character of the Athenians: an executive council of three, rotating on a regular basis among us, that shall be charged with all strategic and tactical decisions, pending review by the full council as opportunity permits.

"In recognition of his many services I propose further that Pericles and his friends be as welcome to serve on the Council of Three as anyone else. I hope this, as well as the manner in which those most troubled by the disaster have chosen to raise their concerns, shall dispel any suspicion of malice, or the sort of political opportunism that is rightly despised by all good citizens. For however different our methods, we all have the same aim. We expect only victory."

Cleon then took his seat beside Xenophon—the one who had argued most against the division of the fleet. From the way they sat together, it was clear that Cleon had at least one ally in the council. Were there others lurking, not yet making their sympathies so obvious, but as ready as he to deal a crippling blow to Pericles' career?

As reluctant to speak as the Olympian was under normal circumstances, he was anxious to do so now. Jumping to his feet, he advanced as if leading the phalanx from the first rank. In his eyes Dexion saw a fire he never displayed arguing over construction contracts and trade policy in the Assembly.

"My friends, I see there is nothing I can say to convince General Cleon to change his mind. Nor should I, for like any citizen, his wisdom is integral to the strength of our democracy. That we debate this question can only assure our victory—either by my removal as Supreme Commander, as he argues, or by the clarification of certain issues that will at last remove all doubt from our collective effort. It is for this reason that I not only agreed to this debate, I insisted upon it.

"First, I must correct our colleague on one point. The

decision that he decries, the one to divide the fleet in order to intercept the Phoenicians, was not made by Pericles. It was made by all of us, sitting together in council just as we are now. Contrary to what some may argue, this is always how business is done in our democracy. No one here is first among equals; no one may arrogate upon himself all the credit for our national policy.

"Now I will not stand here and argue that the outcome was what we all had hoped. The intelligence that inspired our decision was actionable—of that there is no doubt. But we should also allow that the Great King, too, has his sources of information. Should we be surprised, then, at the barbarians' inclination to turn and run when confronted with serious force?"

This drew a chuckle from some of the generals. Cleon and Xenophon remained stonefaced, arms crossed.

"Still, accountability is also an advantage of the Athenian system. The leader does not dictate strategy, but he should accept responsibility when it fails. Anything else amounts to the kind of despotism we can all agree is the end against which we fight. For that reason, and without any further defense, I hereby resign the position of Supreme Commander."

This was unexpected. A flash of panic came over Xenophon's face, but Cleon smiled as if savoring some private joke. The rest looked around in confusion, their eyes imploring each other for guidance.

Pericles continued, "I will make one final point, if I may. While we can only applaud our critic's determination to improve the manner in which we make our military decisions, I believe it would be a serious mistake to replace one leader with a committee. For one thing, I have reservations such an arrangement would ever work. When has any ship benefited from having three captains? The only result, I fear, would be confusion, and the dilution of responsibility that would serve no one's purpose.

"But most importantly, such a measure is unnecessary. For

it is the duty of this council itself to deliberate on how we make war—it is the oath we took, as well as our duty as citizens. Indeed, what need do we have for a council of Three when we have the Ten? As my last act, then, I therefore beg you to mind these objections, as well as to respect the arrangements handed down by our forefathers, and reject this proposal."

With that, Pericles sat down. Menippus rose to take the floor.

"If there are no objections, we will hold the vote now."

"There are objections!" erupted Cleon.

"I agree," Xenophon added.

Callisthenes, who had been silent until then, could take no more.

"Why should we wait? Why should this situation lay unresolved for one hour, when the campaign is at stake?"

"No explanation is necessary!"

To which Callisthenes responded, "I see no reason for us to wait for Cleon to bend ears."

"It is clear," interjected Menippus, "that there is some disagreement on this point. We will therefore vote to determine whether to hold the substantive vote now, or later. All those in favor of voting now, raise a hand."

Six hands went up, with Dexion's joining them.

"The proposal to vote carries. We will now vote on the proposal to replace the position of Supreme Commander with a so-called Council of Three. All in favor, raise a hand."

The count was seven to three against, with Pericles abstaining.

"The proposal is defeated. Now that our colleague Pericles has resigned as Supreme Commander, we need to elect a new one. I nominate Pericles of Cholargus to be Supreme Commander."

"Agreed!" declared Callisthenes.

"The proposal is placed before the council. All those in favor of Pericles' nomination, raise a hand."

And so, all too abruptly, the decision was before him.

Sophocles' first impulse was to support the man who promoted his generalship. Yet how could he forget the cavalier manner in which the Olympian had dismissed his concerns about Artemon's infernal engines? How could he overlook the way the war was cruelly extended, week after bloody week, all for the purpose of sparing casualties? The decision to divide the fleet was, in fact, driven by loss of discipline among men asked to wait too long for victory on a foreign shore. If Pericles was left in power, to what further depravities would this idleness, this cruel and unusual discretion, drive the glorious victors of Marathon and Salamis?

Five hands went up in favor of Pericles: Socrates, Lampides, Glaucetes, Callisthenes, and Glaucon. The nominee did not vote for himself. The remaining five sat opposed—until Dexion looked at Pericles, and saw something in his eyes he didn't expect: a plaintive flicker, a momentary shudder of abandonment, as he seemed on the verge of losing the poet's support. It was a look of panic he had never seen on the Olympian's face before—and it was pitiful.

Dexion's hand climbed by slow, painful degrees.

The meeting closed, Callisthenes and the other loyalists surrounded Pericles to congratulate him. Dexion stood apart, still mystified by how easily sentiment had overridden his reason. And then Cleon confronted him, the man's purple-ringed eyes peering into his.

"That was a fine night's work, scribbler," he said. "Now this accursed siege will never end."

"You don't know that."

"From what I hear, at least *your* wife won't stray," replied the demagogue. "I hope the rest of us are so fortunate."

Pericles caught up with the poet moments later, in the woods just outside the camp. In the faint firelight, he found Sophocles hand and grasped it like a man overboard being pulled to safety. Then, after giving him a kiss, he said just seven words.

"Your loyalty will have its reward."

5.

Some time later two Athenian skirmishers were amusing themselves in the hills beyond Mount Ambelos. Both were the sons of humble thetes, just beyond their legal minority, too poor to afford a hoplite's full panoply of armor. Instead, Timaeus came to Samos with a light shield and spear, and Cleanthes with just a wicker shield his father had fashioned out of the reeds near Marathon. But the latter believed his personal quality surpassed the crudeness of his equipment—and was determined to prove it to Timaeus.

"Throw any rock, then," said Cleanthes, "and I'll throw a bigger one farther than you!"

"You'll regret that challenge," replied the other.

Timaeus stuck his spear in the ground by the butt-spike, and leaned his shield against a mulberry bush. Then he found a piece of limestone that he judged to be the ideal combination—bigger than his fist, but light enough to throw a good distance.

"Stand aside," he said.

Cleanthes watched, smirking with derision, as Timaeus stepped back, swung his arms, and twisted his body discobolos-style. After a few practice swings he unsprung a decent throw, casting the rock into a stand of wild oleander.

"Not bad. Now meet your better."

Cleanthes selected a missile twice as big as Timaeus'.

"Wait, let me see that," demanded Timaeus. Lofting it in his hand, he shook his head. "This is bigger, but not much heavier."

"I never said bigger *and* heavier, fool!"

"You implied it."

Cleanthes reared back and threw. His throw lacked the Olympic grace of his rival's, but it went farther, over the bushes and onto the dirt beyond. Where the rock hit, it made an odd sound, as if the earth was hollow beneath.

"That was strange."

Borrowing Timaeus' spear, Cleathes went to where the rock landed and tested the ground with the butt-spike. It rang like a drum every time he hit it.

Within an hour a gang of diggers was there, swarming over the area with handpicks. Beneath the soil, they found a layer of loose rubble, like the tailings from a mine. Menippus arrived with Artemon just as the workmen came down on the vault of a concealed structure. As they uncovered more of it, Artemon had himself placed at the north end, sighting along its length toward the mass of Mount Ambelos and the city beyond.

"It's Eupalinus' tunnel," he announced. "The head of it, most likely, before it goes under the mountain."

Menippus said nothing, but had a look on his face much like Polycrates discovering his lost ring.

Word was dispatched to Pericles, but before the Olympian could arrive to take charge, the Athenians had pried off one of flat stones that formed the roof of the passage. Excited, they dropped inside. Their exploration had an inauspicious start: one man had to be pulled out immediately, having broken a leg stumbling into the water channel hewn into the floor along the west wall.

As it was described to Dexion, the tunnel was tall enough for a helmeted man to stand upright, but because of the water channel there was room only for the party to go through single file. Undeterred, the Athenians pushed inside, fantasies in their heads of surprising the Ionians on the other end. On they rushed into the empty heart of the mountain, their torches dancing as they ran, their spirited battle cries echoing through the six stades of the tunnel's length. And so they achieved the distinction of being the first Athenians inside the Wall. That they also happened to be many feet underground was nothing more than incidental.

They were three-quarters of the way through the tunnel when their torches lit up a wall of Samian spears. The defenders rushed forward, attacking the faces of the surprised

Athenians.

Dexion heard the sound of this fight all the way from the north end: desperate, high-pitched screams, the bright ring of iron tips on bronze. An Attic voice yelled, "Get out of the water!" Like some giant set of lungs shifting from exhalation to inhalation, the direction of the air through the tunnel suddenly reversed.

"General, should we send more men?" someone asked. Dexion looked up; a shieldman was looking at him, waiting for an answer. He opened his mouth—he would have gone in himself, and alone, if the act would have ended the war early. But he was preempted by the voice of Pericles.

"Menippus!" thundered the Olympian. "What is this? Did you order an *attack*?"

Menippus only stood there with his hand on the butt of his sword. In truth, he had not expressly ordered the assault, but was still responsible for its outcome.

Pericles was rarely so angry in public. With eyes blazing and the cords of his neck snapping free, he summoned Menippus to him like a reproving parent. Menippus obeyed, but Pericles continued to shout into his face as if he were standing on the other end of the Pynx. "Could they have made a better trap for us? Could they defend anything more easily than men coming *one at a time*? Did you order this?"

Speaking in a far lower voice, Menippus managed to calm Pericles down. Dexion noticed, however, that the sound of the battle below had subsided, and that none of the men who went down had returned. Hanging down from above, he peered down the length of the tunnel. Since the passage seemed to jog left about halfway down its length, he could see nothing more than a faint glow in the extreme distance.

He discovered Pericles looking at him with disapproval.

"Send a message to the Ionians. Ask them for leave to collect our dead."

6.

Samian girls had learned that they could count on Eupalinus'
tunnel. War or peace, siege after siege, hundreds of them had
for generations lifted their jars, walked to their local fountain
houses and dipped into an endless supply of cool, clean water.
It had become like a birthright, every bit as dependable as the
arrival of spring. Little need, then, had the Samians for the
contrivances of other, less affluent towns, such as wells and
catch basins for rainwater.

None were prepared, then, when the water ran red with the
blood of the Athenian soldiers killed in the tunnel. As the flow
from the spigots turned foul, the younger girls abandoned their
jars and ran screaming through the town. The Samian men,
convinced by the commotion that the enemy had broken
through the walls, charged fully armed from their houses.
Troops from elsewhere in the city had to be brought in to clear
the streets of bellicose males and ululating females. It was only
a second apparition, as unprecedented as the first, that settled
the unrest: some time after noon, when the day's heat was at its
height, the flow to the spring houses slowed, sputtered, and
stopped. The Athenians had cut the water supply to the city.

Though he was a student of the Milesian school of natural
philosophers, old Callinus had a streak of sympathy for the
tradition that would later be associated with the Cynics. To
him, contrivances like Eupalinus' tunnel were nothing more
than vanities—artifacts of human pride that were destined to
fail. For his part, he always drank as sparingly as he ate, using
only water collected from the cisterns of his own house, or
fetched by his slaves in simple skins direct from springs outside
the city. He would hardly miss the aqueduct. But the rest of the
Samians, who shared neither his philosophy nor his economy,
would indeed miss it.

Callinus went out into the city to see the people's distress
firsthand. They were used to seeing Callinus walk the streets
dressed in nothing more than a thin cloak and the dust of the
road on his skin. Over time, they had come to be amused by

him, pointing and laughing at their "beggar general". With the opportunity lost to break the siege, and the tunnel in enemy hands, the mood this time was as dark as the shadow of Mount Ambelos.

Walking into the marketplace, he saw most of the stands were bereft of customers. The men walked around with their hands playing nervously around the hilts of their swords; the women, whose Asiatic tastes could usually be counted on to add color to the scene, were drably dressed, their jewelry long since surrendered to the cause, their heads shaved to provide caulking material for the navy. In the middle of the market, another pile of hair, collected this time from the heads of the children, was being bagged for transport to the ships.

He was regarding this when the Athenian request arrived to collect their casualties in the tunnel.

"Let them be welcome to that honor," Callinus told the messenger, "if they will send Dexion to speak with me."

7.

The tunnel was just as Sophocles expected—cold. With the flow of water now stopped from the extramural side, it was nothing more than a hole, dead like the anteroom of Hades. As he pushed farther underground, he became uncomfortably conscious of the mass of rock that stretched above his head. The underworld, it seemed, was not only dark and frigid, but a kind of vise, crushing the imprisoned souls within. Chilled as much by such thoughts as by the tunnel's atmosphere, he drew his cloak more tightly around himself as he walked.

By the faint light of his lamp he could see the glint of the ancient toolmarks on the stone. He could also see the glint in the eyes of the rats that turned on his approach, scattering like routed shieldmen before him. The tunnel jogged left, then right; he passed through the place in the center where Eupalinus' two work crews, toiling from either side of the mountain, met at last. The notion of working under such conditions, in frigid, subterranean darkness, lungs tormented by dust, made him very glad he was a producer of plays.

Earlier that morning, Menippus' slave Dorus came to deliver an invitation to Pericles' tent. Obeying the summons, he found Menippus there but not Pericles. The Olympian's pallet was tidy, his armor stacked, his cup and utensils piled neatly for the steward. Without meaning to, Dexion craned his neck to see if their owner was concealed nearby. Menippus looked up from his papers, snorted.

"There's been a message from Callinus. He wants to talk, but only to you."

"To me?"

"Yes, that was my reaction, too."

Of course, there was no question of refusing the assignment. But he had also been considering the possibility of going home to Nais. It was unnerving to have that option abruptly rendered moot—as was the prospect that Callinus, a man he had never met, would decide whether he would ever again see his wife alive.

"You will meet him in the tunnel," Menippus said. "Go alone, and unarmed. I assume I don't have to tell you not to negotiate, just listen to what he has to say. Don't give away the store!"

With Artemon's scribblings, and Menippus' prickly gift for metaphor ("don't give away the store" indeed!), there seemed to be more than one poet on the Athenian side. What sort of man the enemy general was became obvious when Sophocles suddenly felt he was no longer alone in the tunnel. Raising his lamp, he discovered Callinus leaning there, observing him from the darkness.

"Is this an ambush?"

Sophocles' voice did not echo in the tunnel—it congealed into a hollow reverberation that hung around his head like a wreath of smoke. Callinus gave a pained smile, rays of wrinkles spreading from the corner of his eyes.

"If we meant to harm you, Dexion, you would not be alive

now to ask that question."

"Ah, but then the Samians would revert to form, breaking their oaths."

Ignoring the insult, the other opened a water skin and drank from it. Then he offered it to Sophocles.

"I wonder if you can grasp the absurdity for us, to have to bring water into this, the greatest aqueduct in the Greek world!"

"But you must have known we would find it, one way or another."

"Some of us did," replied Callinus. "But some of us preferred to take the counsels of hope."

The poet inspected Callinus' face. With its heavy brow, lively eyes and leathery darkness, it seemed like the face of a marketplace idler—someone who spent the day challenging strangers to impromptu debates in the stoa. But before long he sensed that there was a silence about the Samian that belied the first impression. If he gave off an air of sophistic contention, it was the kind that smoldered from within, as if he were self-sufficient in all wisdom and all foolishness. Dexion racked his memory to find a face to compare it to, and could only think of Aeschylus himself. The comparison made Sophocles feel twenty years younger—and twenty years callower—as he faced the prospect of negotiating with the man.

Then, with Sophocles in mid-appraisal, a vault seemed to shut behind Callinus' eyes, and it was down to business.

"Some people are impressed with your work," he said, "but I must tell you I'm not. What play has ever won a war, or fed a child? You Athenians spend a fortune on the drama, and derive no obvious benefit. It is the curse of the Greeks."

"And yet, I gather you invited me here for a reason."

"If I can say anything for you, poet, it is that you must know the stories of our race. And so I tell you, no city has oppressed the Greeks as much as your Athens. Think of Homer—in ten years of investing Troy, did Agamemnon's army ever surround the city, hoping to starve a free people into surrender? No! They left the city open for all to enter, even the allies of the enemy. I wonder what the poet would say about those who style themselves the heroes of our day!"

"He would say that the Samians compare little to great, when they liken themselves to the city of Priam," replied Sophocles.

"What a pale shadow of that glory you are. Petty, vindictive Athens! What a squalid comparison you make, when you work your engines in the middle of the night on innocent women and children! Did you think we would be awed, to see sleeping babes murdered in their sleep? Tell me how you would justify this, Dexion! Unloose that silver tongue!"

Sophocles flushed when he thought of the Shieldbreaker. He frowned, replied "This silver tongue only moves at the sight of silver."

Callinus dug into a fold in his cloak, pulled out a silver tetradrachm, and tossed it on the floor.

"There—an owl of your own city! Tell me your excuse, now."

"I'm obliged to make excuses no more than you are. You, who conspired against the government of the people, who attacked our fleet by stealth, and who hide from your obligations behind walls! Are these the acts of honorable men? And remember, it is not only the Athenians who have sailed here—we have the Chians and the Lesbians on our side, too. Do they share our arrogance, Callinus? Does everyone, just because they oppose you?"

"Chios and Lesbos," replied the other, almost spitting with contempt, "will sign up for whatever cause enriches them. And you, Dexion, should stick to the orchestra! You make a mediocre politician."

"What proposal should this mediocre politician bring back to his people?"

Callinus shifted on his feet, the disappointment plain on his face.

"You will withdraw all your forces, pledge non-interference

in Samian affairs. After a short interval to restore our fleet, we will return as full partner in the Delian League, contributing ships like before."

"And?"

"And that is all! You haven't conquered anything yet."

Sophocles retrieved the stater and pocketed it.

"That doesn't seem like much of an improvement over your last offer."

"You forget that we demanded restitution for our losses, and a gift for Hera."

"Yes, you could hardly ask for restitution when you've been busy burning your own farms! Fair enough. I will take back your message. But you'll need more than an old scribbler to convince the Athenians to accept such a traitorous bunch back into the alliance."

"You'll have no more trouble than me, convincing the Samians to let Pericles leave this place alive. Remember Dexion, all the world doesn't share your estimate of your own greatness."

Chapter VII

THE SOUND OF THIRST

"For an army, like a city, hangs wholly on its leaders, and when men do lawless deeds it is the counsel of their teachers that corrupts them."
—Neoptolemus, *Philoctetes*, l. 380

1.

The day before Sophocles went to sea he found himself beset by anarchic desires; though he'd sworn to honor his good fortune in deceiving Nais by avoiding Aspasia, he found his thoughts wending toward Pericles' house before his feet followed suit. There was time for one last fall, he reasoned—one last reason to hate himself before the long, cold night. He hid behind a corner, ashamed of himself, until he could approach the door without being seen from the street. When the houseboy showed him into the parlor, he was not a mature man of fifty-five but a child in want, red-faced and desperate to have it over with.

She wasn't alone. Lysicles was there, and from their proximity to each other he could see they hadn't been discussing rhetoric. There was a sheen on her skin that seemed to gather in strength in her eyes, like a cluster of stars standing forth from the twilight. From the way the silk clung to each curve of her body, he believed she must literally have rolled from her bed, pulled on the sheerest thing to hand, and traipsed out to humiliate him.

"May Poseidon protect you," the sheepseller said as he pumped Dexion's arm. "I have half a mind to throw my affairs to the wind and follow you fellows out."

"Yes . . . why don't you?" he replied, perhaps making his antipathy too plain. Lysicles returned a thin smile, then on his way out cast his hostess a glance into which Sophocles read volumes of implications. Aspasia, who was devouring a fig, wiggled her nose at him.

When he was gone, she came up and attached herself to his hip, one silk-clad leg cocked along his midriff. "Thank you for showing up when you did," she said, her eyes closed as she rested her head on his shoulder. "I was beginning to think he'd never go."

"Do you greet all your unwelcome guests dressed like that?"

She looked at him. "You sound like *him*!" she cried, pulling up her hair to show she meant high-domed Pericles. But when she saw the stink all over his face, she turned sincere. "How could you think that! He is his master's dog, and thinks he has the run of the house. But not of me."

He kept his eyes on her until she smiled. "Not that he hasn't asked for it," she granted. "But I can do better."

She led him to her bed. There he found the blankets were unmussed, and if the odor of sheepseller somehow adhered to a woman's body, he didn't detect it. Yet when it was done he still sat up, perturbed in that way he got when a dancer missed his mark, and a performance was ruined. He fingered the scroll beside her bed, thinking only at the last moment to check the name.

"Whose work is this? Agathon? Euripides?"

It was one of his. With that, he crumbled, concealing himself in her arms. She took him in, holding him safe within her perfumed pliance, and whispered, "I worry about you, my poet. I worry about you. How I worry . . ." And there he stayed until they lit the lamps at crossroads shrine, and he pulled himself free in the flickering gloom to wrap himself for the street again, and begin the long walk to the home he loved, but could not abide.

2.

Soon after Eupalinus' aqueduct was cut the guards detected a strange noise from beyond the Samian walls. It was scarcely perceptible at first, making many who heard it wonder if it was only the kind of torment sent by the gods when they make the ears ring in a silent place, or the body throb from some invisible ailment. But then it gathered in intensity, until all the Athenians could hear it plainly from their tents, day and night. It was nothing other than a low, collective moan, resembling the sound produced by the women of a grieving household, but much deeper and wider in scope. Not exactly cheerful, it disturbed many of the Athenians. After a week, though, it was like the hiss of the wind and the chirping of the crickets, so constant it became easy to ignore.

Sophocles fought this temptation. As he lay concentrating on it, he perceived that the sound seemed to rise and fall through the day, reaching its peak in the hottest part of the afternoon. Below its surface the sound had variations, like a theatrical chorus singing distractedly, half in conversation with itself. Yet there were also higher notes in it, higher and more childlike than any heard on the stage.

When at last he understood what he was hearing, he shot to his feet and went straight to Pericles.

This happened to be in the middle of the night. Pericles didn't summon him inside but came out to meet him. With his white bedclothes wrapped around his lank form, and the reflection of the full moon gleaming from his shiny head, the Olympian resembled nothing other than an enormous wax candle.

"What is it, Dexion?" he asked, making obvious the liberality of his patience.

"I can hear the sound of the city suffering," Sophocles said.

"What?"

"The Samians have no water."

Pericles gave him a long look as if to ferret out the joke. But when Dexion stared back without a hint of humor, he reached out to squeeze the poet's arm.

"That can't be. The water's been shut off only a few days, and I'm certain they stockpiled food when they heard we were coming. Would that you were right, my friend!"

But Sophocles was right. Cities were like people—they could try to put a brave face on adversity, striking a resolute silence, but sooner or later their desperation showed in other ways. A starving man might be defiant, but he couldn't stop the involuntary murmuring of his stomach. In a city under siege, when the mass of young or sick or weak of mind swelled beyond a certain number, the expression of their despair could no longer be hidden. It must burst forth at last, rising and merging and spilling over the walls.

"I know you have no reason to trust my judgment in these things," he told Pericles. "But mark my words on this. This war doesn't have much farther to go."

3.

"Do they mean to insult us?" Pericles asked after Sophocles reported Callinus' peace offer. "Or more to the point, do we mean to insult our honored dead by accepting such a proposal?"

The assembled generals looked around, measuring the depth of zeal they were prepared to display.

"Never!" cried Menippus.

Said Creon of Scambonidas, "They spit in our faces."

"Of course, no," Glaucon agreed.

"When I took up my father's shield," said Callisthenes, "I swore I would die before bringing disrepute on those arms."

Glauketes was contented simply to declare, "I trust Pericles."

"They have transgressed the gods and we are the instrument of their punishment," said Androcides.

"The arms of Athens humble the proud," Lampides agreed.

"Unacceptable," pronounced Xenophon.

"It would be a terrible precedent," Cleitophon observed, "for the Athenians to cut and run now."

"We fight on," said Anagyprasian Socrates.

Dexion meant to cast his vote earlier, but was beaten to it by all the others. Now everyone was looking to him.

"The messenger should not be obliged to judge the message. But if you press me, I would say the issue is moot. The Ionians have no water."

"I will not judge Dexion's ear for such things," said Pericles. "It is for greater powers than us to dispense such mercies. In any case, the council has made its decision."

Pericles punctuated the council's "no" with another round of nocturnal bombardment from the shieldbreakers. In truth, no one could have expected anything but a refusal—this Callinus was a stiff-necked fellow, provocative even when he meant to raise a hand. Yet Sophocles found himself negotiating with the gods as the machines rattled into the night, offering to dedicate any masterworks to come to Apollo, Artemis, father Zeus. He entreated Helios to burn up the Samians' water faster. He begged Hermes to put one of Artemon's bolts through the chest of Callinus. What a simple antidote that would be to their collective curse!

The Ionians made their response the next morning. Just after the sun broke over Mount Mycale, a party of ten Samian shieldmen appeared on the walls opposite Pericles' tent. They brought with them half a dozen Athenian prisoners, naked and bound, and a smoking brazier. The handles of metal tools hung over the side of the brazier, their business ends roasting over the coals. Curious, some of Pericles' men came closer to see. This time, no archers rose to drive them back; Callinus wanted his enemy to have a good view of what happened next.

A Samian picked up one of metal implements. From a distance all could see the end of the tool glowed hot—it appeared to be some kind of cattle-brand. As the first Athenian prisoner was forced to his knees, the Samian approached him with the iron. The prisoner struggled as his captors held him down. The brand was centered against his forehead, and the man screamed as the metal sank into his skin. His tormentor held it there a good long time, driving it deep as if he meant to disfigure him down to the very bone. Those who witnessed the sickening act remembered seeing the little puff of gray smoke, accompanied by the wet hiss of molten iron quenched by the prisoner's flesh. The display was repeated five more times that morning.

When they were finished, the Samians pushed the prisoners back out of sight and tossed the iron from the wall. Pericles had it retrieved. The design of the brand was a wide-eyed, recumbent owl, patterned after the emblem on the Athenian tetradrachm. Dexion wondered whether it was just dumb spite, to torment Athenians with the symbol of their own city. Or did the Ionians have in mind a more trenchant comment on Athenian avarice—rendering them, in effect, into versions of their own currency?

The distinction scarcely mattered as the Athenian camp ignited. Soldiers with swords went around looking for Samian prisoners to torture, but there were none. Instead, a mob gathered in front of Pericles' tent, demanding the outrage be avenged by taking the city immediately. The Olympian, knowing full well that he must seem attentive to the people, came out and attended to what they had to say. And he stood for hours more, facing every speaker, keeping his mouth shut as the crowd's rage was spent on everything that had frustrated them since they'd arrived: Samian arrogance, slow food shipments, frigid nights, trench duty, gnats, generals who expect too much, generals who expect nothing, holes in tents, bad wine, blockade duty, ungracious villagers, infrequent mail, no decent market, no blankets, no hunting, no women, no end in sight.

"Pericles, you know there's nothing we won't do for you!" cried one fellow who seemed to have experience speaking in the Pnyx. "Give the order, and we will tear down their walls stone by stone! Say anything, but don't let this farce go on another day! Have mercy on us—let us kill and die like men, not waiting here like dogs!"

The great man nodded as if he had taken all of this to heart. Then he replied, "Make no mistake. I hear you, dear citizens. And believe me, if there was any other way, I would oblige! But even if you could convince me to sacrifice your lives, you could never make a hundred dead enemies worth a single one of you. Nor would I make another generation of needless widows. That is something no command can change!

"But there is one thing you can tell me," he said, his eyes half-lidded now, his tone shifting from the declamatory to the seductive. "I may be wrong, but are there not a few prisoners from the enemy ships being kept on Tragia? I wonder what they're doing right now. Lounging on the beach, perhaps? I wonder what they'd say if they were brought here, to bear witness to the savagery of their countrymen! Wouldn't that be something to see?"

He didn't have to repeat the suggestion. A ship was sent to fetch the Ionian sailors that very day. Meanwhile, Athenian ingenuity was set to the task of fashioning some suitably humiliating cattle brand for them. Dexion saw the candidates in a pile before Pericles' tent—among them, a *sigma* for Samos, an *alpha* for Athens, a cartoon of a vagina that could have been the evil eye turned sideways. The consensus went at last for a shape that was much like a pig's snout seen in profile, meant to suggest the distinctive rams of the Ionian samaenas. In this way many of the craftsmen who had worked on Pericles' splendid monuments occupied their time, devising better ways to degrade the enemy.

Dexion and Poristes didn't watch the show put on by the

Athenians that night. Instead, they sat on the hill over-
looking the strait, sharing a wineskin. Alas, the screams of the
victims—all thirty of them—were impossible to miss as they
rose over the camp.

The captain opened a fold in his cloak and spat in it. "What
have the Athenians become, that they do such things?" he
asked. "Are we Persians?"

"I think the Great King would have had that wall down
already, if it cost him ten thousand lives."

Poristes raised his right arm. "Then hail all-powerful
Artaxerxes in his crooked hat! His father may have failed to
enslave the Greeks, but Greek freedom will finish the job in
the time of the son."

Laughing, Dexion asked "Fool, do you know what you're
saying?"

"Too well at this time of night. Now pass the skin! And
there'd better be more in there than lees and spit!"

4.

The spectacle of Greeks disfiguring each other should have
disgusted Dexion. Under normal circumstances, he would have
resisted it any way he could—if not by arguments in council,
then with verses scratched in secret. To be sure, he was
saddened, and disappointed that the brotherhood of Athenians
and Ionians had fallen to such squalor. He was worried that the
ill-feeling between them would never be overcome. But he was
not disgusted.

In place of Poristes' moralism, or Pericles' resolve, he was
instead strangely exhilarated. Now that is was clear he had little
influence on events, he surrendered to the feeling that had
lurked beneath the surface of his fear. The war was, in fact,
such a unique eruption of awfulness into Greek affairs that it
seemed as if he was watching a tragedy. Just when he had
convinced himself that men could not be more stupid,
History—the governing technician—proved otherwise. In the

face of deliberate starvation, mutilation, and shieldbreakers, what license could he deny himself in art? He felt a whole world of improbability was fair game now. The prospect made him tremble; in the face of what he might accomplish, he felt awe.

Polyneices and Antigone almost began to write itself. Innovations, such as a split chorus and exchanges of masks between characters, seemed possible, even inevitable. He contemplated putting things before the audience—such as a kiss, or a violent death—that had never been staged before. As he took dictation, Bulos' face showed the disapproval he thought befitted such vanities; instead of thrashing him, Dexion inwardly took satisfaction in knowing that his vindication was certain. Yes, some of his countrymen would resist change as they always had. But after hearing what happened at Samos, what Athenian could deny that a new day had dawned in the life of his city? What was impossible now?

This perverse thrill was marred by only one thing. Since the first two letters had arrived from Photia and Nais, he had heard nothing more from home. When he needed time to order his hurtling thoughts, or when Bulos' arm needed a rest from composing, Sophocles would go down to the beach to meet the supply ships.

These were round-bottomed merchantmen too heavy to be run onto the sand. Instead, they anchored some distance off-shore and unloaded their cargo onto barges. Standing there in his general's cloak, he would be among the first to help the shieldmen haul these boats from the surf. Delighted by the sight of a general getting his hands dirty, the Athenians would demand the mail pouch right away, searching for Dexion's letters even before their own. When there were none, the whole crew was disappointed.

It was on one of these trips that he caught sight of the *Antigone*. She parked well up the strand with her hull canted for scraping. In this way she looked at him somewhat cock-eyed, as if tilting her head in mid-question. When she spoke this time, it was in Aspasia's voice:

ANTIGONE: And so you are here again, to look on your handiwork! On what occasion do you risk exposure, Sophocles?

DEXION: My handiwork? Aside from an imprudent creation of a certain character, for what do you blame me now?

ANTIGONE: Why, everything! Look at how these men respect you, a mere poet. You have succeeded in your ambition, for not even Aeschylus was so loved by his shieldmates. Yet what a price you have paid! How profligate you've been with the blood of fellow Greeks!

DEXION: I indulge in nothing but foolishness, in listening to you.

ANTIGONE: Hypocrite! You wrote my story—you know what it is to stand up to power. Are you so enamored of glory that you'll see the Athenians disgraced? Why do you remain silent when Pericles tempts disaster?

DEXION: I don't know what you are talking about.

ANTIGONE: You deceive yourself, while a higher law is transgressed. The warnings were plain—didn't you see the eclipse? While the Athenians congratulate their ingenuity, and strike vain poses, the goddess grows angry. Not even the king of Olympus would willingly invite the wrath of Hera! What will save the Athenians when she strikes? Yet there you stand, knowing full well the disaster you must meet, thinking only of your own affairs. Self-deceiver! For what has all your art been, if not to raise your voice now? Or was it all for another purpose—to serve your vanity?

Dexion rolled over in his cot. The moonlight shining through the tent fabric rendered the wall as luminous as a pan of milk. The camp seemed quiet around him, but the silence was strained, like a bowstring about to snap. Under the murmur of the evening breeze, there was a clicking sound as a shieldbreaker crew wound the firing mechanism.

DEXION: There was a time, tormentor, that your words carried weight with me. You've caused me much pain, cost me many nights' rest. But you should know now that your time is past—that your arguments make no more impression than raindrops on Polycrates' walls.

ANTIGONE: You are Aeschylus' superior in this at least: the way you mix flattery and untruth gives your deceit a pleasant odor.

DEXION: Go again to Pericles with my objections, you say. But why? If we offend, isn't this the cost of power? Remember the play, when the Chorus sang, "And through the future, near and far, as through the past, shall this law hold good: nothing that is vast enters into the life of mortals without a curse." Athens is great at last, and befitting her will be her glory and her punishment. It is not for a mere poet to foil her proper fate.

ANTIGONE: Take care, O Sophocles, that you take to heart your own words!

DEXION: I do nothing else. It is not for us to apply our timid judgment in such cases. Great in their time were the sons of Zeus and Peleus, yet Heracles put on his poisoned cloak in the end, and Achilles meet his arrow. Today no single mortal can match their glory, but cities of men can. Athens has been chosen for eternal fame—as long as men exist, they will remember her like an old man cherishes the memory of his youth. Yet for that honor her men are doomed to die, her walls cast down, her power humbled. It is a fate I can see now as clearly as the end of this war.

ANTIGONE: I see you have changed, poet, for you espouse the foolishness of Creon. But be warned: ruined walls and dead men are not the only curses reserved for you. For this arrogance, this presumption to see clearly what is not for mortals to see, you will suffer special torment.

DEXION: Still trying to turn my head, are you? Be gone now, witch! You have no more power over me. And if you speak to me in the future, I'll give your words no more thought than I give the wind.

With that, the Aspasian Antigone fell silent. The canted ship was, once again, just a ship, and Dexion never heard the doomed princess speak to him again.

5.

The soldiers on the hillsides were spread in every position idleness could devise. Some, off-watch, slept in midday, hunkering in the shelter of hills and shepherds' walls to escape the autumn winds. Lying there, they looked like casualties of some rout, deposited where their pursuers had caught them, until they twitched, reaching into the recesses of their tunics to scratch the welts made by the bugs that infected every crotch in the camp. Some literally buried themselves in dirt to escape this torture: they had their line-mates pile on their bodies the rich

Samian loam, which had the added advantage of being as soft and warm as woolen blankets. After this treatment only the heads of the buried sleepers stuck out, with round river-cobbles for pillows.

Other men sat hunched beneath their overcloaks, sets of knucklebones or clay dice between them, or making wagers on the first ant to escape a circle they had drawn in the dirt. The long, cold, dull days inspired much experimentation with the cook-fires. An increasing variety of birds, rodents and lizards were prepared and sampled, often with novel dressings (roast agama with wild mustard, acorn, and evaporated sea-salt, anyone?) These men would look up as Dexion approached, their boredom relieved by momentary curiosity as he asked, "Has anyone seen Iophon of Colonus?"

None had. Diversion over, the men's eyes would vanish behind clouds as the poet general passed them by. Did any army on the cusp of victory ever seem so dispirited?

After the first try he saw it was useless to send his servant to find his son. Bulos was loathe to ask around, afraid that the soldiers would take their boredom out on dainty slaves. As unreasoning fears went, this one had some justification: with women in such short supply, abuse of slaves was rampant in the camp. Not even the property of aristocrats was safe. Slaves now went in groups to the stream for water, and nobody sent them out at night for anything less than dire reasons.

Sophocles scoured every corner of the camp for the full distance all around the city walls. He stuck his head into tents hosting day-long drinking parties; he asked around the spear-sharpening circles held by those who imagined they were hardcore killers; he went out to the latrine ditches where, amid a stench so powerful it made him faint, the thetes toasted each other with vinegar. Iophon had always been elusive, but Dexion imagined that, with persistence, he would find him in the end. But the boy was nowhere to be found.

Now he was becoming angry. Avoiding one's parents was nothing unusual for youths his age, but all the fruitless inquiries were beginning to make Sophocles look foolish. As the errand dragged on, he had imaginary arguments with the boy. *I'm glad my father didn't live to see what an irresponsible wretch I've raised!* he raged. *I would have given you important news of your mother! Have you no respect for her?* To this, he imagined Iophon would give a theatrical roll of his eyes, put down some foolish ram's head drinking horn he had bought in a junk shop, and ask the matter with Nais. *I don't think you deserve to know!* Sophocles would retort, then turn on his heel and abandon him the way he never could in reality.

Then he saw wide-bottomed Menippus strutting up the crown of a hill with his entourage. It occurred to Dexion to ask where Iophon was; he had, after all, accepted responsibility for the boy. When Dexion hailed him, Menippus paused, turned, and seemed to recognize Sophocles. He waved. Dexion waved back—then watched the man retreat beyond the high ground. "Menippus, wait!" he cried out, driving himself up the hill. But when he got to the top, he was confronted with twenty ranks of identical tents and no clue where Menippus had gone.

The man had clearly run away at the very sight of him. Furious, Dexion addressed a shieldman who happened to be passing by.

"You there! Did you see where Menippus went?"

"You just asked me where Iophon is," replied the hoplite, his eyes laughing at him.

Sophocles withdrew, wrapping the ends of his cloak around his shoulders. His dignity would allow him to search no further. In a way he didn't yet understand, Iophon had to be responsible for this humiliation. The boy would pay the price soon enough.

6.

He was back in his tent, indulging in a sulk worthy of mighty Achilles, when he heard them calling his name.

"Master, someone to see you," announced Bulos from behind the flap.

"If it's that ungrateful brat, tell him I have nothing to say."

"It's not Iophon."

Dexion came out just in time to see four shieldmen from the beach arrive with triumphant grins on their faces. He stood hand on hip, at a loss to understand the occasion until the leader reached into a fold in his cloak and brought out a sealed scroll.

"This was at the bottom of the pouch," the man said. "You missed it."

Sophocles took the scroll. "So I see," he said, inspecting the seal. The wax was impressed with a falcon—the glyph for Horus, which was also the name of the scribe/paperseller who had drafted Photia's first letter.

He turned to take it inside, but was brought up short by the expectant expressions on the faces of the shieldmen. "By Hermes blessed," the poet saluted, not knowing what else they needed to hear. But that simple formula was enough. A soft light of satisfaction broke over them, as if a tiny sun had manifested.

What was he supposed to do with this kind of honor? The admiration of comrades under arms was different stuff than the repute of writing fine plays. The latter was at the end of a long, intensely exhausting process that, frankly, he thought deserved prizes. And his audiences obliged with cash, livestock, and gratitude. When the festival season was over, he was recognized in the streets, but this was always as a prodigy, not a hero. Poets could win renown, but never glory—unless they picked up a spear like any other citizen.

A military reputation was earned in just a few heated moments, and felt nothing like civic gratitude. It was, rather, a brotherhood of shared experience. Athenians throughout the camp believed they had a secret in common with Dexion. Yet this kind of fame already seemed more durable than any other. He could already imagine meeting the same shieldmen decades thence, their figures shrunk by age, squinting at the bulletins posted at the altar of the Eponymous Heroes, and finding the same conspiratorial grins on their faces as they shambled up on blasted knees to recall old times.

He unrolled the letter, which read:

22nd Pyanepsion

Dear Father,

We hope this letter finds you in good health. The most wonderful news has reached the city in the last few days, of the heroism you showed in a battle at sea! You should know that the whole city is very proud of you, no matter what certain people say in the streets. I hear them out the window sometimes, and on my way to the market, and would tell them how petty they were, if I had the gift of your golden tongue. As it is they shut up when they see the daughter of Sophocles in the streets, carrying her basket in a way that speaks as well as words.

Dexion smiled—how good the Greeks were at being jealous! And yes, he imagined there must be a way to bear a basket that expressed contempt for all that. He must remember to ask how she did it, so he could use it on stage.

You should know I've gone down to the water every morning to see if the *Oropus* has come back with your answer to my letter. It has not, but I found another ship to send this message: we went back to Clitus, and for the price of just a sack of last year's olives, he gave Mother a philtre he uses on sick mares. It worked. She is eating now, and sits up in her bed. Yesterday the midwife came and felt how the baby lies and said it seems healthy, though I have my doubts because mother's appetite is not what it should be. She is recovered, but I feel she could be sick again in a moment. I know it is terribly selfish to wish you were here to give your strength to this house, when you are accomplishing great things for the city. Is this permitted for a daughter?

So that is my news. I hope your answer to my last is only delayed because with you and Iophon away and mother so delicate I feel alone. I will now go down to the ships to send this letter and check for your reply.

—Your daughter, Photia

Bulos came in with flint and a sack of coals. As he began the process of lighting the brazier, it occurred to Dexion that the smell of roasting meat could be a potent weapon if allowed to waft over the starving city.

"Leave that alone," he said as he rolled up the letter. "I say let's cook dinner outside this evening."

Bulos' head shot up as if he'd come under arrow attack. No member of a household, after all, was more adverse to a change in routine than the slave. He opened his mouth as if to object, but the look on Sophocles' face dissuaded him.

"Yes, *general*," he replied.

7.

The poet woke the next morning to the sound of jeering. Sitting up, it seemed to him as if the entire camp was collected in front of his tent, whistling in that way audiences did when they wanted a play cut off before the end. It was a sound he had dreaded all his life, but had never expected to hear now, in this place. He threw off the blankets and pulled a cloak over his naked body. On his way out, he had a vision of the whole Athenian contingent gathered around the flap, armed with pits and rotten fruit, ready to pelt the scribbler who dared presume he could lead men in circumstances that mattered.

But the shieldmen were facing the other direction. When they felt Dexion approaching from behind them, they stopped whistling, stepping silently aside without turning to meet his eyes. In this way—like some honored ghost—he passed through a crowd of thousands, joining Pericles and Menippus at the head of the assembly.

The Olympian was portrait-perfect, magnificent in crested helmet and armor. He alone looked at Sophocles; in his eyes Dexion could see something like compassionate pity. Menippus, for his part, was as absent in spirit as he was physically from the hill where the poet had chased him a day earlier.

"Is there something wrong, then?" he asked. Pericles made an odd, open-armed gesture in reply—and that was when Sophocles saw a paper in his hand.

"We have another message from Callinus."

The rest of the Greeks were looking toward the wall. A small group of Samians were gathered up there, this time around a single figure who was seated with his arms behind his back. From that distance Sophocles couldn't see who the prisoner was, but he could *feel* it plainly.

"I don't understand," the poet said. "Is this show intended for me?"

Pericles opened the message:

The Athenians have three days to accept the settlement, or the life of Dexion's son is forfeit.

Then Pericles lifted up something that had been rolled in the paper: a lock of shining black hair that, at first glance, he thought must be from the scalp of Nais. But that was, of course, impossible—she was far away, and her head had not looked that way in years. The hair must be Iophon's.

This thought came with no particular emotion. Instead, he was thinking with absolute clarity, as when he picked up the spear during the Ionian sally, or when he attacked the Ionian ships off Tragia. He turned to the other generals and there, on their faces, saw all the emotion he would have expected in himself. Glauketes' eyes shone from incipient tears. Xenophon had managed to contort his face into something resembling the Creon mask he had commissioned for his play. Only Menippus, it seemed, stared back with something like equanimity.

"I don't understand why my son is a hostage," Dexion said, "when I left him in the care of Menippus."

To which the other replied, "If it helps our colleague, I will accept the blame. But it would be no more true to say that Sophocles handed him over himself."

This, at last, cracked Dexion's calm. "Is that what you feared to say, Menippus, when you ran away from me yesterday?" he cried. "Is this how you accept responsibility?"

"The boy went too close to the enemy during the battle," retorted Menippus, more to the other generals than to Dexion. "Was I expected to control the son, when the father could not?"

The poet had his hands around Menippus' throat before anyone could stop him. As Sophocles' thumbs collapsed the man's windpipe, he pushed Menippus to the ground, using his knees to punish the man's stomach and groin. He held on with such ferocity that tips of his knuckles were slashed by the edges of Menippus' helmet. The blood, the smell of fresh olives on the man's breath, and the look of terror in his eyes, all worked to aggravate Dexion's rage. When half a dozen pairs of arms managed to pull him off, it was Pericles' face that pressed against his cheek, speaking to him from a place so close his voice might have come from inside Dexion's skull.

"Leave him—he's a fool. A fool. Leave him now."

Whether it took a minute or an hour for Sophocles to regain his composure, he couldn't tell. They'd brought out a couch from one of the tents for him to sit on, and hustled the bruised and heaving Menippus out of his sight, when it occurred to him to read the message with his own eyes. Pericles handed it over without hesitation.

The letters formed up on the page in block-like style, like a shopping list. The lock of hair the Ionians enclosed had a dry substance adhering at one end; examining it, he saw the substance was blood. *The Athenians have three days to accept the settlement, or the life of Dexion's son is forfeit.* A sliver of pain pierced his heart—what had they done to the boy already?

Dexion looked up at the barbaric tableau on the wall. None of the figures had moved since his altercation with Menippus. Having had a good look at Callinus during their short interview, he could see that the Samian general was not among them. Then two thoughts occurred to him. First, that in Nais' weakened condition, any bad news about Iophon was likely to kill her. And second, that he had faced Callinus in the tunnel *after* Iophon had been captured, and so while they were speaking, the dog had already known how deeply he was prepared to hurt Sophocles. He had known it, and probably already formed the plan in his mind. What a precious example of Ionian treachery! What galling mendacity! In his rage, he imagined using his bare fists to reduce Callinus to a smudge on Eupalinus' chiseled floor.

Pericles watched the poet's face warily, not speaking until Sophocles' eyes meet his.

"I don't have to tell you, no settlement is possible. You know that."

Again, that sense of falling into disaster, into *awe*, filled him. And for that moment, even more than when he faced rejection in the theater, he felt a sense of openness, of vulnerability, that swept away all the petty cares that afflicted his mind. He was Creon at last, about to lose his family; he was Philoctetes, and Ajax, and Antigone. He was charging one of the seven gates of Thebes, knowing the fate that must befall him. He was holding the red hot iron in his hand, ready to plunge it into his eye sockets. He was alive.

And through the future, near and far, as through the past, shall this law hold good: nothing that is vast enters into the life of mortals without a curse.

Pericles, the mourner-in-chief, put a warm hand on his shoulder. For an instant, he seemed about to say something, but remained silent.

"So you see, for once there's nothing you can tell me," the poet told him, smiling. "Nothing."

Chapter VIII

The Back Hand of Fortune

"Ships are only hulls, high walls are nothing, when no life moves in the empty passageways."
—Priest, *Oedipus Tyrannus*, l. 56

1.

Lucky Polycrates at last met his end at the hands of a treacherous Persian. How the tyrant of Samos, who was by then the most powerful of all the Greeks, was bested by a low-grade schemer named Oroetes is an oft-told tale in Ionia.

One day Oroetes, satrap of Lydia, happened to be pursuing his usual vices in the company of his friend Mitrobates. Now Oroetes and Mitrobates had competed against each other in all things since they were children. When Oroetes mastered the bow, learning to hit a target at three hundred yards, Mitrobates did the same with the sling, becoming the best with that weapon among all the King's young nobles. When Oroetes wed a Median princess, Mitrobates attached himself to one of the leading families in Babylon. And when King Cyrus had made Oroetes satrap in Sardis, Mitrobates worked every lever of influence to achieve the same, getting himself appointed governor of Dascyleium.

After this, Mitrobates got the better of his friend. On the

ascension day of King Cambyses, Mitrobates made the young king a gift of several islands in the Sea of Marmara. This earned him precious recognition at court. Oroetes, for his part, looked abroad for easy conquests of his own, but there were none, for all the mainland of Anatolia was already in his hands, and Samos, lying just offshore, was too powerful to challenge at sea. It was on this point, which he knew full well galled his rival, that Mitrobates chose to needle Oroetes.

"Of course, all of us respect you as a man," he said as he lounged on the goldspun cushions of Croesus' palace in Sardis, "though I've heard it said that you are not the true master of the west, as long as that Greek usurper thumbs his nose at the Great King."

Oroetes held his temper, calling instead for more aromatic firewood to perfume his loggia.

"It is a curious story," Mitrobates went on, "how Polycrates took control of the place with, what, just a handful of troops? How difficult could it be to take it again, with no more men than you have in your personal guard?"

Again, Oroetes did not rise to the bait, but chose to show off the opulence of his table by cutting open the roast pig. A roast lamb reposed within, and inside that, a duck, which in turn sheltered a pigeon, sauced and raisined.

Mitrobates continued, "But you are right not to consider it. The Greekling has become too powerful for the likes of us. You have enough to occupy you here, I say."

Oroetes said nothing. But in his heart the satrap conceived a deep hatred not of Mitrobates, but of Polycrates, whom he now imagined existed only to humiliate him. And so as Polycrates went about his charmed life, building and hunting and feasting as he always had, his neighbor to the east was hard at work conceiving plans for his downfall.

His trap was sprung when he sent a letter to Polycrates. "It has reached our attention," Oroetes wrote, "that the tyrant of Samos wishes to become the master of the Aegean. This is surely a worthy goal, but one that cannot be achieved without ships, which cost large sums of money. Know that we are prepared to assist you in your purpose, if you agree to aid mine. I have learned that the Great King in Susa means to dispose of me and my family. If you agree to take my household into exile, I will make you a gift of the King's treasury in Sardis. This will give you enough wealth to rule not only the Aegean but all of Greece. As proof of my sincerity, I invite you to send your most trustworthy man to inspect the treasure with his own eyes."

To Polycrates, this offer was only right and proper, given the good fortune he had always enjoyed. He therefore sent his envoy, a man named Maeandrius, to Sardis. The treasuries there were always impressive by the standards of the Greeks. Not wishing to risk a refusal, Oroetes made them still more splendid by filling eight trunks with stones, and topping them up with a few inches of gold. Maeandrius, who was honest but also a fool, was so dazzled by what he saw on the surface that he didn't think to look deeper into the chests. He then returned with the good news to his master.

Not all the Samians were so easily deceived. When Polycrates began his preparations to go to Magnesia to meet Oroetes, his daughter Chryse came to him with frightful portents. In her dreams, she said, she had seen her father suspended in the air, his dead body being washed by the king of the gods. Polycrates laughed, and thinking that the gift of some precious bauble would improve her sleep, gave her a pair of ruby earrings. But Chryse came back the next day with an equally dire vision— this time of her father's body hung by the feet, scourged and dripping a liquid the color of rubies.

Chryse's doomsaying incited fear among the courtiers in the palace. The tyrant, who was thinking only of getting his hands on the gold Maeandrius had described, therefore became angry with his daughter. "Be careful of spreading such nonsense in my court!" Polycrates warned her. "For if you are wrong, and I return unharmed, I will punish you with loneliness for the rest of your life."

"Let it be done, then," replied the girl. "For I'd rather spend my days unmarried and childless than see my father suffer."

Triply-blessed Polycrates sailed away to Magnesia anyway. No sooner had he arrived than his escort was disarmed, and he was seized by the guards of Oroetes.

"Villain, know that you have lived your last day in defiance of the Great King!" declared the Persian.

Polycrates, who still believed that nothing very wrong could happen to him, laughed out loud. "Yes, you make a fine joke, my friend, though I think you go too far in doing it in front of my servants."

The tyrant's blindness sounded to Oroetes ears like the most impudent of insults. He therefore subjected Polycrates to such tortures as only Persian minds could devise. He was tied, lashed, and blinded. His bones were broken with stones. He was hung upside down, nailed to a hunk of wood, and finally garrotted. As a crowning insult, his body was punctured in a thousand places. All this was done in full view of the nobles who accompanied him to Asia, as a warning to any that might harbor similar ambitions. It was not missed by the Ionians that Chryse's visions had all come to pass: when Polycrates was hung upside down he was washed by rain from Zeus; when his dead body was disfigured, his blood did not run from the wounds but oozed out, still and shining on his skin like thousands of tiny rubies.

But the most chilling sight of all, said the witnesses, was the look in the victim's eyes when they were breaking his bones. For it had finally dawned on him that this was not a joke, but a cruel reality from which he had thought himself immune.

In this way did Olympus withdraw its favor from Polycrates, who built like a god, outshone all the other Greeks, and was the first mortal man to dream of mastering the sea.

Oroetes did not long survive his victim. By the time King Darius came to the throne in Susa, the satrap's long record of arrogant acts had made him notorious. Darius sent secret orders for Oroetes to be killed by his own guards. The orders were fulfilled with prejudice, and the body destroyed so no trace was left to be honored by his family. Polycrates' bones, meanwhile, were dug up and surrendered to the Ionians, as a benevolent gesture to the new satrapy of Samos.

Bereaved, Chryse willingly took upon herself the curse of loneliness with which her father had threatened her. She refused all proposals of marriage, and when her family plotted to turn her over to Polycrates' brother, she fled to the mountains with her father's remains, never to be seen again. For years after, goatherds told of hearing the mournful cries of a girl, audible when the wind blew down from the high pastures.

2.

With the arrival of winter the Athenians were more or less trapped on the island. The storms that increasingly rose up from the sea made them reluctant to launch their vessels. Rations were tightened as they saw fewer supply ships from home. Everyone, from humblest slinger to general, stalked the beaches half-mad, thinking of the plenty he was missing because of the intransigence of the Ionians. Many of the less-experienced shieldmen had never missed so many city festivals in a row. Competitions were held to distract them, but athletic rivalries only increased dissension in the ranks. Anyone walking the camp would have heard Pericles cursed under many a breath; toasts were made to his death, even as it was understood by all that only he could lead them out of the impasse.

The only bright spot in the dismal season was the example of noble Dexion, still facing the prospect of his son's death a month after receiving Callinus' threat. The poet went about his usual business as the first three-day deadline approached—inspecting the siege works, distributing supplies, mediating disputes. His face was immobile. He slept outside his tent, sitting up, his face turned toward the Samian walls. At dawn on the third day he stood alone in no man's land, a tempting target for the Ionian archers as he waited for the execution party to mount the walls. He had a note delivered to Callinus, expressing neither hope nor anger, demanding only that his son's body be delivered to him when the deed was done.

Callinus replied that a boy so young should not suffer so quickly for the foolishness of his elders. He set a new deadline of one week. When this was endured by Sophocles with equal courage, he set another of two weeks, his demand accompanied this time by the severed tip of Iophon's left index finger.

This, at last, drove Sophocles to Pericles' tent. The Olympian was prepared for him, intending to deny any negotiation—until he was surprised to see the poet fall to his knees.

"My friend, we have known each other for a long time," began Sophocles. "In the days of Cimon, they said I had thrown in my lot with the aristocrats' camp—but we both know that wasn't true. I produced the *Agamemnon*, and they said I lampooned your character, until they saw *The Bow of Odysseus*, and even the dullards could understand my respect for you. I saw then the quality of man you were, and what you could do for the city if you had the opportunity to lead. That time did come, and I've never had an occasion to regret my judgment—until now.

"I beg you to release me from this ordeal. If you will not deal with Callinus, at least let me go and exchange places with my son. My death would at least be in accord with the responsibility I took when I accepted the generalship. But Iophon's time has not yet come for taking risks. The future of my family is at stake. His mother lies ill, and I fear she won't survive such a blow. Will you sentence her to death, as well as our unborn child, just to satisfy your hatred of the Ionians? Must the future be sacrificed for the necessity of the moment?

"We both know what your answer must be, what Athens' answer has always been. Our city chooses the future. If you do otherwise, you are not the Pericles I thought you were, and you make me fear the fate of everything we hold dear."

Pericles looked down at him with an expression of cool compassion, seeming as much to revile the poet's desperation as he pitied his plight. When he spoke, his voice was in the opposite of his public mode—quiet, plain, without flattery or exhortation.

"I am hurt, dear friend, if you truly believe that I act out of something as unreasoning as *hatred*. Come now . . . have I ever been that kind of man? If you so badly misunderstand me, what hope do I have that anyone else is with me?"

Stepping forward, he extended a hand to pull Dexion to his feet. Then he kissed his friend on the cheek, put his arm around him, and began to declaim in his typical rostrum style—albeit from two feet away. "You are wrong to so despise my motives! For of course our enemies are free to say what they want, to sow discord among the people, and therefore to maintain this illusory freedom of which they are so proud. Wiser men than they know the truth: only one thing will keep the Greeks free of empires like that of Darius, and that is an empire *of* the Greeks. And what is more, the only city to lead such an empire is Athens. Sparta can scarcely spare the men to control her own territory. Corinth—she is rich, but a whore, unable to summon the resolve for such a task. Thebes? Is there any doubt she would turn Mede again, if the choice faced her? Is there any other city as despised as she?

"And so it falls upon us—and I tell you it is not a responsibility to be welcomed. What did you think it would take, Dexion, to keep the Greeks safe? What can we fail to sacrifice, to keep an empire? Now that we have it, we dare not let it go, for that would be more costly than if we never tried. That is why the Samians must be punished—not because we hate them, or act out of spite. It is nothing other than a rational calculation."

"Is that all we mortals are to you, then—figures in a calculation? Is that why you oblige me to bury a son?"

"That can't be helped now. What I can promise you, though, is that we will make the Ionians bury more of theirs."

"And have your calculations included the fact that the city will fall soon? You forget that I can hear them, and that no one is better at judging the mood of crowds. Callinus is desperate because he can barely control the democrats in the city. The children are suffering. I can hear their mothers crying over them in the night. If you truly profess to hate wasting Athenian lives, why leave my son to die when the conclusion is foregone?"

Pericles let him go, retreating several feet until turning to confront him again. "I respect your knowledge of these things, Dexion. You may well be right. But under the circumstances, your word is simply not enough. I'm sorry."

They looked at each other.

"May I take my son's place?"

"You are a far more valuable hostage than Iophon. It would be a poor trade for Athens."

"A poor trade for Athens . . ." Sophocles repeated. Then, dropping all pretense of respect, he tore off his scarlet cloak and hurled it to the ground. Pericles watched this with a weary air, as if reminded of mortal frailties he had succeeded in transcending.

Sophocles was about to leave when the Olympian seized his arm.

"Yes, you may hate me if you want, but never disrespect our city. It is my reasoning that vexes us both. And who knows? Maybe one day I will also lose a son to war. Look forward to that day, Dexion, if the thought consoles you."

The thought did nothing for him. Returning to his tent, he sat and looked at his writing tablet, but the prospect of picking it up sickened him.

There was a noise outside.

"Bulos?" he called.

Silence.

"Bulos, I don't want to see your face right now. Go fetch water."

He heard the noise again—the scrape of a spear point against the stony ground. Dexion shot to his feet, ripped open the flap: two shieldmen were standing there in full panoply. He recognized them as guards from Pericles retinue. As he glared at them, they stared back with a softness that was almost solicitous.

He left his tent and strode north, to where Eupalinus' tunnel had been discovered. His minders seemed to allow themselves to be left behind. But when he reached the site, he heard the metallic clap of greaves, and the hollow ring of a bronze butt-spike sheathed in earth. He turned, and found Pericles' men posted behind him again.

And so the Olympian was taking no chances that Dexion would flee into the tunnel to exchange himself. After all, that would be a poor trade for Athens.

3.

Waiting yet again for the appointed time was a torment that made Sophocles despise his very life. Each day that stretched before him, interceding itself between the present and the advent of his relief, became an adversary. If he could, he would have mowed all the dismal hours down with his sword. But Time's phalanx had no back rank. When hours became enemies, they massed on an endless plain, maddening in their resolve to exist, all demanding a small piece of his soul as he endured each one.

Of the progress of the siege he no longer cared. If anyone had asked, he would have reported that the miserable sounds from the city were dying away. The decline was subtle, but unmistakable, suggesting a steady, pitiless attrition. The children went silent as they starved, and after they were gone the mothers grieved with the last of their strength. Though it was winter it was a very good season for the flies.

It was obvious to him that the stubbornness of Callinus and his party was growing less and less relevant as time wore on. But whether it was out of fear or awe at his sacrifice, or just because Pericles ordered it, no one asked his opinion.

And so he was left in his tent to brood over his memories of his life with Iophon. He remembered, for instance, that the boy had been only four when he took him walking for the first time in the garden of the Academy. The place had been recently decorated with plane trees at Cimon's expense. What had been a somewhat unsavory zone at the edge of town was now a park, offering relief from the heat of Colonus in high summer. Fathers brought their sons on festival days, letting them scamper free through the plantings, giving them their first taste of games in the gymnasia.

Young Iophon only seemed to want to run, though. He took to his tiny heels at every turn, his father trailing behind as he shouted warnings about criminals and jackals. As the boy ran, he would simply repeat his father's words without slowing down, declaring in that small voice (and the poet smiled as he recalled this) that the woods were not safe, that scorpions dwelled under rocks, that the red berries were not for eating but the mint leaves were all right.

Iophon turned back to him once, pointing at a distant conical mass in the northeast of the city. "That is Wolf Hill," said Dexion, who was ever handy with such answers. "It was created after Athena made the Acropolis. She had material left over and was carrying it away when jealous Poseidon sent a crow to startle her. The mountain marks the place where she dropped the rock."

But the boy was already off to the next distraction—an anthill that he found every bit as impressive as Athena's handiwork. Sophocles himself became engrossed in a scroll of verses by the soldier-poet Archilochus. The work was good, with so much to savor, that when he looked up it was too late for him to prevent Iophon from inserting his little hand into a snake hole.

He was bitten in an instant. From his screams, and the look of the wound, it was impossible to tell if the strike would kill him. Sophocles carried the writhing boy the five miles back to Colonus, fearing his negligence had cost the life of his only son. He didn't know whether he should rush the boy to Nais or suck the venom out himself. He was on the verge of panic when he reached home, until his wife, with just a single look, told him that the bite was not poisonous. And with this good news, Sophocles collapsed with relief, believing that his own life had been saved, while Nais looked on with amusement and, somewhat more deeply, with vague worry that her husband's self-recriminations were justified.

From that day on, he avoided the Academy, and could never bring himself to pick up Archilochus again.

The day appointed for Iophon's execution was uncommonly warm for Elaphebolion. Though the time dragged by, he was seldom aware of the exact date—there hardly seemed a point. But when someone mentioned it was the ninth, he couldn't help but realize that, far away at home, the City Dionysia had begun. It would be the first time in decades—since he was a cadet, in fact, stationed at the fortress at Rhamnous—that he would miss the entire festival. With no entry that year from Dexion, what an opportunity for Aristarchus, Thespis, and that skulking dog, Euripides! The flush of competitive jealousy felt like the return of an old friend too long gone, making him forget his misery for a moment.

But then he glimpsed Poristes, meaning to pass unnoticed, giving his stricken friend an awkward salute on the way to the latrines. No one, not even those he considered close, had treated him in normal fashion since news of Iophon's capture had circulated. To have a sword hanging over his life—to know the day and time of his son's demise—had a paradoxical effect, making Dexion something more than just another grieving mortal. He was blessed now—singled out by fate, which was another way of saying he was cursed. As they stood in his vicinity, the minders Pericles had sent fingered the strings of blue beads they kept in the caves of their shields.

The Ionians made no announcement when the deed was done. There was no tableau staged on the walls of Polycrates, no grisly souvenirs sent to prove they'd kept their word. Instead, there was only a deliberate uncertainty, a cruel suspension between hope and despair. Yet what else could anyone expect in such a war? If there was any doubt before, it was dispelled. With the defeat of the Great King, the barbarians were not extinct, but only changed their faces. It was now the turn of the Greeks to lose their minds.

All he had left of Iophon now was the severed fingertip Callinus had enclosed with his last warning. Sophocles kept the shriveling, rotting thing in a small wooden box meant for holding incense. As the flesh shrank, turning more black every day, the nail attached to it seemed to grow longer—a semblance of continued life he found perversely comforting. But the illusion wore off. The leathery skin soon cracked, then parted; a sliver of gray bone was laid bare. At last he could take no more, and built a small pyre in the sand outside his tent.

It was meant to be a plain, family memorial; the simple farewell of a father passing his boy to the embrace of the gods. As he gathered kindling for the flames, he saw Bulos watching from a distance, and then Poristes. When the blaze was high enough, a crowd of shieldmen watched silently as he put the finger in the pyre. There was just time to say a few words— nothing more than to name the gods that would receive him— before the last free remains of Iophon ascended as smoke. He tried to keep it in sight as it lofted over the camp, over the walls and the ships, thinning and rising as it merged with the wider gray of the winter sky. It was hardly visible at all when it was caught at last by the wind, speeding off to refuge in the west.

4.

The siege dragged on another two weeks. All developments
pointed in the Athenians' favor. Despite the unsettled weather,
a second squadron of Chian warships arrived, swelling the
allies' already lopsided advantage at sea. Artemon put aside his
poetry to solve the problem of the shieldbreakers' notorious
inaccuracy. The mechanism's vibration on discharge, he found,
could be damped by mounting additional weight on the flexion
arms, which he clad in bronze sleeves custom-made by the
armorers. The result was not nearly as accurate as archery, but
it was an improvement. Instead of having no idea where their
shots would go, the firing crews could now venture a guess, or
posit a range. Ionian lookouts on the walls were surprised to
hear the massive bolts whistle past their ears, or send up
splashes of sparks when they hit the masonry. Enemy bowmen
could no longer line up with impunity to fire on Athenian
scouts.

"It may not be me, and it may not be anyone alive today,
but someone will perfect the machine," Artemon predicted.
"And when he does, it will be the end of cities."

The suppression of enemy archery paid off when, for the
first time, two Athenian scouts reached the foot of the wall in
daylight. Their intention was to examine a small gate that
looked somewhat more pregnable than the others. When they
reached it, they were disappointed to find that the wear and
tear they spied from a distance was nothing more than super-
ficial scuffing. One of the scouts knocked on it to hear how
heavy the planks sounded. Then he gave it a push—and was
astounded to watch the gate swing open.

What happened next became a story told around Athenian
army camps for as long as the city fielded armies.

The scouts, who had no armor and were armed with only
short swords, poked their heads inside the Samian wall to have
a look around. The door opened on a broad commercial street,
with permanent storefronts and raised pavement for pedes-
trians. Under the circumstances, however, the stores were

closed, and the street was empty except for a few Ionian shieldmen standing a post on the corner. The Samians looked in disbelief at the Athenians, who made obscene gestures in return. Then one of the guards put a horn to his lips and blew the alarm.

With an initial advantage of six to two, the Samians managed to push the scouts out. One of the scouts, thinking quickly, wedged the sharp end of his sword in the door. His comrade, meanwhile, screamed for help from the Athenians watching open-mouthed from a distance.

Help came, with the Athenians gaining the upper hand in numbers. As the besiegers charged forward, the Samian archers were ordered onto the walls to shoot down on them. This, in turn, gave the shieldbreaker crews scores of new targets. From the near silence of just another morning, the war had roared to life in a few moments. Oarsmen on ships patrolling the straits heard it, as did the Milesian lookouts on Mount Mycale, who spoke of it in terms like "eruption" or "dambreak". Somewhere on the other side of the island, a villager in a mountain hamlet heard the tumult and realized for the first time that a war was being fought nearby.

Pressing hard, the Athenians managed to open enough of a space for armored men to slip through the gate. One, two, and then three of those brave hoplites went down, until a fourth managed to keep his feet, and swinging a torch in the Ionians' faces, drove some of them back. He went down, too, but the fight now passed within the threshold.

Like the army of Polycrates facing the Spartans, the Ionians made a battle of it by assembling all their able-bodied troops. Hoping to trap the Athenians in just one quarter of the city, they erected impromptu barricades out of carts, doors, window shutters, and furniture from the houses. Though the Samian streets were broad, they weren't wide enough for the Athenians to attack the barricades in strength. Under fire from the shieldbreakers, the archers took to the roofs instead, shooting down on the invaders.

What the Ionians lacked this time, however, was a figure like Polycrates to rally them to truly heroic resistance. The barricades, being built out of light materials, collapsed under the weight of the men fighting on them. The final blow came from within: the Samian democrats, at last seeing their chance to affect the outcome of the war, pelted the defenders from their upper-storey windows with pots, kitchen utensils, flaming coals, even costly flasks of oil. The spectacle of their own citizens fighting for the enemy deflated the morale of the Ionians. The barricades were forced, and the Athenians, like idle demons drunk with the prospect of malice, poured glee-fully into the city.

It was the two hundred forty-ninth day since Pericles led his army to the beaches of Samos.

5.

The way the siege ended prompted an obvious question: how could it be, many wondered, that a contest as bloody and hard-fought as any in living memory could be decided with such a small but disastrous blunder? It seemed implausible. It seemed inglorious. The alternative—that the door had been deliberately unlatched by someone inside, possibly a democratic sympa-thizer—was a marginally better story. But no one in the captured town came forward to claim credit for the act. Perhaps he was killed, shrugged the fabulists, in the confused hours when the Athenians took the city.

Whichever way it was staged, then, the final act of the play left the audience dissatisfied. Despite legends of astounding wealth, the city was in desperate straits when the Athenians sacked the place. There were corpses everywhere—dried, deflated husks of human beings, left to lie in honor in their houses if their families survived, otherwise piled up in alleys and storerooms by a populace too famished to bury them. On some streets, the stench of rotting bodies was absent; on others, it went beyond mere charnel house offal, striking the senses with the force of a weapon.

The domestic prizes were few. Over the months of the siege most of the Ionians had collected their valuables and hidden them. Alas, the secret caches of the dead were lost forever. As for that other sort of prize, the impact of Pericles's blockade on the children of Samos left the city with precious few young boys or girls to take captive. The boney, hollow-chested remains of the mothers—the ones that still lived, that is—were barely worth the trouble of violating. Many of the soldiers, starved for female entertainment, held their noses and did it anyway.

The few hundred Ionian males still able to lift a sword surrendered en masse. As the Athenians took over the marketplace, a few old men stumbled out to greet the liberators. "Where's Callinus?" asked the first officer on the scene. The men pointed to the council house. Investigating, the Athenians found the most prominent members of the oligarchy spread around the bowl-shaped hall, their bodies in various attitudes of permanent repose, their blood dripping down the steps and pooling in the pit. Callinus himself was discovered lying across three seats, his throat cut. On his chest and spilled on the floor was an armload of his most treasured scrolls.

The soldiers came out and asked the next question. "Where's the treasury?" Rushing off, they found they were too late—Pericles' city guards already had the place surrounded.

"You're free to try the houses," said the chief of the guard, "but this place is off limits."

This didn't go over too well with the thetes who believed they'd earned a lapful of bullion. Had they not neglected their fields for a full season? Had they abandoned their wives to the attentions of the wastrels left behind in Athens, just for a few household baubles? The shoving began right away, giving way to a riot as more irate shieldmen found their way to the treasury. The victors got down to fighting each other until reinforcements from Pericles arrived. A hotheaded Acharnian pulled out a sword, announcing that his honor had been besmirched; opponents followed, leading to a desultory battle. When it was over, twenty Athenians lay dead in the market of Samos. More died that afternoon, after the war was over, than in all the time since the Ionians had sallied out to break the siege.

Sophocles entered the city within an hour of its fall. There was, he realized, a chance that something remained of his son to honor. With Bulos trailing behind, he rushed through the unfamiliar city, bursting through the doors of likely places, interrogating exhausted Samians without pity for their own sufferings.

"Where are the Athenian prisoners?" he barked at last at a woolen lump lying on the steps of the Athena shrine.

"I don't know," came the reply from beneath the torn overcloak.

"Where's my son?"

"I had nothing to do with that."

Frustrated, Dexion raised his walking stick and whacked the starving wretch. The impact did not make the fleshy slap he expected, but a disturbing *click*, as if two bones had been knocked together.

He went on. As he searched, he tried to be alert to clues that might lead him to Iophon, but not to anything else. If he had looked or listened or smelled too closely, the evidence of suffering would have driven him away. He was particularly afraid to see the children—the pale, hollow-cheeked three- and four-year-olds with hair absent in clumps and eyes tormented by flies. These would stare at him from windows and doorways, most often naked, their faces filled not with anger or reproach, but with a cautious hope of basic human kindness that rent his heart. He averted his eyes at the slightest sign of them.

He crossed paths at last with a pair of Athenians rushing in the opposite direction. One had a massive rucksack that clanked as he ran; the other was holding somewhat less booty, but cradled a tame ferret in one hand. The animal, which wore a jeweled collar, was clearly a pet pilfered from some un-guarded house. The poet eyed it warily as he asked where the Athenian prisoners had been kept.

"There's a prison behind the council house, Dexion," answered the animal lover, "But there's not much left."

"Just tell me where it is."

Sophocles found some Athenians already standing outside the prison, milling and staring, holding their cloaks over their noses. They noticed him coming from some distance away, and parted to let him through. No one spoke.

The bodies were lying in neat rows in the courtyard. For lack of flowers, the Athenians dressed them in pine boughs, which softened the odor but lent the scene an eerie neatness, as if the prisoners had conveniently expired on a single funeral bier. Sophocles passed from one to the next, inspecting them all, trying to discern Iophon's features on each blackened, gaping face. He thought, how similar all men look in the throes of bodily corruption! As similar as newborn babies to each other, it seemed.

Dexion came at last to a body that was not branded on the forehead. Looking down, he saw that it lacked part of one finger below the last knuckle—and he knew. Sophocles' heart sank, and he fell to his knees before this repulsive thing that he knew must be Iophon, but that looked more like some distant memory of his dead grandfather. The tears rolled free now; confronted with the body, he could do nothing to stop them. All at once he felt heavy, pulled to the ground, head bowed to wash the curled, shrunken feet of his boy. For the first time in many years, he was playing a script he had neither written nor read, and he didn't give a thought of how it played to his audience.

The silence that commenced when he arrived deepened into something quieter still: a whispered, reverent hush in the pres-ence of the sacred. What Dexion would suffer, to bury his only son, was appointed him in full measure, without regard to fame or his services to the city. Though they were reminded time and again, the men of Athens were surprised when heroism proved no immunity from the Fates.

Chapter IX

HYDRA

"O to be wafted where the wooded sea-cape stands upon the laving sea. O to pass beneath Sounion's level summit, that we might salute sacred Athens!"

— Chorus, *Ajax*, l. 1215

1.

On the last day of the trip home, the fleet benefited from what navy hands called the "Aeginetan wind." This was a suddenly refreshed pace, a lightening of the oars, as the bows completed the great right turn around Cape Sounion and the men began to pull north for home. The new Temple of Poseidon, smiling toothy white on the cleft chin of Attica, was better than wine for the oarsmen's spirits. Dexion, too, felt his bottom lighten at the sight of the familiar coastline. Rising to his feet, he found himself naming the little coves and villages under his breath as they slipped by. Though still in mourning, his heart skipped a beat when he got his first direct sight of Athens: the reflection of the early afternoon sun on the helmet of the Acropolis statue of Athena Promachos, towering free and gathering brilliance like a tiny dawn.

Poristes, seeing that his passenger had left his bench, came up beside him. He had become so used to silence from

Sophocles that he'd forgotten to position his unburned side, with his good ear, toward the poet. Perceiving his mistake, the captain turned, facing inboard as he leaned against the arrow screen.

"When we were called to sea, we left so quickly my wife and son couldn't see me off. Now I expect no one will miss our return."

"Fortunate for you," came the perfunctory reply.

"They'll come for you most of all," said the captain, patting the other's shoulder. "Officer of the deck, slow us down! Let them wait a little longer for the hero of the day."

The pipers reduced the cadence, cutting *Antigone*'s pace through the water as her sister ships rushed on toward the sheds.

Poristes' chatter now put a worry in Dexion's mind: if Nais was not at the Piraeus waiting for him, would it mean she was already dead? Would it mean the news about Iophon had reached her already, and that she couldn't look him in the face? What would Photia's presence—or her absence—mean? When he was back on Samos and anticipated being this close to home, he imagined he would be relieved. With a prompt tie-up and clear streets, he would be in Colonus that very afternoon. But now that he was here, his hunger for resolution had grown, until the Saronic Gulf had grown to the dimensions of an ocean, and home seemed an insuperable distance beyond. He took his spot on the bench again, a look on his face like a condemned man awaiting the dawn.

The first fishing boat reached the *Antigone* just as it came abreast of the harbor at Munychia. It was filled with young men in their party clothes, wearing eyeliner and rouge, toasting the ships out of silver cups. The pilot must have been as drunk as the passengers. The boat kept wandering into the path of the ship's oars, obliging Poristes to scream at him to keep clear.

One of the revelers passed a skin of wine up to an oarsman on the top tier. Poristes saw it and ordered him to drop the gift in the sea.

"But sir, they say it's Thasian!"

"Officer of the deck, either toss the skin overboard or toss the man."

The oarsman disposed of the wine. Poristes leaned to Dexion, saying "We must keep order now—most of our accidents happen with the end in sight."

Debarking, they were greeted by a waterfront crowded with faces. At Piraeus, the fleet's successful return was always an occasion for an impromptu festival. Citizens and foreigners showed up in their best clothes, drinking, singing, waving streamers bearing the colors of their tribes. Smoke and sparks from the vendors' carts hung over the scene, rising until the offshore breeze caught and carried them over the ships. There was a history of fires on such occasions. The magistrates in charge of the sheds kept crews standing by with water buckets, to keep the Athenian fleet from being burned by its well-wishers. But there was never a question of keeping the people from celebrating another victory.

Dexion was mobbed by his fellow citizens from the moment he stepped ashore. If Nais or Photia had come there was no way for him to know. He could see no more than an arm's length ahead of him as hands converged from every direction to make contact. He was patted, caressed, pinched, and goosed; someone doused him with perfume. He was sunk in a dull roar of jabbering voices, out of which he could make out a few random utterances:

". . . surprised if you ask me . . ."

". . . could have sacrificed his own son!"

"*Antigone*! How amateurish!"

". . . better than Aeschylus . . ."

". . . stuck with the program."

"Who's to say?"

"We need more like him!"

Soldiers were posted to keep order, but many of these stood by as the crowd swelled around Dexion. He shouted that he needed to get through, but his voice was lost in the din.

At last Poristes cupped his hands around his mouth and cried, "By the gods, move aside! Dexion has a sick wife!"

That deck-voice, which was known to cut through the loudest of storms, did the trick. A few of the celebrants took it upon themselves to bring out the walking sticks with the brass handles. Sophocles saw blood spurt from broken noses as the self-appointed escort started swinging, crumpling the laggards and shoving aside all obstacles.

The poet turned to thank Poristes; his last glimpse of his friend that day was of the captain placing a loose fist to his temple in salute. Dexion did the same, holding the pose until the mob closed around Poristes. Only at that moment—and not the hour of victory at Samos, or his first glimpse of the city—did he feel that a long diversion in his life was behind him at last.

A sizable crowd followed him all the way to Colonus, narrowing behind him as the thoroughfare got tighter, shouting ahead so all the people would know the hero of Samos was in the neighborhood. On the Street of the Armorers, women and children stuck their heads out of second-story windows to witness his passing. An old woman leaned out to dump a chamberpot in the gutter, saw him below, and held her fire. In the scant moments he was in front of another house he saw a young lady brazenly lift the hem of her tunic for him. He was shocked. It was too gloomy in the house to see anything, but the dramaturge in him admired her timing.

And then he was home.

The abruptness of his arrival gave him pause. He recognized the little gate, the meandering fence in front of the garden, and the timber cornice of the house beyond, but it all bore a troubling air of unreality. The prancers behind him stopped prancing, and the pipes left off piping, as the crowd stood silent in the street, seeming to share in the poet's confusion.

He pushed open the gate and stepped inside. As he did so, the admirers left behind did him the courtesy of keeping quiet. The peace allowed him to hear a sparrow somewhere nearby give the same desultory chirp he heard every day in his tent on Samos. There was no sound at all from inside the house. For all he knew, Nais and Photia could have been at Piraeus, looking for him.

He proceeded, a little stiff-legged, through the garden where he had spent so many hours. The pink oleanders were blooming around the pit where he collected rainwater, as they did every year. The old milling stone under the plane tree was exactly as he remembered it, as was the stump where Bulos worked and the little bench where he lay down to dictate his verses—though the latter was in need of a fresh coat of paint. The beds of the kitchen garden could have used weeding.

As for any Greek, the model in his mind of such home-comings was that of Homer's Odysseus, returning to Ithaca after twenty years of warfare and wandering. The story had been retold to him since before he could declare a memory of it; he had thrilled to the adventure since he was a schoolboy, and had returned to it many times in his adulthood to admire the perfection of its bardic verse. In the master's version, the hero was deposited asleep on the beach by his escorts, the Phaecaians. Athena, wishing to conceal him from his subjects until she could instruct him on the proper way to deal with the suitors afflicting his house, caused Ithaca to be shrouded in fog. When Odysseus woke up, the landscape was so strange to him he had to ask a stranger where he was. The passerby was, of course, the goddess herself in disguise. When she lifted the fog at last, the fact of his homecoming burst on him like an unexpected gift. Odysseus, the prince of liars, had an honest emotion at last, falling to his knees to kiss the ground.

Sophocles had not been away twenty years but only nine months. His war had been hard-fought, but by ordinary men, not heroes. The only goddess he had seen was Pheidias's Athena, and that only distantly, from at sea. The recognition of his home did not inspire him to fall to his knees. Instead, after so many months of anticipation, the place seemed vaguely diminished to him: how small his old world had been! After traveling such distances, and seeing such things, was it possible that his satisfaction with home would never return?

Abruptly, he became conscious of how confused he must seem to those watching from the street. Without further delay, he strode to the door, pulled it open, and stepped inside.

2.

Photia had her eyes on him the moment he entered his wife's quarters. She rose from her couch and, bearing with her an air of pensive sadness, seemed to manifest in his arms without crossing the space in between. He held her, feeling how insubstantial she seemed, how bird-like and sharp her shoulder-blades, for as long as she appeared to need it. When she pulled back, he was shocked at what he saw: in the nine months since he left, his daughter had aged ten years. What had been smooth when he set sail was now fraught with lines. If there was no gray in her hair yet, there was gray enough behind her eyes, in the wan smile she attempted for his benefit. He raised a hand to place it on her head, just as he always had done since she was a child—and found himself hesitating, leaving the hand suspended as it covered her from view.

He completed the gesture, causing her to close her eyes in relief.

"I wanted to go down to the ships to meet you," she whispered.

"No need."

"Her bleeding started again, so I had to stay."

Photia turned to the bed, to Nais who was lying there, watching them. The spectacle of the reunion of her husband and daughter seemed to give her no delight. But as he bent to kiss her cold forehead, Nais reflexively raised her arms, pulling him toward her. They remained that way for a while as Photia turned away, pretending to be distracted.

He had seen his wife on the verge of labor twice before. This time, however, it seemed as if she was able to deliver herself into Hades. Her skin was not just unhealthy, not just pallid, but stark white, as if she had laid a coat of cosmetic lead on her face. The slick of sweat that covered her gave nothing like the moist glow of imminent motherhood. Instead, it was like some cold emanation from a corpse, shedding the last humors of the body. Layers of bedclothes were pulled up to her chin, leaving nothing for him to see of the rest of her except the swell of her belly. Yet even under all that she shivered visibly.

"You are here," she said.

"I am."

"That's good. It's all been too much for the girl."

Photia opened her mouth to object, but Sophocles silenced her with a look. In truth, he wasn't concerned with what Nais said, but how it exhausted her to say it. The effort just to utter a few words caused her to grimace with exertion.

"Be quiet now," he said, refolding the covers over her. "I'll stay with you now."

"What's that smell? Are you wearing perfume?"

"It was an accident—on the street."

She summoned a smile. "Isn't it always?"

He stroked her cheek for the few moments it took her to fall asleep. Then he went back to stand beside Photia.

"Where is Bulos?" she asked.

"Coming with the baggage. What did you mean before, about her bleeding?"

"The midwife says there is blood flowing into the womb. Not all the time—it starts and stops. It gets worse when she moves, so she must stay quiet."

"And the child is healthy?"

"It seems so."

"Is her time close?"

"It could happen today."

A temptation rose in him to ask the question any Athenian husband would ask—is it a boy?—but he quashed it. Instead, he pushed her gently toward the door.

"I'll sit with her now."

"I should help you—"

"You already have!" he said. "Now go. Take the bed in my room if you want it."

She relented. But then another worry occurred to him, and he had to stop her before she closed the door.

"Wait! First tell me—what have you heard about your brother?"

Like a boxer deceived by a feint, she winced at the mention of Iophon. The expression on her face told him all he needed to know.

"The news came a few days ago," she said. "They said it was treachery, and that you bore it well."

"Does your mother know?"

Her tears came now, loosed by the dread that she had failed him. "I was afraid to tell her!" she confessed.

He looked on her with an affection he had seldom indulged. Over the years, when work had not preoccupied him, it was Nais, and when it was not Nais it was Iophon. For Photia, dear undistinguished Photia, he had seldom spared a thought. Now that they were joined in a way he never feared possible, his neglect turned to remorse. "You were wise," he said, reaching forth to give her a parting squeeze he knew was grossly inadequate. But it was all he could spare in his exhaustion, and he let her go.

3.

The second of the Twelve Labors assigned to Heracles was to kill the Hydra of Lerna. This was a noisome sea-creature of many heads and poisonous breath, set to guard the entrance to Hades. Approaching the swamps of Lake Lerna with his nephew Iolaus, Heracles protected himself from the monster's deadly fumes by covering his nose and mouth with his cloak. He lured the creature out with flaming arrows. Then, raising a farmer's sickle he had brought for the work, the hero reaped a harvest of the creature's many heads. But for every head Heracles loped off, two more grew back on the same neck. Realizing that he could never complete the labor by force alone, Heracles called for aid from Iolaus, who used a torch to burn the stumps before the heads regrew. In this way the mortals defeated the deathless monster. The last head, which could not be killed, they concealed forever under a boulder.

But Hera would not let the Hydra rest. In her hatred of Heracles, the bastard child of her husband and the mortal woman Alcmene, the goddess was prepared to go to any length of spite. Summoning her daughter Eileithyia, goddess of childbirth, Hera bade her to place a drop of the monster's poisonous blood in the womb of every mortal woman. Eileithyia could not defy her mother, yet she knew that obeying her would mean the end of mankind. She therefore went to Olympus to find Themis, the goddess of heavenly justice, and put her dilemma before her.

"This is not a problem for one unused to judging," answered Themis. "Instead, obey your mother, but leave it to me to decide which women will get a fatal dose of the Hydra's blood. In that way, both your duty and mine shall be fulfilled."

Eileithyia dispersed the poison. She left it to Themis, however, to decide how much to infect each mother, based on the impieties of fathers one generation removed, or a hundred. But as Themis set about this work, she realized that with so many fates to be decided, she would never have occasion to enjoy the diversions of Olympus with her fellow immortals. She therefore turned to Tyche, daughter of Ocean and Tethys, and said, "Sister, I wish to banquet as any goddess should, but this task weighs heavy on my time. Won't you relieve me, then, so I may sit by the throne of my consort Zeus and take my share of his board?"

"I see the size of the burden you have taken," replied the goddess of chance, "and pledge to you now that it shall never rest on your shoulders alone."

From that time onward, no matter how outwardly strong a

woman seemed, and despite all the arts of midwives and Asclepiads, childbirth struck down a fraction of all mortal women. And ever after, the question of whether it was Themis or Tyche, Justice or Chance, that loosed the monster within has bedevilled those left to grieve.

When the time came for Nais to conceive her third child, the Hydra found its purchase along a scar left on her womb from the delivery of Iophon. The flesh, which was thinner there, put up little resistance as the placenta sank its roots deep. The skein of arteries drank greedily of the mother's strength; it grew so thick that it split the uterus, invading the space of her abdomen. If a doctor had committed the impiety of cutting her open and looking inside, he would have seen a snarl of vessels bursting through the rent scar, spreading out to infest the kidneys, the liver, the intestines. An observant eye would see the serpent's arms were irresistible, but also delicate: the slightest movement would tear them, releasing still more blood into the mother's body. From the ends of each severed vessel two more would grow back in its place.

The doctor would marvel that she had survived as long as she had. And he would know that when the inevitable moment of labor came, the contractions would tear the Hydra apart, spilling its noxious blood as surely as the scythe of Heracles.

4.

Sophocles sat with Nais for the next three days, snatching whatever moments of sleep he could on the bench beside her. Photia had to push him out to eat or bathe. In that time Nais' moments of lucidity became shorter and fewer; at one point she woke up to ask what had happened at Samos. He began to explain, careful to leave out details that might upset her. But two hours later she seemed to rouse again and asked him, in a clear and strong voice, why he had not yet left for the war. That night, she grasped his hand with an abruptness that made him jump, and with coquettish eyes he had not seen in some years, said that yes, she would agree to marry him.

The poet watched with a heavy heart as she veered from the woman he knew to an incontinent stranger. Alas, drama on the stage was one thing, but drama in his family quite another. When Nais called out for Iophon, telling him to stop loafing and turn out from his bed, he could finally take no more. He came out to the garden, blinking in the sudden brilliance of the afternoon. There he discovered Bulos lounging on his composing bench, his tunic hitched around his waist, contentedly scratching his balls.

"What are you doing, you dog!" he cried. "Get up, or I'll see you breaking rocks in some shithole in Laurion!"

Bulos gained his feet just as Sophocles' fist cracked across his temple.

"Master, forgive me! I had no idea."

"Shut your mouth! Get your worthless self over there and clear those weeds! And when you're done with that, scrape this bench and paint it!"

The outburst worked like a tonic for his mood. Leaving Photia with Nais, he went out to the gymnasium for the first time since his return, then got a good meal at a tavern he would never have patronized under normal circumstances. As he came out, he saw someone familiar going in. This man, after recognizing Dexion in the gloom, grasped his hand and held it.

"So it is you," the younger man said, a pained expression on his face that was as close as he came to honest admiration.

"Yes, me. Belated congratulations, dear Euripides, for your first prize this year."

"I don't count it, because you were off doing greater things. If no one has told you, let me be first to say it: Athens has seen no better servant. Not even Aeschylus."

Dexion made some incoherent scoffing noise and attempted to wave his hand in dismissal, but Euripides would not let it go. As Dexion searched his rival's face, it occurred to him that Euripides was serious. This was his first taste of acclaim that was beyond all precedent for a poet, and beyond all reason. The prospect frightened Sophocles more than a fleet of enemy warships.

The next morning a caller came for him in Colonus. Coming out, the poet saw it was Pericles' scribe, Evangelus. The slave uncovered his right shoulder, folded his arm under his ribcage, and delivered a bow worthy of a Medan courtier.

"I see your master knows better than to send Menippus," Sophocles remarked.

"The general requests the favor of Dexion's attendance at the memorial ceremony."

"Memorial?"

"For the fallen at Samos. The master will recall the announcement of it on the Altar of Eponymous Heroes. It was posted three days ago."

"I haven't read the postings," replied the poet. "And I have no time for such nonsense."

"The ceremony is in seven days. Perhaps you will be available at that time?"

"Tell your master, and Aspasia, that they don't need me to admire their handiwork!"

Clearly disconcerted, Evangelus performed another, somewhat less elegant bow, and wandered off with his lips moving, as if continuing the argument in his imagination. In truth, Sophocles had rebuffed the slave without thinking at all about the consequences. To waste a day in Pericles' shadow was inconceivable while Nais was in such dire condition. He also felt a deep, unreasoning revulsion against the memory of his infidelity with Aspasia. Indeed, the image of her left behind in the comfort of the Cholargos farmhouse, composing and polishing Pericles' victory speech while citizens fought and died to earn the conquest, seemed to him to border on the obscene.

He returned to Nais' sick room. His wife was asleep, though fitfully, with her eyeballs flitting under her lids and her breathing ragged. Photia sat beside her with a clay spindle and a basket of rude wool.

"I'll sit now," he told her, picking the basket off the floor.

"No, let me stay."

"It's a fine day—go out to the Academy and enjoy it while you can. Do it for me. Now."

5.

The vigil ended four days later. Nais was roused from sleep by the spasms that came with increasing frequency. Throwing the blankets aside, Photia found the mattress soaked with a mixture of clear effluent and blood; Nais's water had broken, and the bleeding had started again.

"Bulos, fetch the midwife!" she cried.

The next few hours seemed to unfold as quickly, with the same air of dread, as any cycle of plays he'd staged in the Theatre. The only coherent words Nais spoke was at the very beginning, when her eyes suddenly fixed on Dexion.

"Did you let him go to the market again?" she asked, frowning.

He grasped her hand and held it until the midwife arrived. The latter was a prodigiously heavy woman of forty, with great, red, sun-chapped forearms and a bristly moustache. In her arms she carried a bundle filled with implements that seemed more suited to the kitchen than the birthing room: a spatula, wooden tongs, a jar of pig tallow, a vessel for water, a bronze mirror, some bolts of cloth. Sophocles had seen the woman around the nearby streets for years, but had not realized until that moment that she was the local midwife. When she saw him, she jabbed a finger at him.

"You, get out."

"Let him stay, Melitta," begged Photia.

"This is not going to be like dancing to the flutes. It's going to be bad—and I won't spare him a second look if he faints."

"I understand," he said.

With that, she set to work. Forcing Nais' legs apart, she used the tongs to probe the birth canal. As Photia used the mirror to focus the daylight, Melitta peered and prodded, ignoring the flow of milky liquid studded with clotted blood that bathed her forearms. The next contraction forced Nais' legs together, around the midwife's ears. Melitta didn't move, continuing her examination until the contractions ended. Pulling back, she said "She looks ready. But it's hard to see anything with all that blood."

When the poet remembered that day with the perspective of many years, it seemed as if the passage from methodical preparation to horror took only an instant. Nais was in an almost constant state of agony, alternately screaming and clamping her jaw shut so hard the roots of her teeth bled. The midwife tried to shorten the ordeal as best she could, reaching in to grasp the baby's head, but it had hardly crowned when they all saw, with rising despair, the blood filling Nais up from within, turning her body black. Melitta ran out of dry cloth; Photia ran through the house, tearing up bed sheets, tunics, wall hangings. The midwife pulled Nais's bottom down to the edge of the bed and forced her hips up and open. "It's working," she declared. "I can see his ears!"

The flow seemed to redouble; a patter, then a torrent of liquid hit the beaten floor, like the sound of a worsening cloudburst. Photia cried, "Bulos! We need dirt! Bring dirt!" as Melitta struggled to keep her footing, and Sophocles saw his wife pour out the substance of her life. In all his days he had never seen so much blood—not when an ox was sacrificed at the altar, not from all the spear wounds he had seen on the battlefield. This was like the abundance of a festival drinking party, of cheap wine shared out for public consumption in a common mixing bowl. But for all that flowed out of her, he could see there was still more under her skin, pooling in dark circles that expanded before his eyes.

She clutched at him; her eyes rose to him as if she had something to say. Leaning down, he asked "What is it, dear one?"

"Do you think this is . . . ?" she began in a dry, cracking voice.

"What did you say?"

He leaned closer, putting his ear against her mouth. She said nothing more. Worse, he no longer felt the sensation of her breath against the hairs of his beard. He looked into her eyes. They did not focus on him, but seemed fixed on some spot over his head. She did not blink.

"Nais!" he cried.

Someone said, "It's time for him to go."

Bulos appeared with a bucket; he saw Photia's soft eyes, her hands on his shoulders. He was being propelled away from Nais's twisted form as he called to her, desperate now for one definitive act, one gesture of recognition. For it was confusion he felt now, as they shut the door in his face. He was confused that she had been the center of everyone's attention, with him at her side, holding her hand, and yet he could no more arrest her departure than fix the instants between the breaths that seemed to come faster, shallower, less distinct.

He had been seated on the floor for some time—it seemed to him hours but it was only minutes—when he heard a newborn cry. He had not expected the sound, seeming to him as incongruous as children's laughter in a slaughterhouse. The door rattled on its wicker frame and out came Photia naked, swaddling the infant in the only clean garment she had left: her own chiton.

When the little one looked up at her, his eyes looked through her in the same way Nais had in her last moment.

He asked, "Is she gone?"

She looked down to peer into the baby's eyes, awake and alert in those first minutes of life, then at Dexion, who only wished he could close his for good. Then she smiled.

"Iophon is here," she said.

6.

To the luster of Dexion's war-heroism, the gods thus added the pathos of the widower.

The following days passed with the unreality of an interrupted sleep. Taking to his bed for the first time since his return from Samos, he entered a state that was neither conscious nor restful. His body seemed to sway as if the bedframe was the hull of the *Antigone*. He saw corpses, from Callinus's determined repose to shriveled Iophon to Nais, stilled in mid-utterance. He glimpsed the living, too: the midwife coming out of the birthing room, her arms drenched to her elbows in blood, her mouth forming the words, "The Hydra—she still lives." He saw Photia and her steadfast, incomprehensible love, and the face of his infant son rising to the daylight, breaking the surface of a lake of venous, sickly purple.

On the third day he climbed to his feet. Staggering on stiff legs to the front of the house, he expected to see Nais at any moment. He thought to see her at the hearth, boiling water to soften the barley, or in her spinning chair, or folding laundered tunics into an olive-wood box. Then he saw her corpse on the front table, lying with flowers around her head and with her feet pointing at the door—and he remembered.

Meticulous cleansing gave the place the atmosphere of a tomb. A death in the house had polluted the dirt on the floor, and the grease stains by the cauldron, and the fingerprints on the doorjamb. All that life was gone now—swept away and replaced by monkshood in proper little bundles, and the acrid stench of some medicinal incense he could not name. A pan of those flavorless ritual cakes was cooling by the hearth. Nais's funeral was no more than a few hours away.

Continuing through the door, he came out into the garden on what turned out to be a cool and pleasant summer day. The blossoms nodded and the doves rustled just where they always had, their eyes wide at the world. The vegetable beds, he saw, had been cleared of weeds, and his composing bench shone with its coat of fresh paint. Testing the surface with a finger, he found it was dry. Depositing his bones upon it, he was suddenly, surprisingly old, yet also at peace with his exhaustion, knowing well how the Fates had tested him.

The poet was hardly alone in his loss. Had he inquired, he would have learned that three other women died in childbirth that day in Athens, and forty more that month. He might have inquired, but never would. What else could he learn but what he already knew? As long as souls were encased in bodies, it was their lot to suffer. The world was not made for the success or happiness of mortals. Indeed, to presume otherwise was to invite the kind of punishment that was meted out for untoward expectations.

He had lost Iophon and Nais, but he was not abandoned. He had a new son. His name shone undiminished in the city. For all he was forced to endure, his eyes were still open. He was no Polycrates, striding oblivious toward his demise, passing from success to utter disaster in an instant. He would mourn Iophon and Nais, of course—that ordeal had hardly begun. But he knew there was still some distance for him to look down on the victims of true tragedy.

The gate slammed shut, and he looked up to see Photia coming up the path. Her face covered with a white mourning veil, she had the infant bundled in her arms. Bulos, looking much set upon, trailed behind with her marketing bag and a rope strung with one small water flask for each of the nine springs around the city. These were for the final lustrations of Nais' body.

Photia hesitated when she saw her father lying there. Rising, he scratched and gave her a bored look—the only expression that would convey some reassurance, without being as ill-suited to the moment as a smile. Taking the message, she brought the baby to him. He was then confronted with the child's squashed, sleepy face, which seemed to glow faintly from the play of sunlight on his downy head. For the first time, he had a good look at his features: they were his mother's, with a hint of the elder Iophon's crease between the eyes.

"He grows stronger every day," she said, her veil clinging to her lips as they moved.

Sophocles didn't answer.

"I know it was wrong to give him that name, without your word," she went on, her voice unsteady. "It was just the whim of a stupid girl—call him what you wish—you don't need me to tell you that. . . ."

He had never liked her vacillating chatter. What she needed was obvious, and he gave it: he took the babe from her and held him long enough to betoken recognition. In her happiness, Photia fairly leapt from her skin; the child, uncomfortable in the poet's awkward grasp, wet his swaddling.

"I thought Iophon was a good name before," he declared. "I see no reason to change my mind now."

She seemed to restrain herself from speaking further as she took Iophon back and pressed him against her breasts. The child rooted against the fabric.

"Have you found a wet nurse?"

"A woman down the street had a daughter on the same day," she replied. "We owe her for three days."

"I'll send Bulos over with the money," he said as he fell back onto his bench. It occurred to him that the most exhausting thing a man could do was not to work or fight, but to spend excessive time in his bed. He continued, "And I think it is time to remedy an oversight in your education. You must learn to read."

Photia stared at him open-mouthed. As if wafting over on a perfumed cloud, she brought her elated self toward him, and planted a kiss on his cheek.

"To read! That would be a debt I could never repay. Thank you, Father."

"Don't be so sure it's a blessing," he said.

Photia turned to him again on her way into the house. "Oh, and they've been asking about you in the market. That little lizard Evangelus, and that person I'm not supposed to mention but whose name starts with *mu*. They want to know if you'll be at the city memorial."

7.

Sophocles saw little point in staying away when the event arrived. He was grieving, to be sure, and tired beyond accounting, with the beginnings of a pounding in his skull that promised to dog him for days. Yet there were hundreds of families all over the city who had also suffered losses, and who would come to the memorial anyway. For a public figure like him not to show up would play to the public as arrogance, not discretion.

To a calendar already loaded with festivals, the city added public funerals as needed. Though they were supposed to be solemn, they were popular events. The poorer families of the war dead liked them because their sons got a lavish send-off at public expense, and the masses liked them because they were good for a morning off from field and factory. The city paid for the grandstands and the bunting. Patriotic streamers of the tribes and the city hung from every cornice and draped around all the stone phalluses at the roadsides. Rich men such as Cimon and Nicias advertised their good citizenship by donating herds of cattle for the sacrifices. As the meat roasted and the people listened to the featured speakers, smaller entrepreneurs supplied the wine and the hand-food. If all went as planned, the Athenians went back to their daily routines with bellies full, heads buzzing, and hearts fortified with fresh testimony to their own greatness.

The people gathered in the graveyard just outside the Double Gate. There, the sumptuous graves of previous arrivals, with their marble spires and urns freshly scrubbed for the occasion, and the precious carved vignettes of departing soldiers and ladies dressing for the underworld, provided a fitting (and free) backdrop for the proceedings. The gods, in a compliant mood, lent them a cloudless morning and a sun that cast shadows of knife-edge purity, flattering the reliefs and rendering the chiselled apex of every gravestone into a sundial.

The organizers had set up the dais to face the gate and the city beyond. Now that he was sitting up there, Dexion understood the power of this choice: the speaker, if he was a citizen and a man, could not help but be inspired by the spectacle of tens of thousands of Athenians gathered around him. Because the event was open to women, foreigners, and resident aliens, it attracted more spectators than any meeting of the Assembly. It exceeded the audiences for plays, dwarfed Olympic crowds, and put processions at Delos in the shade. Indeed, few cities in all the Greek world were populous enough to attract such a throng. In its sheer bulk it spread in all directions, covering the gates and the city walls, crowding the roofs, filling the trees. When it roared, it was as if the great Earthshaker was ripping open the husk of the world.

To this Pericles had now added a final, crowning ornament: above the walls, glittering at the city's heart, rose his renovated Acropolis. Only in the last few weeks, as they removed the cranes from around its periphery, had the full glory of Athena's temple been revealed. Once decried as an eyesore, as the Olympian's monument to himself, the nearly-complete building silenced its critics. Instead of looming over the city, it seemed to float in the late morning heat, regular in its lines but shimmering in the distance, like the echo of some metrically-perfect hymn. He had not visited it yet. But if he did approach it, he could only imagine such perfection dissolving like a mirage before his eyes.

To a poet like Dexion, whose works were by nature ephemeral, responsibility for such a permanent spectacle lay as much beyond his experience as the levelling of mountains or the diversion of rivers. It was something more proper to the power of the Great King, who dug a canal around the Mount Athos and whipped the sea when it displeased him. Yet this was not the deed of some monarchal maniac, some pompous potentate. It was the work of Greeks like himself.

The ten generals of the Samos campaign filed onto the dais in deme order. This put Sophocles second in priority after the obscure figure of Anagyprasian Socrates. An ovation began when he appeared, and continued after he sat down. Parsing the applause, he perceived that he was most popular among the humbler classes—the thetes, the foreign-born artisans, the slaves. The aristocrats, when they acknowledged him at all, did so only politely. The idea that a mere versifier would take such an important place in government had never sat well with them.

It was bad form to show up one's colleagues by encouraging or acknowledging such acclaim. Instead, he sat stone-faced, listening as the cheering slackened for the next two generals who came up, peaked again, along with catcalls, with the arrival of Pericles, and subsided through Cleitophon of Thorae.

They endured something close to silence as the generals sat for a moment, their helmets resting on their knees with the visors facing all in the same direction. (Lampides had to reverse his at the last second.) In that time Sophocles searched the crowd for Aspasia. He found her in the very front, slightly off center to the left. Though she was wrapped in a plain cloak with her head covered, there was no mistaking those eyes as they stared back from the refuge of her feminine obscurity. Just as he spotted her, she shifted her hood back, revealing more of her face to the light. As she looked at him, she bore the serenity of someone who was sure that she alone, among all those around her, knew what was about to happen.

The crowd shifted as Pericles rose and took the rostrum. Like Aspasia, he had dressed down for the occasion—no rings, no conspicuously bleached linens. Instead, he wore just a buff-colored tunic and his general's cloak gathered behind his shoulders. He raised his right arm as if to salute his fellow citizens. The effect was as if he had laid a blanket on the proceedings, muffling all sound. For a moment there was nothing to distract from him, not the twittering of a bird or the rattling of a wagon in its ruts, as Pericles opened his mouth to speak.

8.

"Athenians! It is incumbent upon the man charged to stand in this place of honor to attempt to do some justice to the deeds of our gallant dead. For it is deeds that constitute the guts and sinews of our political body, not words, which come and go like the wind from Zephyrus' cave. The men we honor here today have made their statement by the sacrifice they have lain at the feet of the people. With what we say here this morning, and our devotion to their memory, we can only hope to laud them without exposing the inadequacy of mere words."

The voice that came out seemed honed for the occasion: precise but never precious, powerful enough to carry to the back of the crowd but not hectoring. No one achieved this balance as well as Pericles. It left everyone in the crowd, including the most hostile partisans, listening with looks of pleasurable distraction on their faces.

"It is often said on occasions like this that the Athenian system stands alone in the world. And it cannot be denied that in both the breadth of its support among the people, and its power to inspire uncommon quality in the common man, it is unique. But it would be wrong to say, as certain critics do, that because the people rule in Athens our city is not ruled by the best of us. For this is the advantage of our democracy—that the justice of our arrangements motivate the best to rule, and the others, by their ballots, to lend their consent to be ruled. What need have we, then, for the petty tyrannies of past ages, or those high-handed cliques of magnates who dominate in other places? What need have we to choose between second-best alternatives? We alone have squared the circle. We have fashioned a system that inspires excellence, not through fear, not through the dead hand of tradition, but through the only quality that makes for enduring strength: justice.

"For evidence of this, look around you. See the splendor of what we have achieved since the Mede burned the altars of our ancestors. Witness the abundance that pours into our ports, and the respect Athenian arms have earned among the Greeks. Look at these things—and then look deeper. See that the buildings, inspiring as they are, and the trappings of our out-

ward wealth, which far exceed that of any other city, are merely
reflections of the quality of her people.

"Most important of all, look beneath the soil here, in this
hallowed place. See where the ashes of your ancestors lie. It
would be unseemly to neglect the many by recalling the names
of only a few. Instead, we honor them by remembering the
places that are forever marked by their deeds: Marathon,
Salamis, Plataea, Mycale, Oenophyta, Tanagra—and Samos.
We recall their heroism, and marvel further at the vigor with
which they made their sacrifice. We Athenians are never
sparing in our defense of freedom, never selfish, because
through our efforts, we lend breath and limb to the best
aspirations of the Greeks. In this way, as much as in the
excellence of any edifice or book, we have become the school
of Greece; we teach her how excellent she may strive to be.
For proof of this, look no further than the achievements others
claim for themselves, yet owe much to the men who lie here.
For would the Lacedaemonians have made their stand at
Thermopylae, without the example of Marathon to inspire
them?"

On reflection, few in the crowd could take seriously
Pericles' candied rhetoric. Only some were properly educated,
but all of them knew that claiming Athenian credit for
Thermopylae was, at the very least, a presumption. But on the
public side of the gap between what citizens told themselves
and what they said out loud, his words played like music.
Sophocles felt the discrepancy himself: skepticism at the
speaker's simpleminded flattery that, after passing through the
contorted passages of his heart, manifested as a patriotic puf-
fing out of his chest, and a smile on his face. It was there, in
the way the speech flirted with his scorn yet counted on his
instincts, that he felt the influence of Aspasia.

"We will not name their names," he continued, "lest we
laud a few and forget the rest. They are all equal in their
sacrifice now, from the greenest hoplite falling in the first
moments of the battle to the heroes who first broke the

Samian walls. Whether they fell on foreign ground or into the depths of the sea, their brothers have made sure they have all come home. It is, after all, our way. We never hesitate to cross the battlefield when our hand is forced, and every man goes home to rest in the Attic soil that gave birth to this, the purest of all races of the Hellenes.

"Thanks to them, we have put down the adversary, and moreover, the worst kind of adversary—the one which has betrayed his oath of alliance. What quarter, what kind of forbearance, should such an enemy expect? I say none, for the gods are surely on the side of the righteous. Yet again, the Athenians light the way for the Greeks, for we did not make Samos a graveyard for her transgressions. Instead, we left their city intact, their people alive with the freedom to rule themselves. That too, is our way. For as long as our neighbors live in peace with each other, and contribute their share to the common defense, Athens will ever be a friend and a partner. That is our pledge to the Greeks.

"As for you, the living—it is your peculiar curse that you must now live on with the good fortune these men have vouchsafed to you. It is a responsibility we will all face for the rest of our lives, to endeavor to be worthy of those who now lie beyond indignity. We have among us the finest examples of this sort of citizen—the servants of the people who never lost sight of the goal, never lost faith, and saw our ship of state here, to safe harbor."

And although Pericles seemed to be speaking of all the generals on the dais, he turned to look at Dexion alone. The crowd, perceiving that this was his moment, raised a cheer that seemed to bloom from the dust of the ground to crown the heights of Mount Hymettos. Sophocles, flushing, cast his eyes downward. Keeping a modest demeanor, he let the sound of their acclaim fill every corner of him, driving out all trace of grief or doubt. The ovation was so sweet that he was prepared to believe it was just as Pericles described—the war had been fought with a singular vision that had never been challenged.

For was Cleon himself not applauding, his face turned faithfully to the rostrum, deriving whatever public glory he could from his proximity to Pericles and Dexion?

"It is to be wondered how many of us can aspire to this kind of courage. For it is one thing to see a father or a brother off to war from within our own walls, safe at least in the knowledge that his sacrifice, if it does come, goes for a greater purpose, and is suffered in the company of his brothers in the line. It is never easy, yet we may take comfort in a cause that lies right before our eyes, in the safety of the land all around us. But how many of us can look at the loss of an only son, in a manner so barbarous that we know the very hour of his death? How many could manage an hour of sleep knowing this son would die alone? I say few of us would have the strength to look on that prospect, and not flinch. You all know of whom I speak."

More applause, again in a manner that seemed intended for no one but Dexion. This time even the nobles dropped their reserve. Pericles, meeting his eyes, gave him a wink. Sophocles looked down at Aspasia. Though her eyes were concealed by the shadow of her hood, her lips were curled into a smile of almost maternal satisfaction.

With that, Pericles had given him what he only half-understood he wanted for himself. Aeschylus had charged the Persian line at Marathon and attained a lifelong honor to match his achievements on the stage. Yet he was only one soldier among many others in the battle. For his role in the siege of Samos, a war for the security of everything built since, Sophocles of Colonus had been singled out for praise in front of his entire city.

It was the kind of coup that would make any gods-fearing man anxious. Yet between the tremors in his gut, Dexion could not help but think, *Let that pipsqueak Euripides match that!* The thought shamed him even as it hatched in his brain, but there it was, as irreducibly Athenian as nuisance litigation and red-figure pots.

"As for the women of the fallen—let their role be as it always has been. For if even the finest words cannot redeem their loss, they cannot begin to encompass the importance of their example, both as widows and mothers. Therefore let silence attend the women of Athens. Indeed, let the fact that they provide no cause for praise or blame be their monument.

"The law demands a few words be spoken today in honor of the dead," Pericles rounded up. "The responsibility has fallen upon me, and I have done it as well as I am able. It is now up to you, the survivors, to answer in deeds what the departed have achieved by theirs. Remember their names. Tend to their graves. Rear your sons, so that they may answer the valor of their fathers. To that end, the state will shoulder the cost of their education—an Athenian education, for which these men have foregone all to assure to their posterity.

"And so our observances are done. Now that you have lamented the dead, rest in the knowledge of that you have discharged all requisite custom, and go your separate ways."

With the end of the speech there went up a brief cheer—sounding more like a shout—that seemed to acknowledge Pericles' *pro forma* dismissal. As the crowd resumed its distractions, and the vendors and the souvenir-smiths converged from the margins, Pericles turned as if he wanted to say something to Dexion. But before he could open his mouth, he was distracted by a lone figure that approached him on the dais.

Sophocles was slow to recognize that it was Photia who stepped forward. Dressed in her best chiton and gold rings and earrings that once belonged to Nais, she had never appeared so grown-up to him, so much the confident and beautiful matron of Athens. With one arm she crowded little Iophon to her breast, and with the other she summoned the Olympian down from his perch. Bemused, Pericles bent to receive her.

"And how may I serve you, my dear child?" he said, smiling.

"Yes, you deserve some kind of glory, noble Pericles," she declared in a loud and steady voice. "You have presented us with many dead citizens today. Not to celebrate the defeat of barbarians, we see, but all to subdue an allied and kindred city. Thank you, great general. Thank you."

Photia turned away, leaving a chasm of silence behind her as the crowd gaped, and the smile died on Pericles' face.

9.

If it was the virtue of woman not to be spoken of, then a seventeen year-old virgin had become the least virtuous woman in Athens. For the next few days little else but Photia's remark was discussed in the marketplace. To the vast majority, that she dared indulge her sarcasm on such a solemn occasion represented not just an insult to Pericles, but an affront to every citizen. One did not impugn the war when the ashes of its victims were not yet warm in the ground. It went without saying that political speech from the mouth of such a person, a minor who had not yet even borne a child for the city, was especially intolerable. A rumor went around that it was Dexion who had put his daughter up to the act—for how else would such a notion enter the head of a mere girl?

Those who hated Pericles or abhorred any war to maintain the Empire welcomed her message. But its timing, and the shape of the messenger, put them in a quandary, for such obvious disrespect would only seem to discredit them. The least risky defense, therefore, was to deny Sophocles was behind his daughter's misdeed. The debate in the stoa came to hinge on this question of Dexion's involvement. The actual substance of her remark, on the very nature of what the war really achieved, was conveniently forgotten.

"I can only guess what possessed you to make such a spectacle of yourself," Sophocles told her. She was standing in front of him in the husband's quarters, hands crossed in front of her like a bound prisoner. Afraid that his anger would get the better of him, he had waited until two days after the incident to speak of it.

"Father, I—"

"No, I don't want to hear your voice," he commanded. "Don't compound your error. It is bad enough that you would shame your family in front of the whole city. That you would now presume to contradict your father is more than I can bear."

And so she remained silent as he rebuked her, rarely lifting her eyes above the floor. Her gaze met his only once, when he described how, thanks to her, Iophon's sacrifice was forever tarnished, as it would never again be recalled without also raising the distasteful memory of his sister's arrogance. At this, she shivered.

"You would have done well to listen to Pericles before you opened your mouth," he concluded. "Did you think you mattered enough to dare criticize your betters? Did you think anyone would listen? If you did, then I am ashamed to have raised such a stupid daughter. Come now—answer me! Account for yourself!"

When she looked up this time there were tears standing in her eyes. Opening her mouth, her voice failed. She swallowed, tried again.

"Father—I can only say that you give me too much credit, for I did not think at all. I only said what came into my head. Now it is as you say—I have discredited us all. If I could go out into the town and tell everyone that I only spoke for myself, I would. If that is what you wish, command it. If you want me to pack my things and leave this house forever, I will. Only do not think I meant to harm my family. That would be the end of me."

He stared at her, waiting to hear more. In the past, she had produced longer, circuitous soliloquies on the question of whether to go to the springhouse in the morning or the late afternoon. That she stood before him now, manifesting Laconic virtue, only made him more exasperated.

For if he was ashamed now, it was not only because of her disgrace, but because of his own conduct. What a hypocrite he had become! With what gross self-satisfaction he had sat on that dais, celebrating himself with the likes of Cleon, while only a few months earlier he had voiced similar doubts. The army had indeed brought back the remains of every fallen soldier from Samos. All of them, that is, except for a piece of the celebrated Sophocles of Colonus, lost along the way.

"I don't want you to leave this house," he said in a soft voice. "Your brother needs you. But I think you'll understand why I withdraw my offer to teach you your letters. Perhaps in the future you will think about the consequences, should more thoughts enter your head."

Her jaw tightening, she nodded. On her face there was suffering, yes, but also resignation, as if the prospect of learning to read, now gone, had never seemed quite real to her.

"You may go," he said. "And send Bulos in after you."

"Yes, Father."

When Bulos appeared, the poet commanded, "Bring me the scrolls of *Polyneices and Antigone*, and the scraper."

"Do you mean to erase something?" asked the slave.

"Just do it."

In a few moments they were settled again in a familiar position—Sophocles on his bench under the plane tree, Bulos seated on a stump with his papyrus scrolls and all the other attributes of composition. It seemed to him all too easy to imagine that they had never left that yard, never sailed across the sea to confront what happened at Samos. But that, of course, was a child's way of thinking; they had indeed left, and stayed away for longer than he ever thought they would. And what happened, did.

"Scrape all the pages," he commanded.

"Master—are you sure?"

Was he? The question was moot, because these were not issues that turned on proof or certainty. What he knew was that the conceit implicit in *Polyneices and Antigone*, that the princess' resistance to the will of the State could be reduced to the consequences of an illicit love-affair, now seemed absurd. It repulsed him, and not only because it was a piece of psychology that might come from the stylus of Euripides. With Photia grown, with a strong back and handsome face and womanly hips, and taking up the responsibilities of a wife in his house, the timing felt wrong for a play that contemplated the temptations of incest. The wages of such abomination, certainly—but not the temptations. On that subject he had another idea to pursue.

"And when you're done scraping," he said, "I have another title for you to put at the beginning."

Bulos took up the wax tablet and his pen. "Yes? What is it?"

"Let it be called *Oedipus the Tyrant.*"

AUTHOR'S AFTERWORD

The war with Samos is discussed in some detail by Thucydides (*History*, 1.115-117) and Plutarch (*Life of Pericles*). Although it has received relatively scant attention by modern scholars, it was no mere footnote in Athenian military history. Samos in the fifth century BC was a wealthy and powerful military power in her own right, one of the few states capable of challenging Athenian naval supremacy in the eastern Aegean. The process of subduing her was a nine-month, see-saw affair that required a series of naval battles and a bitter siege of her capital, led by Pericles himself. Contemporaries compared the hard-won Athenian victory favorably to the conquest of Troy. More ominous, perhaps, is the ruthlessness and savagery exhibited by both sides, which sadly foreshadowed the opening of the Peloponnesian War a decade later.

It seems inconceivable to us that a poet like Sophocles would be given responsibility for an army. A modern analogy might be for some eminence of US letters, such as John Updike, being given a division-level command of American forces invading Iraq in 2003. The analogy fails because it doesn't take into account the much different role of the military in Athenian civic life. Unlike in early 21st century America, every free-born, able-bodied male in ancient Athens received military training. Generalship itself was more of an ad hoc occupation than we can imagine today, with our military academies and officer corps staffed with career professionals. In antiquity, to be a citizen was virtually tantamount to being a soldier, and to lead men in battle was the prerogative of nobility. This is perhaps still true in a reverse sense: while we currently do not pluck our generals out of the ranks of CEOs and politicians, it is perfectly acceptable now for a general to become a CEO or political leader.

The comparison with modern America is apt in other ways. After the defeat of the invading Persians in 479 BC, Athens enjoyed a post-war boom. Moving out from under the nominal leadership of Sparta, she became the biggest, richest, and most powerful state the Greek world had ever seen, dominating her world in ways prefiguring America's traditional mixture of commercial power and military muscle. The alliance she forged to defend the Greek world from further Persian aggression, the Delian League, encompassed the Aegean. Under the leadership of Pericles, the alliance came more and more to resemble an Athenian empire, with its "partners for peace" resigned to paying tribute instead of ships and troops for their defense. (Samos was an exception, providing ships instead of money.) Rebellions against Athenian authority came to be met with ruthless intervention, which were often justified as restorations of democracy. (Pericles would have well appreciated the rhetorical force of today's military euphemisms, such as "Operation Enduring Freedom" and "Operation Restore Democracy.") While modern neo-cons mull clever-sounding comparisons between the USA and ancient Rome, students of ancient history know better: America's global hegemony more closely resembles Periclean Athens than the Roman Empire.

The novel presents a brief sketch of Aspasia, paramour of Pericles, tutor of Socrates in rhetoric (if Plato's *Menexenus* is taken literally) and perhaps the most famous woman of classical Athens. But who was Aspasia, really? I am indebted to Madeleine Henry's monograph *Prisoner of History* for my

perspective on Aspasia scholarship, such as it is. Alas, I could
not follow Henry in inferring that she was a plain, hapless,
chaste and all-around unremarkable war refugee. It strains
credulity (or at least mine) that such an ordinary soul found her
way into the beds and hearts of some of the most powerful
men of her time without at least some talents to recommend
her. Considering the low status of women in ancient Athens,
and the specifics of her personality aside, it is perhaps Aspasia's
greatest achievement that she appears in history at all. We may
forgive her a little unscrupulousness in getting there.

The ancient sources provide few details about how the siege
of Samos ended. The implication is that the war was one of
attrition—the defenders were simply worn down by Pericles'
patient, casualty-averse "anaconda" strategy. That treachery
also played a role in Samos' fall, as I portray here, is unattested,
but plausible given the state of siege technology in the mid-5th
century BC. (The conveniently unlocked door is borrowed
from a real incidence many centuries later—according to some
accounts, during the 1453 siege of Constantinople by the
Ottoman Turks, the Kerkoporta Gate was not breached by
force, but deliberately left open.) In fact, treachery and
starvation were almost the only ways to subdue a well-fortified
city in antiquity. It was not until the ascendancy of Macedon in
the later 4th century that the advantage at last began to swing
toward the offense.

Historical literalists will object to my giving the Athenian
army siege catapults (here, translated literally from the Greek as
"shieldbreakers") in 440 BC. I'm aware that the advent of such
devices, beginning with flexion-based artillery, is only attested
by the early 4th century BC—two generations after the siege of
Samos—and credited to the tyrant Dionysius of Syracuse, not
the Athenians. On the other hand, Diodorus Siculus (*Library*,
12.28) and Plutarch (*Life of Pericles*) report that Pericles
deployed "siege-engines" at Samos, "out of admiration for
their novelty." These accounts are generally understood to
refer to battering rams, not catapults. Yet given Pericles'

aversion to Athenian casualties, and his interest in shortening the duration (and cost) of sieges, it is at least plausible that he would have been interested in long-range artillery. It is also likely that if the Athenians had anticipated Dionysius, their innovations would have gone unrecorded. Unlike in later Hellenistic and Roman times, there was not much specialist technical literature in classical Greece, and much disdain in the literate classes for the putterings of mere mechanics.

Finally, I want to thank my agent, Jeff Gerecke, for his tireless efforts to find this project a home, and Rod Hunter of Bella Rosa Books for believing in it. I'd also like to thank my wife, Maryanne Newton, and Professor David Hollander of Iowa State University for examining the manuscript. Any errors that remain are entirely the author's responsibility.

ABOUT THE AUTHOR

Nicholas Nicastro was born in Astoria, New York in 1963. He has worked as a film critic, a hospital orderly, a newspaper reporter, a library archivist, a college lecturer in anthropology and psychology, an animal behaviorist, and an advertising salesman. His published novels include *The Eighteenth Captain* (1999), *Between Two Fires* (2002), *Empire of Ashes* (2004), and *The Isle of Stone* (2005). His writings also include short fiction, travel and science articles in such publications as *The New York Times*, *The New York Observer*, *Film Comment*, and *The International Herald Tribune*.

Printed in the United States
78353LV00002B/128